CONCEPTION

ALSO BY KALISHA BUCKHANON

UPSTATE

Praise for *Conception*

"The work of a gifted young novelist." —*The Washington Post*

"Readers . . . are richly rewarded." —*Chicago Sun-Times*

"A poignant, heart-wrenching novel." —*Kirkus Reviews*

"[H]eartfelt and affecting." —*Booklist*

"Much like her acclaimed debut novel *Upstate*, Buckhanon is again at her best." —*Mosaic* literary magazine

Praise for *Upstate*

"A moving and uplifting story of love and hope in the face of adversity." —*Publishers Weekly*

"*Upstate* starts out strong and never lets go." —*Chicago Tribune*

"A realistic love story that's set against an urban backdrop as gritty as its characters are memorable." —*People*

"A sensitive portrayal of young lovers that moves beyond gritty urban fiction." —*Essence*

"Captures the faithfulness and tenacity of young love." —*Entertainment Weekly*

"Packs a swift, head-clearing emotional punch." —*Elle* magazine

"Filled with tragedy, despair, and hope." —*Toronto Sun*

KALISHA BUCKHANON

CONCEPTION

ST. MARTIN'S GRIFFIN ⚏ NEW YORK

CONCEPTION. Copyright © 2008 by Kalisha Buckhanon. All rights reserved. Printed in the United States of America. For information, address St. Martin's Press, 175 Fifth Avenue, New York, N.Y. 10010.

www.stmartins.com

Design by Dylan Rosal Greif

The Library of Congress has catalogued the hardcover edition as follows:

Buckhanon, Kalisha, 1977–
    Conception / Kalisha Buckhanon.—1st ed.
        p. cm.
    ISBN-13: 978-0-312-33270-9
    ISBN-10: 0-312-33270-X
    1. Teenage pregnancy—Fiction.   2. African American women—Fiction.
I. Title.

PS3602.U264C66 2008
813'.6—dc22

2007040441

ISBN-13: 978-0-312-54514-7 (pbk.)
ISBN-10: 0-312-54514-2 (pbk.)

P1

For Brenae, Isaiah, and Jaylyn

ACKNOWLEDGMENTS

My agent, Tracy Sherrod, I love you! Monique Patterson: I love you too, and thank you for being patient with me as I attempted to write this novel! Thank you to her assistant editor, Kia DuPree, for jumping on board and loving this book. I'd also like to thank the following for providing a quiet place to write: Andrea Holmes, in whose Bronx co-op I "accidentally" wrote the first chapter of this book; Robyn Gorbett, whose isolated Thawville, Illinois, trailer forced me to finally get into it; and the wonderful staff of the Orrington Hotel in Evanston, Illinois, in whose charming hotel I was able to achieve that first temporary ending. And a very special thanks to my manager, Felicia Pride, without whose assistance I may have never been able to get my life together in order to finish this book. I'd like to thank friends Erica Botts, Billie Burrell, Judith Trytten, Joseph DeLouise, Rob Walker, Erica McClendon, Ebony Madison, and Tara Betts for many reasons that they know of.

I would also like to thank the Alice Bernice Kaplan Center

for the Humanities at Northwestern University, where I workshopped the first half of *Conception,* and the University of Chicago Creative Writing Center, in whose Emerging Writers Series I read from the book for the first time. I must express gratitude to the following writers for their advice and support of my work and young career: Sapphire, Achy Obejas, Bayo Ojikutu, Harriette Cole, Terrie Williams, bell hooks, Sonia Sanchez, Kenji Jasper, Bernice McFadden, E. Lynn Harris, Terry McMillan, Sofia Quintero, Pittershawn Palmer, and especially Professor Dorothy Roberts, whose book on Black female eugenics, *Killing the Black Body,* proved to be an invaluable inspiration. Thank you to the following members of Achy Obejas's writers' group: David Driscoll, Patrick Reichard, Elise Johnson, and Sarah Frank.

And finally the St. Martin's team, and all of the reviewers, reporters, readers, bookstore professionals, publications, libraries, teachers, colleges, high schools, and youth organizations who made my first novel, *Upstate,* such a blessed success.

PART ONE

FROM THE INSIDE *looking out, life doesn't appear rose-colored when you know most people—including yourself—may one day die just like a rose: dried out by trouble and time, fragile and shriveled, scent faded to odor, color bled away, shrunken parts vulnerable to each and every touch, head bowed and apologetic in demise. Now I know better than to mourn when my life ends before it begins. How much more graceful to be cut from a bush and turned upside down immediately after bloom, preserved for a near eternity before a crumbling explosion of blossoms too ashlike to ever be put back together again. I'm content to remain like a flower seed, tumbling in and around and throughout the earth, languishing in possibility and potential because birth always brings the consequences of confusion, sadness, disappointment, then death.*

But I could be a Black child soon. One day. Maybe. I haven't been born yet, but I want to be. I want to live in the world: clothed, fed, loved, guided, educated, magnificent, important,

essential, and good. I want to contribute, do something impor-
tant that might make the world go round just a little bit easier,
change a few other lives when I finally get to live my own. But I
must be born first. I've had chances, but I never made it.

Suddenly I see myself at six years old, jumping rope in a
windstorm. Always before I come back, flashes of a future startle
me right before I awake. These scenes in my mind break the
promises they make; I'm never born so I never get to see them
happen in an actual life. This time, I see I'll have red, green, and
black beads hanging on the end of my cornrows, locked in place
with a tight tip of aluminum foil. When I bounce up from my
toes the beads smack me back in the face. An old woman, maybe
my grandma, opens the front door and lets her cooking smells
out. She hangs from the tattered screen with her purple duster
flying open just enough to see all the brown stardust scattered
between her breasts. Who is she? And why do I mind her? She
has a cotton white rag wound around her head. She doesn't
have to move her mouth to get me to throw down my rope.

If I have to tell you one more time . . . *is what her eyes say.*

I think about smacking my lips. I protest silently instead,
leaving the rope she bought for me on the sidewalk, knowing it is
vulnerable to the wind. Who is she? Will I ever find out? The
roses planted in front of the house the old woman always dreamed
of calling her own are being ripped from the ground, along with
some planted basil and the dandelion weeds I give her for the
dinner table on Sundays. Tiny, fast-moving black ants disperse
and swirl because the wind has demolished their sand castles. I
hope more don't come out of the ground and start biting my legs
because they are now like all the grown-ups I've known, furious
they have worked so hard for nothing. I ignore the gusty cur-
rents of dust and open my mouth to taste the dirt. Then I catch
my old woman a rose as it shoots past like a kamikaze. My palm
closes around a menacing thorn. I walk up to the dull, leaning,
one-story yellow house with the flower in my hand and a little

blood running down my wrist. Behind me, I see a rusted chain-link fence with circles like a honeycomb. I imagine bees on their way to sting me, then I hear the bark of a big dog coming from somewhere inside. But I'm not afraid of any of this. People are the only things which disturb me. I don't like when this woman twists her mouth at me, like she's wondering why she ever liked me in the first place. I want to make her happy. I want her to think I can live forever, rise in smoke if I was burned and not even hundred-mile-per-hour winds are strong enough to carry away my ashes. So I don't cry although it hurts. Instead, I hold up my hand and say, "Ma'am, look at me. Now, I'm just like Jesus." And I really wanted to be.

For as long as I had known of myself, earlier than this dream vision of a blustery day that hasn't happened yet, I was a dark soul floating through the arcane, craving the journey of birth, fashioning a life from God-given visions and my own make-believe. From the forever sleep I've awakened, in many times and many places, only to be forced to close my eyes and simply wait, forever and again. It was 1992 when it seemed ready to happen for sure, in a winter on the cusp of millenniums, in a no-name Pennsylvania town on the road from Chicago to New York City, when a girl named Shivana Golding fell in love with a boy who was not my father. She was strong enough to conjure the courage to embark on a quest less hopeless than being a magical but completely invisible Black girl on a crowded street in Chicago. She was fifteen, already aching for a purposeful life: to be a mother was a calling.

All the women who had conceived my soul but lost my life in the past had believed the same. And there were many before her—the sweet Yoshi, the spitfire Darlene, and the tragedy, Tawana. But faith alone had not been strong enough to anchor me to their wombs. I never grieved when I died; I tried again, though I wasn't itching to find myself dropped into the vicious worlds I saw waiting for me through their eyes. When the months crept on and I grew older inside Shivana than with any others in the past, I started to believe I could see my face on the outside of my dreams. It was up to me to convince Shivana to want to see my face on the outside of her own dreams.

I knew I was eventually meant to make it—one day. I just wanted it to be a day when my life would be right. Until that day, I found solace in imagination's peace, the pondering of the "what ifs": What if the women had been White? What if the women had been privileged? What if the men had been taught how to love them? *To those questions, I drew my own conclusions. I wish I could have shared them with all my mothers, if they could have heard me. And if I had found out, in time, how our shared story would finally end.*

BACK TALK.

That's how it sounds when a little voice inside of you splits your thoughts in half. Splashes the half-empty glass against the mirror you think through so you can consider it was fuller than you had thought. Makes you look past the tiny beads of your perspective to finally see yourself, and everyone else, as a shredded design in a kaleidoscope: complicated, unpredictable, subject to change but no less beautiful because of it. Sometimes, more beautiful because of it.

I heard something speaking to me, could tell something was trying to talk to me, and still tried to ignore everything I heard. I don't care who she is, how much money she has, where she comes from, how good she believes her man is, or what the circumstances of her own coming into this world were. Every woman is going to have some questions when she finds out she has another life inside. And she will have doubts. And fears.

Deciding on the life of somebody else isn't the best place to be when you're deciding on your own.

And so that's where I was when I started hearing and knowing things I otherwise shouldn't have known. That's where I was when the whole world started to make some sense, become a little more focused and narrow. That's where I was when I really saw and understood where I was in the world, in the order of things. I wasn't a mote in God's eye. He probably couldn't have even found me had he looked for me through a microscope. I was living on the South Side of Chicago. I was barely passing school. I was poor but didn't know it. I was never happy, or around people who were. I was going through slow motions that had already been set for me and that nobody was trying to accelerate. I was dreamless. I was unable to imagine me beyond the day I was in at the moment. I was sad about all the sadness around me. I was indifferent. Then I found out I was pregnant.

I look far back to remember our stories. And though my mind knows I am not looking back centuries, my spirit feels like it was that long ago. I always felt like a grown woman and an old soul, even before I became a mother. A grandmother used to always say, "Girl, I swear you act like you been here before." *Here* was America, the North, Chicago. Now that I am no longer there, but here, with mature and wiser eyes I have a new perspective on just what being there meant, and I now know I was tougher than I gave myself credit for. I confess. I took advantage of youth's luxuries: sulking, learning, misbehaving, dreaming, falling in love. I was always a sassy little thing and a treasure chest of contradictions; I straddled the fences between being rambunctious but withdrawn, brilliant but inarticulate, spirited but defeated. And now, finally and only after much time to think about it, I can laugh when I think about those last couple months of my life in that foggy and crazy-weathered city. A new perspective makes it hard to tell the story how it really was, because maturity wants to twist the details into a version of the truth that lets me off the hook. But I can't leave out all the mistakes I made and the wrong I did. Despite even the parts of the truth for which I'm ashamed, I still feel like life turned out alright.

It's hard to remember when exactly it began, why I left, how I ended up where I did and how I did, in the way I did. There may not be enough time to really start at the beginning, to remember or tell it all. But I guess if I really had to think back as far as I could about how and when I could tell somebody was fighting me, arguing and debating and challenging me, pushing me to grab a hold of my life, screaming at me though I couldn't see the source of the sound, it would be a couple days before that somebody could have even been there. It would have been the fight, I think back. Because whenever I go back to think of all I could have done differently in those last months, it starts with the last fight with my mother. The change that changed me forever really started then. Some man may have burst a seed of life inside of me, but I know now it had always been there.

ONE

WHENEVER ME AND Ma fought, she always went for my hair.

When she was younger, everybody talked about her long, black, silky, *Indian in the family* hair. My hair's bright rusty red color is one of the few things my father ever gave me, but I wished I had taken after my mother when it comes to texture and length. Maybe if I had, my life would have been different. Better, easier, calmer. Everybody talks about her "good" hair and whenever they do, she has to remind them how her only child, a girl child at that, wasn't so lucky. And the hair isn't the only difference between us. I'm short with a voluptuous butt and big breasts; she's tall, hippy, with the small tits I haven't seen since thirteen. Now she's going gray and bald at the same time. Her hair is always balled up in a bun that looks like a steel wool pad. Most of the time, she wears a scarf.

She hadn't asked me first, but she came into my room wearing my long Fendi head scarf that I had just bought from my favorite African man selling things on Forty-seventh by the El.

She asked me if I had eaten all her Danish butter cookies, the cheap ones that come in the round blue aluminum tins. Actually, she told me I had eaten them. I didn't even know she had bought any Danish butter cookies; I wouldn't have eaten them all anyway since I only like the ones with the hard sugar dots on top. But trying to explain anything to Ma after she's made up her mind is a waste of time. I lay down and tried to ignore her, but that never worked. When I didn't answer her, she grabbed my Afro puff of a ponytail and twisted it tight in her hands. I could feel my scalp burning hot like when I left a perm in too long, only her pulling made it worse.

For as long as I could remember, I had let her hit me, slap me, or do whatever else she was going to do while calling me every name in the book. But this time I don't know what happened, what came over me. I don't know if it was because my breasts were sore because I was waiting on my period, but I fought back this time. I put my knees up, then for the first time since I turned thirteen and she started fighting me like she had fought men, I hit my own mother back. She held me down on my twin bed with one hand and started slapping me openhanded with the other. I heard her screaming at me, cussing me out because she was surprised. I think she was a little scared too, or maybe nervous, so I was glad. I felt tears coming, but I held them back. My throat lumped up while words came up from out of my stomach, out of my heart, out of my mouth, and into my mother's twisted face:

"Keep your hands off me . . ."

That was a couple days before my aunt Jewel came back, and that's how those police who came busting through the door after the neighbors called found us—two grown women screaming the same thing over and over, and neither one of us shameful enough to cry. That was when I knew my mother's life and mine had to change.

. . .

MA AND I fought before I got pregnant; I left because I knew it would get much worse once she found out. I never *planned* on getting pregnant when I was fifteen; it just happened. But isn't that just how it always is? At least if you're young and Black, or old and Black for that matter. Planning pregnancy was for White women; every woman I had ever known just got caught—caught up in some man to the point where she was foolish enough to drop a load for him, believe all that "carry my seed I'm gonna love you *and* my child" sweet talk. You can keep foolishness and stupidity a secret, but a belly swelled will always tell the truth even if it isn't a whole one. The whole truth is that the child was an even bigger accident than the relationship. And a pregnant woman or one who already has kids by a man who's no longer thinking about her never, ever tells that truth—not even to herself.

I knew the story well. I had seen it, heard about it, been warned about it; my own father left so I was a victim of it. Any gathering of two or more women made me a silent witness to the deep wounds men left behind. Later I was guaranteed to be kept up well into a night listening to my hardened mother, still young, who vowed a crowbar couldn't get her stiff legs open again—let alone a man.

The story was always the same. At first he cooks her breakfast in the mornings, rubs her feet at night, pinches her cheeks like she's his child herself, and rubs her belly every time she walks by. He stands outside with his chest stuck out and brags to the neighborhood regulars that he "got a shorty coming." He buys her ice cream, comfortable walking shoes, and a thick pink robe to sit on soft skin he rubs down with the *real* baby lotion, after she takes the Calgon bubble bath he ran. When he makes love to her, he's soft and careful. They lay tight like two spoons in a squeaky bed, listening to Luther or the Isley Brothers or Chaka Khan when she was still with Rufus, and when she starts crying because she's turned away from him and she thinks he won't know, he can tell she's scared he'll leave her just from the tension stiff in her back. So he massages her spine and her doubt, wipes away her tears, and whispers, "Baby, *I promise,* I ain't going nowhere."

He might mean it . . . until she swells so much from both water and baby that she couldn't pull her grouchy lips in if she tried. Or until she has it and her wrinkled, dark, sagging stomach won't snap back to that smoothness he used to love to bump up against. I've seen them stay until the baby's first blown-out-of-proportion birthday party or maybe even later, but something about being called "Daddy"—never mind husband—seems to choke men these days. They shove off their women and kids like suffocating pillows smashed against their faces, cutting off not only their air and vision but the rest of their lives.

At least when somebody's suffocating, you can tell: you see their faces turn blue, their lips quiver, their eyes buck, and their throats jerk. But when a man is mentally packing his bags, the suitcase is never out until he's already standing on the other side of the door. He suddenly gets shy whenever they have a little time alone, silently fusses with the food on his plate much more, *if* he's even still eating her cooking at all. Then his nights at the corner bar start dragging on longer than they used to, well into the hours they used to be shattering headboards and calling each other's names. Suddenly the mama he complained about when they first got together becomes strangely needy, and she starts hearing the excuse a man gives a woman he wants to have sex with without having to spend the night: *"I gotta do something for my mama."* Exactly *what* is never explained, but she looks at him with puppy-dog eyes anyway and says, "Okay, baby, take your time." It's all over by the time she starts first dropping hints, then actually saying, *"You need to start bringing some more money into this house."* If the kids are lucky (and I wasn't), they'll be too young to remember the arguments filled in by the swish sound of flying objects, the lightning-bolt crack

of slammed doors, and of course the face slaps. Finally the story
ends when a Greyhound bus or loaded-down car hits the highway, and the woman is left staring into a window rather than
out of it.

I know the exact moment my baby came inside me: it was on
October 11, 1992.

That was the night I met Rasul, and the night Renelle Washington came home early from work with a new surprise birthday
cake for her husband Leroy. An Entenmann's German chocolate
cake, thirty-six candles standing up sharp and wicked like pitch-
forks. The whole sixth-floor apartment still held on to the burnt
stink from Renelle's earlier attempt at "homemade" cooking.
Three months into another birth, she had tortured a Duncan
Hines chocolate box mix into volcanic rock that morning; its
nasty failure predicted the baby's fate.

Leroy and I whispered about the cake while he lay on top of
me on their black leather living-room couch, finding his way,
unprotected, into my silky young softness for the second time
that night. We had been doing this behind his wife's back for
months. He made my heart beat fast and my blood race through
my body so strong and hard my baby's heart started beating
too. My baby screamed and glowed red when it roared to life inside me, but Leroy and I didn't see or hear or know.

"Forget that burnt cake . . . this all the chocolate I need right
here," Leroy whispered to me, and I didn't know how to respond. I was just fifteen then, still spoke only when spoken to,
tried not to curse in front of grown folks or wear clothes that
hugged my shape too tight. I still wanted to be a child, but my
body just wasn't having it. So I said nothing at all. I just lay
there in a slick mist of our sweat. My head slid closer and closer
to the arm of the leather couch until I was bumping it hard. I
made tiny, quick sounds until, dizzy from the friction, I stopped
him.

"Leroy, that's too hard."

My pleas only excited him.

"All this body, and you can't take it?" His grubby hands with their dirty fingernails pinched strong at my hips, right on top of stretch marks gilded by a recent growth spurt. He rocked inside of me with even more force.

I said no, but he ignored it. I had to push the word out and around his tongue when he finally kissed me, a half hour into it, for the first time that night. Kissing was something I knew how to do, something I liked, something I had practiced and prayed for, the only thing—really—I had wanted in the first place. My girlish noises became natural and smooth, no longer pained and hesitant. My lower back lost its arch with each twirl of our tongues. My breath evened out when I felt Leroy crushing deeper and deeper into me. So I took my hands from his back to his tough hair, but then he just slid them back down to his fast-pumping behind. He sensed my thaw and started the frantic movements that would move my head up again. He didn't have the sense to know my inexperience demanded he kiss me like we were slow dancing.

I knew the hard arm of the couch was inching closer, so I shut my eyes and braced for the thump. I put my tongue deeper and deeper into his throat, imagined I was finally taking some control. A throb of pleasure took over in my silky softness, and I melted. When Leroy hurt me, I liked it just a little. There were seconds here and there when I would actually move with him. I'd dig my little hands with their bitten-down green glitter fingernails into his back, make a two-inch radius circle with my hips to give myself a quick flash of something warm, electric, and confusing. I imagined the man on top of me was instead a boy at school who would never look my way. My instinct was to be embarrassed, but before I could blush from shame, a feeling I had never ever felt before spread out from my middle like waves. I felt red all over from something else. My tiny moans became sharp cries. I didn't worry I would wake up the two kids sleeping down the hall because I had forgotten them. I fell deeper in love with each cry, with each and every one of his charges toward my immature womb.

And just when Leroy had lifted himself up with his arms and started to brush his wiry hairs against my tiny spot just right, he released me. It was over. Renelle got off work at 11:00, and I saw the time on the VCR clock was 10:45. Leroy knew we would need time to get our breath back to normal, for the sex to dry from our complexions.

"Did you like it?" he asked me that time, just like every other time we finished.

"Uh-huh," I said.

He stayed on top of me, unlike every other time we finished.

"You gonna make me fall in love with you, girl," he said.

I halfway smiled.

"Bet you think I can't fall in love with you, huh?" he asked.

"I don't know . . ." I hunched up my shoulders. "What about Renelle?"

"Renelle," Leroy whispered, pressing himself deeper into me. "Yeah, Renelle."

His eyes went to a faraway place.

"Sometimes, you know, two people ain't got nothin' in common no more," he answered. "When the love is gone, well . . . I don't know. I love her, but I ain't wanna get married. She did."

I said nothing. I was stiff. This was strange; he never talked to me like this after.

He just kept talking in a slurry mumble that made me think he was going to fall asleep on top of me. That couldn't happen. Leroy was heavy, and I was scared to get caught.

"Don't know, Vana . . . I been in Chi all my life. Ain't never been nowhere else. Feel like it's only so far I can go here. Fighting a million other niggas for these goddamn City of Chicago jobs. Throwing gabage, driving buses. Shit, if it was something else for me to do here, I woulda done it. I want to see something different, do different things. But all Renelle wanna do is work, get a house, work some mo', get a car, work some mo'. I don't know. It gotta be somethin' better than this . . ."

I soaked up him and his sleepy talk.

"Guess she just thinking 'bout the kids," I said, and I rubbed the back of his neck real soft, real gentle, like he was mine.

That was the mistake. He stopped breathing for a couple of seconds, then twisted out of my arms. After he pulled himself out of me, his pant legs clutched like knowing tripwire around his ankles, I could still feel my pulse beating down there. I closed my thighs tight, tight, *tight,* and tried to squeeze the feeling out, like I was ringing a dirty wet mop free of all its germy water. A burn filled my chest and I wanted to cry, but then part of me wanted to keep going, to grow that tiny current into a flash of lightning.

I wondered when next Renelle would walk down three flights of stairs and ask me to watch the kids while she worked her evening nurses' aide shift. Ma never questioned out loud why the Washingtons needed a babysitter when everybody knew Leroy never went to work. I kept it to myself that from three to eleven, Leroy was usually in the streets but sometimes sat in the house and waited for his beeper to go off. And when he *was* there, shadowy, gaunt men and women always stopped by unannounced—scratching, sweating, and negotiating.

"You better put them clothes back on before Renelle get home," Leroy instructed while he walked away toward the kitchen. All of a sudden, he turned back around and pulled it out from between his fly, wagging his thing in his hand so I could smile. My face fell flat again as soon as he turned his back. I wondered then how all this began. I wondered why I first allowed him to have his way with me—because that's exactly what he did. He had his way, and like with everything in life I didn't have mine. I would never lie and say he started out by raping me, because I never told him to stop. I had always just looked up at him, curious and shaken, when he stared down at me with moist eyes while licking his lips. I always wondered what exactly he would do next, because I thought then I would learn a little bit about what it meant to be grown. Yet each time we were finished, I didn't feel any more grown than I had before, only smaller.

In between the roar of me and my baby's blood clashing between my ears, from the back of the messy three-bedroom apartment with its sad, dumpy furniture, I heard the harsh, rattling cough of the three-year-old, Leroy Jr. It wasn't like I cared anymore; it had lingered for months and nobody felt he needed to see a doctor, although I had mentioned it a couple times. The baby and his sick cough had been reduced to an alibi, my reason not to be anywhere near the husband when his wife walked through the door. I didn't know how much longer I could hide or disguise it, pretending fifteen dollars a night drove my enthusiasm for watching two brats who did nothing but beg for sweets and talk back.

Before I made it to Junior's bed, I stopped to check on the six-year-old, Jessica. She was a sweetheart; nerve-wracking because she was always asking questions, sweet because she would do anything I asked her to. It didn't take me long to start calling her Jesse: *"Jesse, go run your brother a bath. Jesse, go make sure that door locked. Jesse, help me clean up this house before your mama and daddy get home."* My mother couldn't help remind me that a woman who couldn't keep a house would never keep a man, so I figured I was doing Jesse a favor by putting her to it early.

I was shocked to see Jesse naked from the top down, her Strawberry Shortcake nightgown twisted up around her narrow chest. I knew she was just one of those hard sleepers who fought herself throughout the night, but I couldn't help but panic for a minute. Once I threw *those* thoughts out of my head, I noticed the Vicks humidifier by Junior's flimsy daybed was out of water. After refilling it in the rusted pedal sink of the tiny bathroom next door, I came back and pulled the lint-covered, flannel black blanket back up around the boy's chest. Then I sat next to him alone, in the dark, on the edge of the mattress until I heard Mrs. Washington arrive home, calling my name above Mr. Washington's inflated guffaws: *"Shivana."*

It sounded like an echo in an empty house—surprising, crisp, soft as a breeze. And like cooped-up apartment dwellers fanning outside broken windows, I had been waiting for that breeze for far too long.

I was way too young to know I was disgusting: watching over a woman's children while screwing her husband was an unforgivable contradiction. After that first time, when I struggled out of a dream to find Leroy staring down at me with his pants already unzipped, I couldn't even look Renelle in the eyes when she paid me for that night. In my own bed later on, I held a hot face towel between my legs to stop the sensation of insides shredded by the sharp end of a rusty nail. I used the same towel to wipe the tears I had cried all night; I had cashed in my virginity long after most girls my age, but I still felt broke. As time passed I didn't know how to end it and once he told me he loved me, I didn't want to. I had been taught right from wrong, but not how to right a wrong. Unlike a mistress in the White man's big house, I couldn't claim self-preservation, custom, or the law to exonerate myself. I was a horny young Black girl unwanted and I thought unloved by anyone else, crushed ego temporarily bolstered by a scoundrel old enough to be my daddy—which maybe he should have been trying to be.

I crept back toward the front room to face Renelle, saw for the first time that almost all the oranging family pictures framed in the light blue hallway were held in cracked, raggedy frames. I smelled the burning candles, wanted to be *Mrs.* Washington—three months pregnant and all—bopping about and serenading Leroy with "Happy Birthday," Stevie Wonder style. After I finished Leroy couldn't stop smiling at his wife, but he peeked at me from the corner of his cat-yellow eyes. I stood close enough to see him spit a little on the cake when he blew out his candles. I didn't know what to do with myself, so I rocked back and forth on my heels with my arms folded tight. I was too worried I smelled bad to do anything else. Before Renelle could ask me to stay, Leroy had pulled a twenty from his wallet.

"Bring me my change next time," he said, grinning and holding on to the bill a couple of seconds after I pulled on it.

I said the only thing I thought I was supposed to: "Okay."

Renelle giggled like it was her birthday. She held on to her husband's narrow hips, nuzzling him a bit before pulling back.

"Baby, you so silly."

Then, without taking her eyes off her husband, "You want to stay and have some of this cake?"

I mumbled no and started toward the door.

"You sure you don't want no cake, Shivana, some to take to your mother . . . ?"

I was already closing the door when Leroy scolded his wife: "You heard the girl say naw the first time."

NEITHER GROWN-UP HAD thought to see me to my door. That's what 1992 had come to: boys were men with that first hair on the chest and girls were treated like grown women long before their bodies said so. Seeing this, I had long forced myself to look straight through, never straight at, all the things I should be afraid of. Like my building.

We took some pride in the fact that ours wasn't an official "project," a category that would have caused us to slur our address or lie about it altogether when we weren't around people like us. Beyond its status as one small step above public housing, there was nothing proud about another bitter, run-down low-rise having the nerve to sit on a street named after Martin

Luther King. The dark brown hallway carpet could hush the footsteps of any deviant. Most of the low-wattage bulbs cased in cheap glass cylinders were too dim to light anyone's path, courtesy of a slumlord cutting every corner as sharply as he could. He only bandaged the boiler, never actually replaced it; winter nights were a grueling patience game while we listened for the radiator's hiss from underneath every cover, sheet, sweater, and coat we could find. There was no trash chute; we had to suffer past or right next to garbage rooms that reeked always, more in summer, even more over the weekends when the building's one super was off. Another quiet, more loathsome odor betrayed the presence of vermin carcasses lodged within the walls. Even the cleanest apartments were invaded by other people's roaches, though most had given up so it's hard to say whose roaches they were. Hash from split-open cigars littered the stairwell, and the offenders left the skunky odor of their weed blunts behind. They put their cigarettes out by mashing them against the walls and then dropping the butts straight down to the floor. The apartments were peopled with old-timers who were set in their ways and newcomers who had lost theirs. Nobody stood out in the hallway and discussed recipes or the weather; neighbors never borrowed from one another. Locked behind evergreen doors lined tightly as mausoleum slots, we daily ignored the sounds that penetrated walls: coughs, sobs, sniffs, screeching babies, whining children, decades-old rhythm and blues, midnight sitcom laugh tracks, over dramatic fucking and arguing. It was a graveyard spread up, not out.

It was no wonder why, by fifteen, I already knew what it felt like to feel nothing. But that night there was this boy in the third-floor stairwell. I wouldn't even know his name until weeks later. He shot an old basketball toward the ceiling with a disciplined flick of his thin-boned wrist. I saw him first from behind when I rounded the landing that dipped from the fourth floor to the third, where my mother and I lived. Without even seeing his face, I knew I had never seen him before. I could tell his legs were long though he folded them into himself like a grasshopper perched to jump. Underneath a thin blue tank top, his muscles curled broad, smooth, and even like a legato along his spine. A red Chicago Bulls cap covered his Afro—knotted black florets just begging for long fingers to cut and curl through to a scalp. I remember I paused just to peek at him longer before I passed. Gray sweats bunched about his knees, the fine sparseness of the hair on his coco-colored legs marked his immaturity. The delectable strength and tone in his calves ignited my electric. As if sensing someone scoping him out, the next time he shot the ball toward the ceiling he lost his cool. Just a little break in form and the ball went in its own direction, back behind him and almost into my stomach. I turned just in time for the ball to miss my middle and hit my side.

"Damn, boy, watch it! Shit . . . goddamn! Ow . . ."

When the boy I liked without first even seeing his face finally did turn around and stand, I was disappointed. He really wasn't all that, not like his backside had insinuated. His face was ashy, acne-scarred; I sucked in my breath when I saw a quarter-sized circle of bleach-white skin marking his cheek like blush slapped on in such a hurry it did more harm than good. He jumped up to help me, said something like "Aw, my fault," then threw up his hand like he was waiting for some secret handshake. But I had nothing better to do with my night than join the rest of the world and shove a Black boy back into his place. A flair for the dramatic was another of the few things my father had given me, so I couldn't accept the apology without letting my annoyance be known.

After I cursed him out loud, in my head I added *clumsy Black ass Negro* but was too scared to say it. He *was* a foot taller than me.

I bent over and shoved his hand away when he grabbed my shoulder. I pushed past him and snatched open the stairwell door without looking back. I made sure to hug my pudgy stomach like it had truly been hurt. I walked slow enough for him to notice, added a little bend to my waist and twist to my hips. I wanted to know if the boy was still watching me, but I sensed he was. I smothered a laugh and wondered if I shouldn't have cussed him out. I couldn't help but look back for him, but by the time I turned around he was already going. I caught one of those brown grasshopper legs before it disappeared round the landing to the fourth floor. Except for his white cheek, I couldn't have told anybody what his face looked like, wouldn't have recognized him if he had passed me on the street. Yet even so, like someone had pricked a voodoo doll in my honor, I *felt* something.

TWO

I **WAS WAY** too tired the next morning to focus on any of my classes. I was more than relieved to get to third-period biology and see Mrs. Carly had stayed her demanding ass at home. We had a substitute and I wouldn't have to do a thing. I spent third-period biology ignoring the dowdy White female sub, along with the two dozen other kids in the class. The other half dozen or so threw paper, smashed chalk, played spades, threatened to leave, chased each other, yanked the window shades, ate no-name chips, juked to beats drummed out with pencils, interrogated this period's babysitter with the usual questions: *You married? Where you live? How you get this job? Can we go outside? Can we pleeeease go outside?* The substitute just passed out handouts on the new unit because she knew better than to try to classroom-manage or, God forbid, teach. When she did speak, to tell us what we were supposed to be trying to read about "reproduction," the only ones who heard were the sad innocents who always sat in the back and never said a word.

I could have easily held a conversation with Nakesha Murray, one of the few girls I talked to, but opening my mouth and maneuvering my tongue required effort I couldn't muster. I lived in my own head most of the time, and found my thoughts wandering to the nights before often. My sexual awakening was not turning out to be the wonderland I had thought it would be. A consequence of lost virginity, my moods had immediately taken on the unpredictability of agriculture. I thought I was in love. My kind of young, stupid, naïve love always flowed like liquid—fast, sloppy, without bounds. No one had taught me or told me about good old-fashioned love. Evenings with Leroy typically stunned me into immobility, my feelings torn equally in the disparate directions of pleasure, shame, guilt, and giddiness. My fresh heart hadn't yet learned how to navigate the tender emotions, so it just stood still and often the rest of me followed: my mind, my eyes, my legs, my voice if I was especially troubled.

I just lay my head down along my shoulder, turned over the black-and-white handout with alien babies curled up from months one to nine, and scribbled notes to Nakesha on the back. For the rest of the period I wrote Nakesha and Nakesha wrote me back, in between unbraiding and rebraiding her raggedy extensions that had come loose.

Girl, me and Leroy did it again last night. It was his birthday.

You nasty.

Why I gotta be nasty?

Mrs. Washington gonna kick yo ass if she catch you with her man.

She ain't gone catch us. We always stop way before she get off.

You gonna get pregnant.

No I ain't. He use a rubber most of the time.

Most of the time? What about the rest of the time?

A few times we don't, but he pull it out.

You stupid.

You jealous.

I don't want no old man.

Yeah he old, but that mean he know what he doin. Not like these stupid boys.

You ain't never been with no stupid boy. You only been with Leroy. He a stupid man.

They probably all stupid.

I wouldn't know.

Don't act like you don't know. Remember Charles, and Darnell, and I forgot that boy name who was your cousin friend? I bet Leroy do it better than all those dogs you been with.

I guess so. You keep on doing it. And my cousin friend name was Darius and he was good. Girl he made me cry.

Leroy make me cry too but I don't let him see. But anyway I'm gonna stop. I don't think I want to do it anymore.

Why?

I don't know. I want a real boyfriend. Somebody to go to the movies with. Somebody to talk to. Least they be sweatin you.

Well as long as you with pretend boyfriend, you need to be taking something.

You right. I'm not trying to get knocked up. But I don't want my mother finding no pills either.

Girl, I'm telling you, you need to go to the clinic with me and get that shot everybody else getting now. If you under eighteen, you ain't gotta pay.

I'm scared to get that shot. Everybody who get it turn fat and baldheaded.

Hate to tell you, but chick you already there.

So. You right there with me.

We could get the sticks. Then we won't be able to get pregnant for five years. This lady came to gym to talk to us about it that one day you wasn't there. That's free too.

But everybody say once they put those sticks in your arm nobody will take them out.

Take em out for what if they in there so you won't get knocked up?

I don't know. If you change your mind, I guess.

Yeah, I guess you could want to change your mind.

Like my Ma friend Myrtle got four kids and didn't want no more but she swole up like a balloon and was bleeding through her pants all the time with that stuff. We saw it in her arm cause she used to make them sticks wriggle like worms. But her doctor said they had to stay for five whole years or she had to pay 500 dollars. So she had to go to the emergency room when she tried to dig em out herself with a razor.

Damn, that's messed up.

See that's what I'm sayin.

So, let's get that shot. They say that's only for about six months. If we get fat and won't stop bleeding, then we won't get it again. I just know I'm not trying to get pregnant cause I don't want to be on no public aid. Cuz damn I do like doing it. Don't you?

Yeah I like it. And I guess having a baby is worse than having a gut or a bald head.

Well let's go to the clinic together and get that shot.

Alright. Let's go right after seventh period today and walk in before it get busy.

Okay. Meet me at the vending machines by the side door right after the bell.

Cool. Peace out.

IT WAS TRULY October in Chicago, because when Nakesha and I stepped outside the school building we shivered under the white sun. That time of the year, noisy blackbirds all joined wings like loud, excited schoolkids on a field trip holding hands. Normally, I didn't even notice them. I looked up, and there they were, making the only letter of the alphabet seen every year in the sky, all over the world. We were walking north, because the V pointed behind us. It was the first time I had looked up at the sky in what seemed at that moment like years.

"Damn, I forgot my sweater," I suddenly remembered, knowing I would have to explain its whereabouts to Ma if she noticed.

"You wanna go back and get it?" Nakesha asked me.

"Girl, I ain't going back in that tired building."

"I'll keep you warm," she said, putting her arm around my shoulder and pulling me in close.

We walked together like this beyond the three-story school building that consumed half a block, past the schoolyard disintegrating to a junkyard, and onto a busy city corner holding over a hundred kids who either had nowhere to go or did not want to go where they could. The hour after school was a chaotic and dangerous maelstrom, a time when disagreements sparked during the day were able to finally escalate into full-blown physical confrontations. Luckily, police cars remained until the multitude thinned. It was a tense hour, but if anybody had learned how to watch their back it was me. More than a few kids had been shot and killed over the years. Their shredded faces and chests were enough to frighten the innocence out of us, but weren't enough to earn a sound bite on the evening news. Perfect, permanent maroon circles on the sidewalk marked the most violent victims' falls, and after a few sorrowful weeks of reverence everybody usually forgot and started to walk over the circles again like they weren't even there.

Nakesha and I had never been the popular girls. We lacked the grades, boyfriends, hairstyles, faces, wardrobes, or personalities to earn notice and respect. Without talent to dance, dress, rap, sing, run, ball, or wisecrack, we were irrelevant to our peers. No matter we were good cooks or secretly interested in science, or that my eyes epitomized "almond-shaped" and

Nakesha's cheekbones surged forward to create an enviable hollow; we were too brown, too broke, too nappy-headed, too quiet, and too mysterious. Getting our hair done professionally was a necessity we couldn't afford, so we were always out of style. In our paycheck-to-paycheck households, a biweekly hair appointment was a laugh-out-loud suggestion we knew much better than to make. We may have owned two or three pairs of brand-name shoes and jeans, but beyond that we only bought the cheaper sweatpants and T-shirts with money we earned from babysitting. About the most we had going for us was our curvaceous bodies: narrow waists and thick bottoms that had cursed us to an everyday torrent of catcalls from men and boys who had no true interest in what we held inside. We sparkled when alone or around other girls fated to this category, but faded out in any crowd that refused to validate our existence.

Such a crowd had built up behind us without our knowing. Patrice Wallace led it, but Fred Ace Spade, Tasha Spruce, Jeanette Towns, and a copper boy named Tavares, whom I used to have the worst crush on, were her willing lackeys. Patrice was a big-boned, roguish, redbone girl with a face like a baby doll but a mouth like Richard Pryor back in the day. Her relation to a small-time rapper named Cognac had catapulted her to notoriety when his single "We Likes It Ruff" stayed at the top of the Coke Top Nine at 9 on 107.5 WGCI for all of the last summer. At the height of Cognac's success, Patrice took on the alias Patty-Cake and cashed in on a collection of boosted designer shoes, purses, and shades; their authenticity, as opposed to the banality of the cheap knockoffs rocked by everybody else, instantly transported her into the realm of the exotic, amusing, and cool. Though Cognac hadn't had a song much less a hit since, Patrice was determined to ride for as long as possible off her status as a mini-celebrity's baby cousin, making sure *no one,* especially not all the boys who had never paid any attention to her before, forgot she had provided the feminine pants and moans that were the song's claim to fame. She abused her position by taunting those like me who still hung desperately to the bottom rung of the popularity pole. She and her followers cornered us in our obvious hiding places: at the back corner tables of the cafeteria, on the way up-top rafters in the gym, in front of smudged girls' bathroom mirrors as we attempted to up our status with greasy beauty supply lipstick, watered down perfume sprays, and messy hair gels letting us down on the "baby" hair promise. A couple years before Patty-Cake and I had eaten lunch with the same group for a whole semester after Constitution class. Now we shared the same biology class, though we had never had reason to speak. Until today.

"*Ugh.* Look at them hugged all up. They must be *dykes.*"

We heard the crack—fighting words, really—although we kept walking like we hadn't heard her talking about (and to) us. To break apart would have been to acknowledge and corroborate her accusation, making matters worse. But cool nonchalance was never sufficient armor against determined heckling; our insistence on staying together proved a defiant remonstrance the bullies couldn't appreciate or understand. The taunting from several voices continued while we walked several blocks, well outside the nearest police officer's view. By the time we rounded the corner where the school could no longer be seen, we had heard them all:

Dyke. Butch. Femme. Lesbo. Pussy-chewer.

I protected myself by going deaf and dumb, an automatic self-numbing I had picked up and mastered with time. I walked hearing only my own footsteps.

"Well, I guess when don't no man want you, you gotta take what you can get," Tasha said.

"Bad enough they pass love notes in class," Patty-Cake

continued, slurring her words while she sucked sour apple
Laffy Taffys from in between her silver-glazed back teeth.

"Uh-uh!" Fred laughed. From that point forward, a dozen
kids with nothing better to do followed Patrice in tormenting
us. I felt like I had shrunk two inches. It wasn't long before
Nakesha and I quietly broke apart and sulked to opposite ends
of the sidewalk.

"They do be passing notes, every day in math, like boyfriend
and girlfriend."

"You mean boyfriend and boyfriend," Jeannette corrected.

"Who got gym with them bitches? Ladies, watch your ass
'cause you might catch 'em in the showers."

"Dripping wet and naked as they please!"

It wasn't even an original crack. He had stolen it from *The
Women of Brewster Place*. That imbecile's reference to a movie
we had all watched over and over again fueled an uproar that
the rest of the closet comics scrambled to upstage.

"Well it's hard to get a man when you look like one," Tasha
observed. "Tavares, don't Nakesha look like a man?"

"Why you asking me?"

"Ahhh . . . you don't want to say it. Come on, Fred, don't she
look like a man?"

"Not really. Her ass too fat for that."

"Naw . . . Shivana got the nice ass," Tavares answered, and I
was repulsed rather than relieved. "Nakesha booty kinda
thirsty, though."

"I'd do 'em," Tavares wanted us to know.

"You do anything!"

"I wouldn't do you."

"Nigga, you *wish* you could."

Patrice made sure to bring the roast back into focus: "Look,
the Garbage Pail Kids ain't hugging no more. We musta hurt
they feelings."

"If you don't shut the fuck up, I'm gone hurt you."

I had said it before I knew I would say it, turning around with flame in my eyes. My lethargy had abruptly ended. Nakesha stood trembling a few feet ahead, frozen and embarrassed. Debating on whether or not she would jump into the fight that was inevitable, her slight inch closer to me was a bold statement of alliance. Wearing crooked-over jelly sandals and no bra, I wasn't ready for battle myself, but enough was enough. Who did they think they were?

The whole heartless mob stopped in its tracks. Its general checked, they did not know the next move. So they fidgeted: hands shot to hips, fingers stifled giggles, necks twisted and jerked in anticipation. Patty-Cake's forehead furrowed with disbelief and disgust.

"You better shut the fuck up and keep on walking with your girlfriend, bitch."

My face had hardened into lockjaw. "Make me."

"Girl, don't play with me . . . ," was the only comeback Patty-Cake could muster. Caught off guard, she oddly veered toward the middle of the sidewalk as if planning to maneuver around me.

"I said *make* me, bitch."

Patty-Cake stopped cold this time. My obstinacy alone was enough to make her second-guess herself. She tried, unsuccessfully, to bring the ball back to her court.

"Why her shoes leaning over like trees ready to fall down?"

"Timber!" Wally shouted, melting their tension into comedy. But I remained still. I sensed the chink in my opponent's armor and used it as my fortress. We stared each other down like the first to fold would implode. I cried inside; the fight had been defused before it began, yet more troubling than a catfight was the fragility of remembrance. How quickly confidences, jokes, and conversation shared—even if only over a lunch break— could become moments too insignificant to dig up compassion.

Patty-Cake and I stared at each other like we were strangers. A single tear slipped out of my eye. I raised my hand to slap it away—hard. So hard a couple kids winced. When I saw their reactions, I slapped my face harder in the same place again. And again. And again, until I felt a handprint smarting on my face. The boys howled while the girls just frowned.

"Oh hell no . . . that bitch is crazy," one girl hissed through Bubblelicious.

"Come on, baby, she ain't even worth it," Tyshon finally declared, jamming an Afro pick into his scalp after wielding it like a harpoon. He grabbed Patty-Cake's arm and led her, finally, past her two targets. Sensing the curtain closing on her latest performance, she began an encore. She flailed her arms and tried to wriggle her torso out of Tyshon's tight grip.

"Naw, don't hold me back. Don't hold me back!"

"Let the bitch go!" Nakesha suddenly screamed, and again the mob faltered. I still had not moved one inch. My balled fists remained tight, my back stiff. Its point made, the handprint's sting vanished swiftly as a poltergeist. I wanted to smile because I had swept them away with just one funnel of my mind energy. It took the short yelp of an approaching CPD car to break the spell the mob had woven on me. The crowd hurried on. Rightfully demoted, Patty-Cake now lagged behind rather than in front. Patricia had not a shred of good-home training left in her bones. She suddenly turned around and spit at the ground. Nakesha and I just stood there with our hands on our hips, daring any one of them to look back, until the crew became a rambling speck against the horizon.

I had been dealt the hand of a life that left the living wondering why they had ever been born. It was a life choked by collision and battles: one after another, rolling up on me as forceful and determined as tides eroding a small island. I wasn't prepared for what was about to happen.

Neither me nor Nakesha felt like talking after that; our trip to the clinic was abandoned without either one of us having to say why, and at the Green Line near Fifty-fifth and King Drive we went our separate ways, knowing we would never, ever put our arms around one another again.

FROM THE VERY *first dream I had inside of Shivana, I was scared her story would end just like all the others. And that the end of her story would be the end of me.*

A new memory . . .

All around me, women hold hands and sing under a sky brimming with clouds waiting to break. This is something I've dreamed before, many times actually, though today I see the women standing on city concrete and not country road or a crop field's soil. There must be colors, but shades of gray are all I see. Six men appear at the mouth of a huge stone church with iridescent white crosses glowing on its graffiti-covered sides: portraits of Martin, Malcolm, and Mandela, a collage of images similar to ones found on a wall in the home of every grandmother who made it through the sixties. Framed by a light on the other side of paned doors, the men stand out of the gray and force me to look, though I'm not sure I want to. Their faces are grim with struggle because they are working hard, and together, to hold up the thing in their hands. I can't take my eyes off of them. I'm fascinated, like I am with all things in the real world. Their labor is like a careful dance, improvised more than choreographed. Their bodies are on one accord. As if their minds are connected, they move, flow, and adapt to one another depending: on whose hands get so sweaty they must let go to quickly wipe them to hold their grip, on whose weight must shift to accommodate another's laxity, on who must push and who must pull, on who must twist or lean as they change direction. Their compass—a heart no longer beating—lies inside the thing they carry. It guides each of them toward the correct maneuvers to accomplish their task. This rested heart is the axle around which the men pivot, slowly and silently out of reverence. Pallbearers never realize how heavy a coffin carting death will actually be, until they must keep it from falling.

I know I am at my first funeral. But whose, I don't know. Though I can't tell my age, I know I am old enough to understand and absorb the sadness. I am shrouded by women with blood for tears, and men who are bleeding sweat. The old woman who weaves in and out of my dreams is here again, her white head rag a halo I follow above a dark plain. I reach out to her because I don't know anyone else there to hold on to. She calms me with a single gaze, says nothing, only grabs my hand to lead me through the thickness. She knows I want to get closer to the heart no longer beating. She knows I want to see inside, both the coffin and the heart.

I want to ask her, "Who are you?" More importantly, "Who am I?" I want to know why visions of the life I may one day live trickle into dreams I share with my mothers. I want to know why the old woman never speaks. I want to know when the coffin carried will be mine, because if I have died then at least I will know I once lived.

This old woman weaves her way in and out of my dreams, with intensity more than frequency. Her face is sometimes blurred, sometimes she is headless and other times she is a talk-ing head. The white rag always appears before her face. Some-times she is younger, but she always comes as an elder. She rarely comes and when she does, she rarely stays, but still I won-der what she means to me.

The pallbearers ease their load into a hearse with no riders, except for one: a mother who has fainted from grief. The police department has sent cars to lead a processional to the burial, but I sense their presence is not needed or wanted on this side of town. Black people not part of the funeral furrow the street like a storm, feeling a part of others' sadness today because they don't know about their own tomorrow. We follow the parade of mourners from the church down a street called Cottage Grove; the black hearse leads us down the middle of the street. With my back turned to the mourners I am able to see color again. The buildings and people who live above them shine with the bright-ness of a shantytown. We walk past used furniture shops with their names weathered away from wooden signs, past chicken and fish joints that we can smell blocks before and after. The old woman leads me to the front of the crowd entering a cement-gated cemetery stretching several blocks, carries me really, like I am weightless, without gravity, in utero. When in my dream we push through the thick of bodies and heat to view a coffin opened for one last, final time, I look inside and still cannot see who it holds.

THERE WAS NO coffin for the first one. The very first girl, who could have been mine and I could have been hers, was Yoshi: fif-teen, just like Shivana, a girl unlucky enough to fall in love against others' advice and her own will. Like me, she was a soul in captivity; unlike me, by slavery and not by thwarted birth. When I first saw Shivana's wide, lucent, fresh baby eyes frag-mented through cracked glass, I hoped for a second that the *ocean had just rediscovered Yoshi, lifted her from its bottom to spit her out to give her back to me once again. And it would have only taken 150 years.*

The old maid Helene's stiff, enlarged, aching, broken, cut, tired, and indigo-stained hands had thrown Yoshi into the Atlantic. Nearby Cumberland Island was the only threat to her journey toward aquatic immortality, the only place she could wash up on land for thousands of miles, but Helene needed to take the chance that Yoshi just might make it on past the Golden Isles and into the open blue forever; in a lifetime and without a miracle, she could never make it far enough to wash up on Asia. Helene had had the help of a couple other women who participated despite their disagreement and disgust. But their matriarch had convinced the wailing women that it just wasn't right to permanently rest a carrying woman anywhere else.

"We gotta set the baby free," she had told them, while they unrolled Yoshi's body swathed in the unmended sheets Mrs. Parnell had donated out of mercy and guilt. "That there inside still gots a chance."

I see Helene, recall that it was she who first wore the white rag on her head, the day she rolled us forever away with a gentle, unnecessary finger push aided by the omniscient guidance of the moon tide. She sits in the high-noon shade of a Georgia oak so deeply rooted its massive, winding trunk was Parnell Estate's most frequent enclave for the slave children's occasional privilege of a game of hide-and-seek. She holds a field hand's fussy newborn in one hand and a crisp, stolen letter in the other. Though she can't actually read the words Helene can't stop staring at the letter, a stone of gloom weighs so heavy in her stomach she doesn't realize every baby she has held that day immediately starts howling. The day before this one, under the cover of dawn, Helene had met the Missus' helpmate, my Yoshi. The crackle of their footsteps on fallen acorns was the only sound cutting the silence. Out of necessity and fear, Helene and Yoshi first kept their voices to a whisper but by the end they were mouthing most of their words. And today, Helene couldn't stop crying.

Last night Parnell's oldest three boys had dug a bowl-shaped hole in the ground, round and wide enough for Yoshi's four-month-old pregnant belly. They had carried her away from the main field and closer to where the stud Hind stayed, both so he could see and so no one else could hear. They had placed her belly in the hole, her face in the dirt, one of their hands on the back of her head, and delivered the twenty cowlicks Parnell had ordered. For theft, he explained, though all she had stolen was the letter that told her she was about to be sent far away from her family. This morning, Yoshi had suddenly stopped moaning as the women (not one her mother, who couldn't stand to see) dressed her wounds. The seamstress Ethel reported how much of Yoshi's blood was splashed throughout the cypress trees and sawgrass near Hind's cabin; she had not seen that much blood since the day in 1829 when a couple mares, unexpectedly wild from the scent of thirty women's moon-synchronized cycles, had stomped to death the babies the working women housed in a shallow trough dug around their part of the sweet potato field. Just three years old, Yoshi had been the only baby spared, though she often dreamed the nightmare but didn't know its origins. This was long before Helene had sat down to watch over the babies. Remembering that day, that blood, and finally Yoshi, Helene could not stop crying.

Her eyesight has faded to a distorted and cloudy gray, so trying to recognize even one word was futile. But she thought she exactly remembered Yoshi's tearful reading, first aloud, then in silence as the reality of the words spilling from her mouth stole her voice. So by the end Yoshi was only moving her mouth, manipulating her lips, but she made no sound. She had arrived barefoot and trembling at exactly 5:00 A.M., the hour whispering women had spread to Helene that she must wait under the oak in order to learn what the young girl had claimed, "I just can't

*keep to myself." Staring at the swirling characters today, Helene
heard the memory of Yoshi sounding out the same words she
could not stop crying over:*

October 11, 1842

Sir Hale:

In response to your recent inquiry concerning the matter of
my deceased father's debts to Hale Plantation and Estate for
various resources borrowed before his death and
bequeathing of all property to my brother and me, I have
devised what I feel to be a mutually beneficial solution. In
hopes of dissolving the current debt (plus interest) of $5000,
which primarily represents the borrowing of articles of
husbandry and farming implements, I am offering you a
choice purchase of one healthy, fertile, young colored girl. In
particular, allow me to suggest our current house girl, whom
records show my father bought in 1830 from an Anderson
Buckley of South Carolina as part of a family, her portion
costing $600. She is currently pregnant and, as far as I know,
capable of further breeding. Her mother had previously
produced six offspring for my father, most of whom he sold
before his death in order to stave off bankruptcy. One of
which, an older buck, I recently sold for $1,400 and just
received a most glowing report on his productivity. But this
one I offer, a perhaps 14 or 15-year-old girl, remains here
and has to date conceived one child. Therefore, I see no
reason why she could not birth six to eight offspring,
especially since she has gotten off to an early start.

Because she is in her reproductive prime, I am sure I
could get close to $2000 if I sold her alone on the market
today. What I am urging you to consider, Sir Hale, is the
opportunity to benefit not only from her productivity but

also from the potential value of her offspring. For such old and high debts these are long-term considerations, I know. However, I am urging you to take into account your decades-long relationship with my father, as well as the future of this property. Its survival at this point is dependent upon the generosity of men like you. I urge you to look within your heart for kindness and mercy, as I am doing all I can to keep my father's legacy alive and to secure the financial future of this estate for my own offspring. I thank you for your many years of kindness, and wait eagerly for your reply.

Sincerely,

Mr. Jonathan Parnell

Once Helene had gotten all the way to the bottom a third time, the newborn started howling again so loud even the swallows shel-tered in oak tree leaves scatter. A six-year-old girl walks toward them, smiles under a mud-coated bonnet, her scratched, ashy, and lanky limbs buried under her shift of compounded refuse.
"Why y'all crying, Miss Helene?"
"We sad, Daisy Mae."
"How you know my name, Miss Helene?"
"Why wouldn't I? I know'd you since before you was born."
And she had known them all, most at least. At seventy-six, Helene was too old for field work but too proud to sit down all day. She had already relegated herself to watching more chil-dren than she could reasonably keep an eye on, long before the senior Parnell came to her and suggested she finally "get some rest." This was shortly after he discovered he himself was moving toward eternal rest. Helene found comfort in the simplicity of her new role. Unable to remember her own childhood before almost seventy years of backbreaking work had begun, she refashioned it through the children she oversaw. The toddlers passed time

giggling softly among themselves, laughing, staring at the moons on their fingernails, winding and rewinding the bandages on their feet that passed for shoes, making toys from buttons, sun-dried mud, and twigs. The older ones roughhoused, waited, flirted, courted, and playfully antagonized those even younger. They stood tall against the horizon outlining the tobacco or sweet potato fields that were their future and their fate, their spines and spirits not yet bent; occasionally, one of them would ask her to referee their stickball game or a round of marbles fashioned from fire-roasted clay. She always happily obliged, setting down the baby she held in a nest of leaves, leaning in close to the game, itching for one of them to beg her for a tip or an opinion.

Long before others knew, Helene had suspected Yoshi might be "in the family way." For one thing the young girl had been craving dirt, tearing in secret at the Johnson grass to uncover the mushy blackness underneath. One day Helene caught her and inquired if she had been receiving her rations. Then Helene took mental note that there was still fullness in the girl's breasts, fleshiness in the face, no hard edges suggesting marrow was just one layer away, though oddly her breasts stayed flat as a bird's folded wings. Helene drew her own conclusions and waited for the girl's midsection to tell. Yoshi's sudden departure from the field and assignment to estate housework was all the evidence anyone needed; after losing too many would-be workers to mis-carriages in the fields, Mr. Parnell had come to his senses and realized that maybe carrying women were entitled to a little bit lighter work. One of Miss Helene's own had come unattached before he made that decision. Yoshi confessed to Miss Helene one day after a now-rare trip far and deep into the field from the big house where she cooked, washed, served, ran errands, and played with sun-haired babies. Over a still-steaming pan of left-over turkey meat clinging to a massive bone, she suddenly said: "Miss Helene, I gots me one inside."

"So I see," Helene said, tearing the meat apart as fast as she

could. Her aged, rigid fingers were not fast enough for the children who had scattered in line; knowing there might not be enough by the time she got to the back, a mêlée had already erupted from too many attempting to cross ahead.

"Who the fella?" Helene asked without taking her eyes off the meat. She knew the answer. She sucked dramatically on the meaty strings caught between her teeth, so as to make its flavor outlast its swallowing so she could save the actual meat for the beggars in front of her.

"It's Hind," Yoshi answered.

Yoshi knew to leave it at that. There would be no announcement, no wedding, no signal or symbol to everyone else, no "taking up," no jumping a broom. Hind's dangerous good looks were fact but his loyalty was legend; with not enough capable men to go around, the senior Parnell had pegged the wide-backed and broad-shouldered Hind when he was just sixteen to be the bullet aiming for the womb of each and every girl over thirteen. No one knew how many he had fathered since, in the ten years that the Parnells had monthly chosen a new girl to spend their evenings away from her family and in Hind's far-off cabin. For the fresh young virgins, the love glow smacked on their faces by thirty days of Hind refused to go away until they noticed another girl packing a satchel and marching in his cabin's direction. Since Yoshi had finished her thirty glorious days, the first couple spent resisting but the last couple spent begging him to let her stay, she had watched a couple girls come back lit up, renewed. Most likely carrying as well. But her glow still hadn't faded, and it had been a couple of months.

"Best get over it quick," Helene warned as the glow shone, stern eyebrows raised to reinforce the command. The children frenzied and elbowed each other at the sight of only a couple slices left. Helene ignored them. She could only do so much with a carcass picked damn near clean by greedy and wasteful White folks, she knew. She continued:

"*Ain't gone be no family. You gots one so best get ready to have some mo'. Hind can't wife you and the child ain't gone never know the daddy name.*"

Shamefaced, Yoshi had walked back to the house. And the last time Miss Helene was to see her, she would be on the crest of the Atlantic, swathed in dingy, torn sheets tarnished with our blood.

Miss Helene had been right. Not about Hind because that no longer mattered anyway, but about me and the ocean. A soul smothered by bloodstained dirt has nowhere to go. Rolling through effervescence, tumbling through tides, 360-degree turns over and over and over again, life reincarnated and swallowing itself whole, her impulse had given me a new chance to be born.

THREE

IN THE CRACKED glass mirror of my building's elevator, I checked my face and found it to be in the same condition it was that morning: ugly. My small afternoon triumph had not been powerful enough to correct that. I saw nothing of the slim, precise, glamorous features of the video girls and stars everybody at school admired: Janet Jackson, Tracy Spencer, Vanessa Williams. I wished my features weren't so puffy, bloated, and dull. As soon as I was old enough to realize what the rest of the world thought was pretty, I started longing for the surprise of green or hazel eyes, a freckled nose, wavy hair flecked with bronze and gold, and red rosy cheeks on a Black girl. My biggest disappointment was a boring complexion: a medium, pecan-pie brown I shared with too many others. I wished I was half-breed light like the girls who were up for homecoming and prom queens every year, but instead I had to settle for a common, muddy tone. I wasn't even colored enough to be called Shaka Zulu, or for the well-meaning Big Mamas to declare me "pretty, to be so dark." I wouldn't have cared about the insults or the compliment sliced in half. Some attention was better than none.

Not a punch had been thrown earlier, but I still felt sore deep down inside. I forgot to push number three when I stepped onto the elevator. I watched the numbers light up to six, felt a slight chest pound as I imagined Leroy stepping into the car. I always hoped to run into him outside the apartment, where I could have at least spent time with him without worrying about holding down my skirt. He wouldn't have dared touch me in the elevator, but we could have talked a bit at least. I would have ridden all the way down to one with him, maybe even walked outside in the sun. Suddenly I realized I had never stood out in the sunlight next to my love, never even walked with him on a street. Never seen him that much, really, outside his apartment. Once, at the beginning of one of my shifts, he was going to make a run to McDonald's for dinner while Renelle was still home; he had asked me to ride with him, but then Renelle suddenly decided to leave early and so I was stuck in their apartment with the children. Almost as if she knew he had his eyes on me. A woman who had a claim on a man could always sniff out another woman who had his nose open.

But still, I wondered what it would be like to make love with someone I could also make a public display with. I saw them all the time, kids my age leaning against each other while they waited for the bus, holding hands on the train amid a crowd of friends, French-kissing in between counting out change on the counters of cheap Chinese food and chicken joints. I was both jealous and pleasured by watching those who couldn't control their lust, though it caused me to doubt my own state of mind. I shut off feelings for my old man when I shut the door to his home. I was sure he did the same, if not sooner. But when I watched others in love, I noticed it was hard for them to control their affectionate gestures. I had recently learned a vocabulary word—*smitten*—and needed to know if it applied to me. Leroy's wife and children complicated matters, of course, but if he really wanted to see me all the time (like he claimed he did) I worried that he could control his desire so well. That if I myself was able to contain it, suppress it, summon and command it, block it out when out of the moment, then was it even really love for me?

The grasshopper boy from the night before stood in front of the elevator door when it opened at six, still carrying that raggedy basketball. His tank top was red this time. He hesitated when he saw me. I sucked in my breath silently, but then stepped from in front of the door and back into the crook of the car to make room. I folded my arms and waited for him to speak. He grunted " 'Sup?"

"You got nerve asking me a question," I spat. I smiled in spite of myself, shifting my weight toward him. He followed my lead.

"You still on last night? I said I was sorry . . ."

"You shouldn't be bouncing balls that late anyway," I told him. "Makes too much noise. You know people do work around here . . ."

I was hoping he would tell me where his "around here" had been before it was here.

"I know, that's why my aunt put me out in the hallway, 'cause I was making so much noise last night."

"Ain't that telling you something?"

He whistled air, not music.

"It seems like somebody's always telling me something."

The elevator stopped on number three. I stepped to the door before it opened, calling back once I stepped outside, "Maybe you should start listening."

This time, I looked back at him. He was standing with his mouth open, a slight smile on his face, obviously amused. The next thing I knew he was jumping out of the elevator and following behind me. I really wanted to know what he thought he was doing. I was figuring out, slowly but surely, that grown men weren't shit. I wasn't about to get tangled up in a young one's web.

"Where you live in here?" he asked.

"You really don't need to know all that," I told him, stopping so neither one of us could go any farther.

"Damn!" he said. "I ain't no murderer or nothing. I'm just trying to meet my neighbors. You know, be friendly and all that nice shit."

I didn't say a word, only folded my arms.

"I guess you ain't friendly," he said.

"It's not that." He seemed like one of the dudes at school who was always chasing some girl but never getting her, either because he wasn't wearing the right sneakers or his fade wasn't shaped up right. Minor obstacles that he wouldn't even realize or care he needed to fix. But even those guys didn't bother to speak to me. I was confused.

"I'm just not trying to make any new friends right now," I eventually told him.

"Not even one who just moved here?" he asked me. I started walking again, slowly. I had the feeling that he would watch me go all the way to my apartment anyway, so I might as well just hurry up and get there. I had to make sure not to open the door too wide. For all I knew, he was a hype trying to case me and my apartment. We didn't have much, but I knew any desperate thug could find ways to capitalize on the older model television, VCR, and stereo sitting in our living room. Not to mention my mother's records and all my cassette tapes.

"Hell no!" I shouted. "You wanna be friendly with me then we can go out, out of the building."

"Where you wanna go?"

I just smirked at him and rolled my eyes. I had never been asked on a date, but I damned sure knew the way to go about it wasn't by me having to tell him he had to take me on one.

"Anywhere," I said, and then just walked away. "I don't need you to walk me to my door."

"Yeah, I guess I gotta come pick you up at your door when we go on our date," he said.

I just laughed and kept walking. I guess he had some pride, because he stopped in his tracks.

"Like on Friday, I can just come back and we can go out somewhere," he said.

"Yeah, yeah . . . ," I muttered under my breath. Promises, promises. He obviously didn't know who he was talking to. I wasn't about to get all excited just because somebody I didn't even know claimed he was going to take me somewhere. He was probably lying, just wanted to promise me some bullshit to see if I would go with him right now and end up fucking him in his boy's bed.

"See you later," I called back.

"A'ight," he said. "Friday night."

And just as I had predicted, he was still standing in the middle of the hallway when I reached my apartment door. He was waiting for me, watching me from behind. Like he *really* liked me, and wanted to see all of me that he could, even my backside slipping into my apartment. I should have been excited, speechless that I was finally getting the attention that I wanted. But that's not what it felt like at all. I couldn't get excited about Friday at seven because I knew how I would feel if I opened the door that night and he wasn't standing there. I pulled my keys out and put them in the lock so that he wouldn't have a second to respond to what I was about to tell him. And I gave him a look to let him know he shouldn't even think of coming over to change my mind.

"I just remembered," I lied, "I got something to do on Friday. So I can't go nowhere."

.   .   .

RIGHT BEFORE I opened the door, I heard the soundtrack to *Lady Sings the Blues* and smelled the scent of Shalimar. These two meant one thing: Aunt Jewel was in town.

I wasn't used to being greeted with tight, sincere after-school hugs. But Aunt Jewel was not like her sister, my mother. She flew from the kitchen where they had been listening to records and smoking Salem cigarettes. I could barely flub "Hey, Auntie Jewel" before I was in a grip.

"Come here, love, and give your auntie some sugar!"

Aunt Jewel talked with her whole body; by herself, she was a congregation. She couldn't stop her shoulders from shimmying or her neck from rolling while she stood before me with arms outstretched, radiant in a snug black rayon dress patterned with dots as orange as California poppies in the wild. She couldn't have known about the swollen tenderness in my breasts, and squeezed shy giggles out of me despite the discomfort.

"Every time I see you, I swear I'm reminded I'm getting old," she said.

"You just seen her last summer," my mother said in between blowing smoke circles. "She ain't that much bigger . . ."

"Well, I don't see Miss Thang every day like you do, Annette," Jewel replied. "And every time *I* see her, if she hasn't grown up she's definitely grown out. Look at those hips!"

Aunt Jewel playfully slapped my behind as Ma sauntered back to the kitchen tucked in the rear wing of our L-shaped two-bedroom apartment. Emboldened by the surprise visit of the one relative who brought gifts rather than grief, I sashayed to the beat of Diana Ross singing "Ain't Nobody's Business" as I followed them. By the time we arrived in the humid kitchen, the record had started to skip. Pearls of blood had finally started to pop out of the flour-coated chicken wings tumbling in a cast-iron pot of grease. Instinctively, Jewel tended to the music and I grabbed a fork to rotate the meat. I knew better than to

let the blood bleed out and into hardened knobs of brown before the chicken was ready. I had not forgotten the stinging
thwacks on my lower back when Ma had once bit into a thigh
that drizzled red. It was my chore to fix us both something to eat
on the nights I didn't babysit, but Ma shooed me out of the way
tonight. She wasn't about to let her apathy toward domestic du-
ties shave even more off her womanhood than her baby sister's
kittenish allure already had.

Me and Ma spent our evenings tiptoeing out of each other's
way, or trying to think of things to say. We hadn't always been
this strained. Before I shot past her height we had been thick as
thieves. Sidekicks whose outfits, earrings, barrettes, and finger-
nail polish were color-coordinated just for the reactions of others.
It had been nothing for us to spend hours watching television,
running errands, or simply digging through curls to massage
each other's scalps. But our honeymoon ended around the time
I got my first period, which showed up early when I was nine.
Four brown dots in the daisy-yellow panties I had showed her
snatched Ma out of recess. Her affirmative sidekick was actually a real person and evolving woman, no longer a doll. She
stopped calling me "her baby" after that, and I started saying
Ma instead of Mommy. Friends and aunts had been no help—
they only told Ma amplified horror stories of their own girls
smelling themselves. Had Grandma still been living, Ma may
have had someone to convince her that a little blood hadn't
turned me into a possessed haint hell-bent on discovering and
pointing out her shortcomings.

"She's still a baby, just musty now—from attitude and everything else," was something Grandma would have advised. But
Grandma couldn't be heard below her simple rectangle of slate
in Woodlawn Cemetery. The whippings intensified to beatings
and finally fights as my mother struggled to maintain sover-
eignty over me though I hadn't yet rebelled.

"They always test it before you have to break down and put a foot in that ass," I heard one after-work drinking friend telling Ma in the kitchen one day. Ma was complaining about my increasing hours on the phone, talking to nobody but girls I wouldn't talk to for long. Later that night the first hard, insulting strike occurred when she discovered me gabbing under the covers. My pride was so wounded I couldn't speak to her for days. Once my silent treatment abated the cloud of tension in the house never quite evaporated. Before she fought me, she had fought her old man—not my father, but this once-promising older guy who had lived with us for a couple of years before suddenly packing just two bags and his stereo equipment.

Soon after that Ma's eyes became sodden sinkholes, blank upon casual glance from those who couldn't possibly know what lie behind them. However, to me they were two little crystal balls peeking into a past I had no desire to borrow from for my future. In them, I peered at a carousel of incidents too frightening to recall, too mystifying for my young mind to confront, too incomprehensible for Ma to forget:

A childhood fall from the almost top boat of an Indiana state Ferris wheel. Injured memory and a permanent, iron-shaped gash smack in the middle of her forehead. A four-year stint in the "slow" class because her talent of drawing and sewing things wasn't considered fast. A brother first lost to crack and now simply lost. The quick stroke death of her daddy. The languid, agonizing, demoralizing demise of Grandma, who refused chemo but discovered death would take its time if that's what it felt like doing. Of course, the still unexplained exit of my father. And the tubes she burned as a result, and because public aid made it free.

She couldn't affect or console my shaky self-esteem when her own self-worth had been chiseled down to the nub by bad skin, bad luck, bad men, and bad timing. In my eyes, Ma's life had been a purr and not a howl; she was a hermit whose visitors had dwindled to regret, anger, and self-hate. So it was my auntie Jewel whom I looked to for hope.

The day Jewel graduated high school, she had run away from her family's overcrowded Robert Taylor Homes apartment and into the arms of a hefty truck driver who promised to show her the Grand Canyon. They only made it to Idaho before she discovered he had a wife, but Jewel couldn't turn back after seeing that, indeed, the grass *was* greener. She had been to college, several actually, but she had never stayed long enough to earn any degrees. She had been an actress, inviting our lazy family to plays in dingy Midwest churches and community theaters. No one ever wanted to go. She had danced on cruise ships and worked at Disney World, but Ma would never let me escape to visit. She had been a medical secretary for almost a decade in Denver, earning just enough to pay her bills and leave the country twice each year. Her postcards from places we could barely pronounce were stuffed down deep in my panty drawer. It was during that decade that we only saw her twice: at Grandma's and Granddaddy's funerals.

I quickly gathered she had arrived in Chicago this afternoon to tell her big sister that, on the ledge of midlife, she was finally ready to "have some babies and lay down some roots." Though she had been there less than an hour, the apartment had already freshened itself off Jewel's jubilant air. Like most femmes fatales, her intoxicating and bewitching scent was the result of her reliance upon and fascination with all things fancy. She carried the long, soft leather pocketbooks people smelled before their owners pulled them out. Hair products with *African, Black,* or *Nubian* in their names were not "effective" enough for Jewel; she preferred her products not only manufactured by White men, as most were, but also bearing their names: Calvin Klein, Christian Dior, Valentino. Her bright, powdery, metallic lipsticks and eye shadows were fragranced in excess, so much so that leaning in to kiss her face was like stepping into a flower garden. When she came back to Chicago she would only venture (in a called-for cab, of course) to State Street's Carson Pirie

Scott or Marshall Field's for new underwear and bras to get her through the latest stay; once, I had opened a stately white shopping bag of flimsy, lacy things and immediately recognized the crisp, clear scent of the big stores downtown that I never got to visit. Jewel wore sturdy shoes too distinguished to harbor sweat and odors, and they held on to their same exact shape even after she removed them; I longed for such shoes—unlike the lazy, clearanced sandals and sneakers that lolled flat and crooked as soon as I took them off, as if they had been holding their breath the entire time they were on my feet.

Aunt Jewel was the one member of my family nobody talked of, but everybody talked about. They cared not to spread the news of her travels, hobbies, or accomplishments. Instead, cousins said she was strange. Elders not used to a woman being single and unhappy rather than married and unhappy said she was gay. City folk too provincial to accept the cosmopolitan rumored her head wraps hid a bald head. Uncles whose barbecue she snubbed out of concern for her waistline called her narrow-hipped and cautioned their meat was just what she needed to sprout the man-traps. She never failed to dress like the place she was going to was much more important than the place she was coming from, so when she visited Chicago folks always wanted to know why she was dressed "up" as opposed to down. Only the little kids recognized and respected her eccentricity for what it was—genius sprinkled with the nonchalance necessary to bring it out. I was one of those little kids, and she was the closest thing to a princess I had ever seen. In her thirty-seven years—twenty of those spent in complete surrender to kismet—she had never ached for marriage. She had pulled many men's creased, bent photos from her wallet, but never labored over wedding invitations. She avoided explaining when the family pressed for juicy details, never divulged if he had asked and she had said no or if he had ever asked at all. She simply discarded their photos and moved on to the next.

But this summer, on a solo excursion to Harlem just to *"cross it off the list,"* she had met a man named Hakim who owned a barbershop in Brooklyn. After just a couple of his visits to her current city—Memphis—he had asked her to play house with him in New York. She quit her customer service job, shipped boxes to Brooklyn, closed out her savings, and found she had just enough to spare a month of leisure with the big sister she had drifted so far away from. Hakim would come to get her before Thanksgiving.

"What makes you think this man is worth you packing up and moving across the country?" Ma snorted as she turned to open aluminum cans of Aldi's sweet corn and string beans. Behind her back, Jewel frowned. She refused to dress down for the sake of acceptance but had no choice but to eat down when she came around us. After tasting everything from calabash to quince in their native countries, she never understood why her family never invested in fresh produce, why we couldn't think to stash away income tax checks for anything more than cars, jewelry, and clothes.

"You've always been a skeptic, Ann," Jewel said. "Shivana, your mama is still as mean as she was the day she came home from the hospital after the Ferris wheel."

That is how friends and family often spoke of Ma—before and after the Ferris wheel.

"The Ferris wheel didn't make me mean—people did," Ma said as she lifted bubbling hot pieces of chicken from the grease. She braced herself for a scorching splash if one should fall, though thirty years of frying chicken had perfected the careful wrist twist I still occasionally fumbled.

"Mama and Daddy made us mean long before other people stepped into the picture," Jewel countered. "Shivana, you'd get pretty mean if you were holed up all the time in the house with a Bible and a broom."

Before I could smile, Ma had started to put me down.

"She's about to be holed up in the house with a Bible and belt," she said. "She's got just as fast . . ."

"Oh Annette don't tell me you're still whipping this child." Jewel stood up and grabbed me. "She's grown!"

I hated being regarded a minor by the one relative whose opinion actually counted, but it had been so long since I had been held tight by anybody. I wanted to melt into a puddle Jewel could scoop into one of her perfume bottles. She could take me on her journeys, release tiny sprays of my spirit into the sky above places I had only seen in the movies.

"Don't spare the rod," was all Ma offered. Jewel sat back down in the kitchen chair whose pleather seat was peeling. She specialized in changing subjects.

"So, Shivana, what you doing in school this year?"

I couldn't say fending off bullies, waiting on books, and feeling sorry for the teachers.

"This year I got biology, English, world history, physical science, gym, and study hall," was all I told her.

"Gym?!? Study hall?!? What about drama, art, pottery, music?"

Jewel's eyes bucked and her voice screeched when she got excited. Ma turned around as fast as if she was going to slap me; she always said I was Jewel growing up all over again. No wonder we couldn't get along, because she and Jewel never had.

"Now Jewel, you know they done cut all that out of these schools," Ma said.

"How could they?" She was back on her feet with her arms flailing. "It's what our kids need. Things have gotten even worse than they were back in our day!"

"I was in the choir all last year, remember?" I asked, remembering how much I had loved to go to music. I took over Ma's seat; my forehead was sweating and the back of my tongue suddenly tasted salty.

"Of course I remember—I drove five hundred miles for your Christmas concert. Do *you* remember?"

I just nodded, wondering if the wrinkled, shrunken, microwaved hamburger I had for lunch was responsible for my nausea. The chicken, Jewel, the nearby garbage room—I had smelled all of it more powerfully than I should have. I should have wondered if I was pregnant then, but the signs are always missed by a young girl who knows she ain't got no business being knocked up. I welcomed the knock on the front door as my excuse to go downstairs for air.

"I'll get it," I shouted as they droned on.

"Annette, how are we supposed to open up the world for our kids if the powers that be refuse to cultivate their minds?"

"Who you askin'?"

"See, this is the problem . . . Black kids need to learn how to imagine, to create! All these schools want to do is give these kids a ball or a microphone. Pipe dreams! No real futures. They did the same thing to us and look at what our options turned out to be. Shivana's a bright girl. She can do anything in this world she wants to do. She deserves better . . ."

"What the hell you 'spect me to do about it without no money to send her nowhere else? Now Jewel, don't come up in my house with that old-fashioned Panther shit . . ."

"This is not the Panthers talking—I been over that stage for a long time. This is me. Your sister. Jewel. Annette, you ought to let me take that child to New York."

"Hold on—now you've lost your ever-loving mind."

"You want her to sit here in Chicago all her life, up under you? Same way Mama tried to make us sit here up under her? This life is too short, Ann . . ."

"Now see, you ain't gotta bring Mama into this . . ."

"Yes I do! I loved her just as much as you, but she didn't want us to do shit but sit here up under her and keep her company while Daddy was out doing God knows what. Died before her time but looked years ahead of it."

"How you know what she looked like when you wasn't nowhere to be found?"

"Mama sat in Chicago all her life walking around the same two blocks!"

"Everybody ain't like you, Jewel . . ."

"What do you mean by that?"

My eavesdropping ended with a louder knock on the door.

"Girl, would you get that damn door!"

Above the music and Ma's scolding, I heard the cough grown to a shaking hack. Renelle Washington and her kids stood in the hallway. Renelle had been crying and the boy's nose was running. Renelle didn't ask if she could barge in.

"Shivana, I'm gonna need you to watch the kids all this week. I might not be able to pay you 'til next month though . . ." She could barely get the words out before she broke down, shuddered, and dropped both babies' hands.

"What's wrong?"

"Girl, they done arrested Leroy."

I slammed the door. Going down for air was no longer important.

There was always enough for everybody when Black women cooked. Ma was more than used to not seeing people she barely knew until all hell broke loose. An unspoken rule, strangers who rarely spoke could default to blood when a shoulder to cry on was needed. So Ma calmly gave up her seat and started to scoop plates after I brought Renelle into the kitchen. I led the kids away from their mother and offered chicken wings to keep them quiet. I made sure to pluck the stiff stray feathers often left behind because they always scared Junior to tantrum. I eased down the faded yellow kitchen counter, stopped at the sink, and pretended to stare out the window even though there was nothing to view but a brick wall. I chewed softly so as not to miss a word. Once Jewel got over the sight of the frantic neighbor and her unkempt children, she took the lead as usual.

"I'm Annette's sister, Jewel . . . honey, what's got you so upset?"

A tear-soaked sigh rippled up Renelle's rib cage before she began.

" 'Bout two o'clock this afternoon, right before I'm getting ready to go to work, the police came knocking on our door telling us they needed to search our house."

"Did they have a warrant?" was the first thing Jewel thought to ask.

"They showed us a paper, but before we could look at it they had pulled out handcuffs and locked me and Leroy to the radiator."

Ma looked ready to faint. Jewel slid a Salem out of its neon-green carton and passed it to Renelle.

"In front of the babies?"

"*In front* of my babies!"

"How the hell can they handcuff you before they arrest you?" Jewel screamed.

"Chile these police do what the hell they want to do, when they want to do it," Ma said. "I just watch 'em every day while I'm on my bus, and I swear on every corner they got some boy throwed over a hood with his pants damned near down. Most of the time, you know it's for nothing. But what can you do?"

"Lord, today . . . ," was all Jewel could think to say. She put a lighter to the cigarette quivering between Renelle's lips, then Renelle went on after a long drag.

"My babies was screaming and crying, 'Mommy, Daddy, what's going on?' I mean, they could have at least let me put them in the room or something . . ."

"At the very least!" Jewel shouted.

"Next thing I know they was going through my house turning over the furniture, tearing our clothes out the closets, breaking plates in my kitchen, pictures on my wall, trashing my house like our stuff was nothing but junk in the alley." Jewel and Annette leaned in close, the climax impeded by Renelle's sobs. Ma passed her a dish towel for the tears and Jewel rubbed her back, shaking her head in disbelief of the law's wretched ways.

I could hardly keep from screaming, "Bitch, what happened to Leroy!?!" I went back to the stove for seconds and into the refrigerator for the Kool-Aid I knew the kids would soon be asking for.

"Next thing I know they was breaking up the tile in my kitchen, and that's when they found it."

"What?" And Jewel, her true idealistic self, really needed to be filled in.

"Well . . ." She was rightfully too ashamed to tell, but she knew she couldn't come into another woman's house and raise hell without resting it.

"My husband had been slinging a little rock—just on the side 'cause we been wanting to buy a house." She sensed their disapproval, and hoped they weren't street smart enough to know that no inner-city police department had time or resources to waste on "a little."

"I knew it wasn't right, I didn't want him doing it. I had begged him to quit."

With no word for or against, she picked up they must be against. I knew my place, which was not in a position to open my mouth. Junior slurped loudly as he emptied his grape Kool-Aid cup and held it up to me for more. I batted his hand away while his mother continued. I shook inside, waiting for Renelle to get on with it already. But the apology, not that she owed us one, had taken over:

". . . the money helped. I mean, with the kids' clothes and the bills. Leroy couldn't get no real job with his leg messed up from that motorcycle accident back in the day. And well, because of his old record. But he was just trying to buy us a house. I thought about getting a second job but I'm pregnant and trying to finish nursing school and working full-time already . . . I just couldn't handle no more . . . But I knew it wasn't right. I should have done the right thing and made him quit. And those people *never* came to our house . . ."

Seeing no end in sight, Jewel finally interrupted: "Where is your husband now?"

Renelle shuddered. Telling the truth always actualized it.

"At Cook County. On ten thousand bail."

"Jesus . . . ," Ma exhaled, and went to the freezer for the pint of Seagram's she kept for these moments. She confined the shot glasses to a high cabinet above the refrigerator so she wouldn't be tempted to retreat to her former pastime of drinking with nobody but Frankie Beverly and Maze. She stood on a chair to retrieve the glasses. Renelle cried soundlessly in prelude to one of Jewel's unavailing monologues.

"Now Mrs. . . . ?" was how it began.

"Washington. Mrs. Washington. Just call me Renelle."

"Now Renelle, I can't say that I agree with your husband pushing dope but that's not my business. I don't pay your bills. I can barely pay my own. But I will say that I find something a lot wrong with the police traumatizing these children. Why does it have to turn into a *Cops* episode every time they want to arrest us? I can't imagine your husband wouldn't have let them just take him down to the station for a little questioning. They could have saved the rough-up for there, because you know when they tell you questioning they really mean battering. See, this is why, Annette. This is *why*! This is why I packed my bags and got the hell out of this city and I didn't let you, Mama, Daddy, or nobody else stop me . . ."

"Black folks get arrested all over this world, Jew Jew, not just Chicago."

"Well, *Ann,* I didn't hear a lot of these stories in Denver." Jewel smarted every time Ma put her in her place with her childhood name.

"You live in Denver?" Renelle cried to the stranger. "I'm sorry, I forgot your name."

"Jewel. My name is Jewel. And I used to live in Denver."

"Denver? Wow, that's far." Renelle took a shot and Ma poured her another. She had finally stopped crying, leaned back, and in anticipation of more shots to come, unpopped the brass button on her faded stonewashed Cherokee jeans.

"Denver is a hike, but I swear you ain't lived till you've seen the sky well above sea level. I loved it. Not to change the subject 'cause I know you're upset, but you know, the West really is uncharted territory. Land and land and more land for miles."

"I wouldn't know," Renelle said. "I been in Chicago all my life. I have family in North Carolina, and Mississippi, and Arkansas."

"Oh, yes, the South!" Jewel exclaimed, savoring the gesture of dangling a shot more than the shot itself. "I just came from living in Memphis, which come to think of it ain't no better than Chicago. It's war down there too with the police. But I can say that more Black people might want to start looking to the Confederate states again. Segregation laid low for a while but it crept up North when nobody was looking. At least down South you can get a decent house and don't have to be holed up in these . . . these buildings."

Jewel always offended Ma without realizing she did. Even if it was just by starting a conversation on a subject that would keep Ma quiet because she knew nothing about it. Scheherazade reincarnated, Jewel began stories I had heard time and time again.

"Shivana, can we go to my house?" I heard Jessica say, but I ignored the child. Everybody else did. Why should I keep trying to be different? Diana Ross masquerading as Billie Holiday became too much when she sang *Southern trees bear strange fruit, Blood on the leaves and blood at the root, Black bodies swinging in the southern breeze, Strange fruit hanging from the poplar trees . . .* She sounded so gloomy and faraway, and I knew from watching that movie so many times that she had cried when she sang it. I stifled an erupting sob with my own shot of Kool-Aid.

For hours the women talked about the sadness by not talking about it, a survival mechanism inherited from humanity and passed down by blood. Like grieving family during a long funeral weekend, their conversation scratched only soft surfaces: old loves, old jobs, the neighborhood's demise, future plans made up on the spot, the music of has-beens. They didn't notice me, my back to them, my face blotchy and wet as I stared at the adjacent brick building's chipped burgundy paint. Hopeless and green, I ached that I hadn't been there, handcuffed to a peeling silver radiator and facing the flared nostril of a cold, glaring gun right along with Leroy. I listened intently while keeping the children out of grown folks' business until twilight, when Renelle finally carried them and a hefty plate of leftovers back up to the sixth floor.

FOUR

WHEN MY BABY came inside me, I started dreaming again.

I would wake up most mornings, the covers on the floor and the sheets twisted tight around my legs like I had wound them myself. Sometimes, whatever I had slept in would be moist with sweat, my overnight shirt sticking to my chest until I pulled it loose. So I know I had to be wrestling with something when I slept, even if it was a nightmare that would not loosen its grip. But after that last night with Leroy, I started remembering what had trickled into my head while I slept. I started to dream about the everyday—my street, my city, people I knew: Ma when she was young, Daddy when he was there.

My daddy was a cabdriver. We never had a car, probably couldn't have kept up the payments if we had. What most men lacked in loyalty they made up for with creativity; along with the required photocopy of his driver's license, Daddy had clipped his only daughter's kindergarten school picture to the one-page application for the job. Once Stately Cab forgave his lack of references (Daddy had cussed out every single boss who let him go), he was able to kill two birds with one stone: he got us some income and a car. Ma quit nagging him for a little while about money and riding the bus. Couldn't stop giggling then, in between staring out the window whenever Daddy drove us around the South Side. This was back when both Stately Cab and their love was brand-new. Ma liked me to lie in her lap back then, used to pat my head with one hand while she tickled the back of my daddy's with the other, until he screamed at her about making him run us off the road. I was too little to resist against her. It got to the point that every time we eased in back of Daddy's cab, playing like we were fares, I automatically assumed the position Ma enjoyed. But I craved the smell of new leather, a rich and foreign scent against the harsh odor of a chain-smoker's only jeans. I would lie on my mother's legs and sniff with all my might, holding my breath to seal in the smell until my chest grew so heavy I had no other choice but to huff it out. I looked for my face in the shiny new door handles, and imagined my reflection was rich. Then I woke up.

Like my perception had suddenly heightened, during the day I would remember the smallest details from these new dreams—like the veins in leaves, or the crinkles around somebody's eyes, or a baby screaming six stories up. I wet the bed for the first time in ten years one night. I had dreamed of magnolia blossoms descending on a never-ending sepia swamp, something I had only seen in movies or schoolbooks but never in my actual, limited city life. Of course, Ma and Aunt Jewel didn't complain when I woke up and volunteered to do the laundry. Another night I dreamed of chocolate cake and woke up with sweet on my tongue and crumbs in my bed. Finally, I confided in Jewel about this. Her reaction was outrageous, as usual. She grabbed the salt shaker off the kitchen table and dragged me into my room by one hand; she chanted words I couldn't make out, flung salt in every corner, cackled, then dragged me right back out. We flew past Ma laughing and wouldn't tell her why.

I didn't understand, until I found out how and why my body was changing, that I was sharing even my mind with this strange new someone else. My daydreams were captured by the night. I saw life as if I walked on my knees, my perspective cut down to a child's eye level, too narrow to be just the baby's inside but too wide to be only mine. Like the food and water going in my mouth, the blood coiling under my skin, even the rations of my own thoughts were diminished.

One night, in a dream where the only other thing I could remember was a coffin, I saw the wide Black face of the lady called Ma'am come closer and closer and closer . . . until a bright light circling her head reached out and swallowed me whole.

FOR THE NEXT couple of weeks we three became a soundless chord. Ma, Jewel, and I went about the same routine every day, played out in different keys. Ma's moods both determined and induced the lows. Jewel—always a high note—balanced us. With Leroy locked up, my feelings steadied somewhere in between. Ma rose every day at 5:00 to make her 6:30 A.M. Chicago Transit Authority shift, sleep-driving through the South Side of Chicago on the #4 Cottage Grove bus. She started wearing her hair down and listening to old records, so long as Jewel was there to talk about "the old days" with her. I endured school, got along with the Washingtons' kids, and waited for Leroy to call collect while I was there. He never did. The unenviable job of explaining Leroy's predicament to his regulars was dropped into my lap, and pretty soon the timid knocks stopped when the majority caught on and spread the word. Jewel slept until high noon, spent afternoons crafting mismatched meals: steak and flan, chili and sourdough toast, tacos and fresh asparagus; one Sunday, we surprised Ma with real butterscotch brewed from butter, brown sugar, and starch. At the beginning of November, Jewel dragged me to the South Side Armory so I could watch her vote for a White man named "Mr. *William Jefferson Clinton*" for president. That was the first time I had seen anybody vote for anything other than those prom queens at school who I never knew. When she came out from under the hood of her mysterious black booth—doing the same dance she had done when I saw her that first day I came home from school—I knew she thought she had done just one more thing to save the world.

Every single night at 8:00 sharp, the phone rang. On the other end was her man Hakim's buoyant New York and West Indian accent. She had showed us a picture of a dark, strong, gap-toothed man with his arms around her, his face beaming like a freshly pressed coin. His eyes were proud, but still had that slight downcast of love. Still the picture severely disappointed us; he didn't look nearly as good as he sounded. Jewel strung the phone cord between her teeth and curled her toes anyway during their hour-long conversations. Nights at last became worth remembering: tapestries of smoke, liquor, Richard Pryor and Eddie Murphy movies, old and new love ballads on the radio's late-night Quiet Storm. Jewel transformed our third-floor hovel into a song uptempo, sealing shut the raw nerves. But the harmony achieved by her coming wouldn't keep the symphony going. The schism in our composition was soon to come.

The first bad note sounded when Renelle unexpectedly stayed overnight at the hospital where she worked and she had to beg Ma to let me skip school to care for her kids. She had miscarried in a staff toilet. A few days later, the baby's lone repast occurred at our kitchen table, over Budweiser, fried chicken, and spaghetti offered in remembrance.

"It just slipped out of me," Renelle told us. No amount of consolation could stop her dry heaves. "It sounded like a penny plopping in a wishing well. I begged everybody not to flush it, but I know somebody eventually did."

Jewel cried like she had lost her own. Me, secretly jealous of the thing further binding her to Leroy, could not find the emotions. Ma hit on a diagnosis I'm sure the doctors missed: "All this damn stress these men put us through."

Once Renelle left and the only light in our place came from the cars and flashing signs of King Drive, Jewel asked me to sleep in my twin bed with her. I had taken up on the couch while she was there, the back pains that resulted better than the bruises when Ma and I were alone. Jewel had told us she needed music or a man to fall asleep, so my alarm clock radio supplied the former. She kept it so low I couldn't tell if Chaka Khan or Mary J. Blige sang "Sweet Thing." I folded into Jewel, my behind cupped into her virgin womb and her hands atop my squid-soft belly.

"I think Leroy don't care the baby gone," I said out loud. "And I don't think he love Renelle."

"And what, girl, do you know about how a man loves a woman?"

"I know he cheats. On her. All the time."

"How you know?"

"Ummmm . . . women call and stop by," I lied.

"He cheats and he stays?"

"Well . . . yeah. They still together."

"Oh, shit. They ain't together bit more than me and the man on the moon."

"I mean, they're still married."

"And that's all they are. Just holding on to love taped together with pity and friendship," Jewel hissed.

"He says he there for the kids," I offered, hoping Jewel would have more answers, hoping I wasn't telling on myself by revealing his confidences. But Jewel's right brow shot out like a tangent.

"Why is he talking about *her* with *you*?"

Had she been on the outside of the bed, I would have broken away and clung to my white wall, curling into myself.

"Don't ignore me girl." Jewel *was* a Golding, after all. She moved back far enough to flick a couple of fingers at my behind. First warning, and there wouldn't be a second before Ma was called in to get answers.

"Ow . . ."

"I *said,* why is that grown Negro telling his babysitter about his marriage?"

"Alright fine, he ain't tell me nothing . . ."

That time, a palm and not just fingers.

"Ow!"

"If I have to ask you one more time, I'm getting your mother. Now I know you have something to hide. Answer me. And look at me. And dammit, don't say ain't."

"You say it."

"I'm grown."

It was 12:37 A.M. What Jewel didn't realize was that Ma would have whipped her too had she been shook up less than five hours before she needed to rise.

I wanted the wall but needed to avoid Jewel's eyes. I stared at the brass doorknob and the wire hanger of drying panties dangling low. I hoped it wasn't true that mothers (and aunts too, I guess) could sniff a little loving out of a girl's panties. It had been over a month since the last time, but I swear our love smell lingered no matter how much Purex, Clorox, and Snuggle I tossed my undergarments with.

"I've been working for them for a while, so over the months he just done told me stuff." I wasn't lying.

"That's a whole lot of *stuff* to be telling a young girl. Shivana, he hasn't tried to touch you, has he?"

"No!" I could face the sex panties no longer, and needed the cold comfort of the empty, chilly white wall. But I couldn't turn around and I couldn't face Jewel. I fixed my eyes on the *Jet* magazine cover torn from the hinges for the sake of keeping Al B. Sure at arm's length.

"Are you telling the truth?"

"Yes."

"Promise?"

I knew I had to look her in the eyes to answer. I squirmed around: "Yes."

Jewel let me go and I sunk toward my white wall.

"I was going to say . . . that no-good Black nigger won't be *in* the jail. I'll make sure he's under it."

Lying there in her arms, I wished Jewel was a big sister and not an aunt. Maybe then, I would have told her I wasn't as naïve as she thought I was, the niece who still laughed at cartoons and could be placated with the promise of ice cream. I knew I wasn't a woman—yet—but I had gotten off to a good start. I had lain with my legs spread waiting for a man to come on top of me, just like I knew she would do when she finally got into the arms of Hakim. Just like Ma before she stopped having the man company that used to make her smile, before she stiffened into the bad attitude that wouldn't loosen its grip. As if she could read my thoughts, Jewel suddenly asked: "You got you a boyfriend, Miss Thang?"

There was no way, without lying, to give an answer that would satisfy her. She wasn't blind—she had two big black eyes wide as moons to look at me every day and see I wasn't what the world thought was fine. She knew no one from the male species ever came by—for me or Ma. She had never had to click over for us while she was talking on the phone to Hakim. If I was lucky, Nakesha would call and we would gossip a little about school—not much, since those who were talked about like dogs never felt qualified to return the favor. So if I told her no, she would want to know why. If I told her yes, she would want to know more.

"Yes and no," was what I decided on.

"Now you sound like your neighbor," Jewel replied. "Either you with somebody, or you ain't."

"I like somebody," I told her.

Why hadn't I seen the Black boy with white cheeks any-more?

"And I think he likes me," I imagined.

Jewel laughed, high and tinny. Joyful. And relieved. Her embrace tightened. Her mouth touched my ears when she whispered: "Does he talk to you all the time?"

I nodded.

"Does he make you laugh?"

This time, a giggle accompanied my head nod. And a tear slid because all I wanted was for my lie to be the truth.

"Does he make you feel like a little girl when you're with him, like all you want to do is take a day off just to play?"

I couldn't respond, or she would have known I was crying. So I just held her arm tight across my neck, my eyes across the room, hating the sex panties, wanting to burn them and forget the times I had worn them, because then I could forget the times I let Leroy take them off.

"Well, go ahead, baby," Jewel said, and though my back was to her the singsong sigh in her voice let me know she had closed her eyes.

"Go ahead . . . fall in love."

THE SECOND BAD note hit when I finally got the call I had been waiting for. After that last night with Leroy, heaviness had come out of nowhere, sat on my eyelids, and refused to budge. I didn't yearn for sleep as much as I just needed snatches of time—on the bus, in my classes, at the kitchen sink washing dishes—where I could just close my eyes to throw off the weight. Now, the brats had to wake me up just to remind me it was time for *them* to go to bed.

One night, Jesse and Junior snored atop me on their black leather couch, their slob collecting in the crook of each of my arms as they lay on either side of me. I couldn't feel their dribble because I had traveled into *The Cosby Show.* I had evaporated from my building, its stench, its tight quarters, its unfriendly and sour neighbors. Instead I now lounged on the grand, floppy sofa that centered the Huxtables' dollhouse: many pastel rooms half the size of my whole apartment, capacious rooms demanding multiple doors that swung in and out with the ease of double joints. I now had fireplaces in my kitchen, bedroom, and bathroom. A high front porch of many steps all my own, rather than one shared, token square of cement at a front entrance. And best of all, a daddy who worked right downstairs. My hair was a thick bush easily tamed by a hard brush and a pink ponytail holder. Without a care in the world, I thumbed through the *Ebony* magazines they kept sprawled on their opulent coffee table. My stomach balanced a tea set plate of sugar cookies and crystal glass of milk, set there gently by my new mother Claire. Her perfect black hair flounced as airy as clean sheets flung up before stretching on a bed. Unfamiliar, cataclysmic music—runaway piano keys tailed by screeching horns—drowned out the cars and conversations from the street.

What snapped me back into my life was a telephone operator talking into the Washingtons' answering machine: *Hello. This is Cook County Correctional Facility and . . .* I tossed the kids to the side and snatched up the phone just as Cliff was breaking up a rough and tumble catfight between Vanessa and Denise.

"Hello? Hello?"

"You have a collect call from the Cook County Correctional Facility from Leroy. Will you accept . . . ?"

"Yes!"

A dry voice—unfamiliar and grating—clicked in.

"Baby?"

"Leroy?"

"Renelle?"

"No, it's me. Shivana."

A pause.

"Oh. Shivana. Hey, girl!"

"Leroy, I been so worried about you. I can't believe they got you! I can't believe they got you . . ." I was so nervous to hear his voice I couldn't go on.

"Don't worry, baby. I got this. I'm gone beat it. Ain't no reason to sweat this shit."

"When you get out?"

"I go to trial next week. I need you to let my wife know."

"I'll tell her. I'll be there. You know I gotta represent . . ."

"Naw naw naw. You can't come now, Vana. Too much drama plus I don't want you exposed to this shit."

Had he forgotten about exposing me to way more than a trial?

"I'm not scared . . . I want to be there."

"Look, this shit is serious. These clowns trying me for priors on top of the present. They talkin' 'bout me going to the clink for a while this time. I just want to get this shit over with so I know where the hell I'm gonna be. I can't stand all this waiting, not knowing what the fuck is up."

"Can I come see you?"

A soggy sigh.

"I'm gonna beat this and I'll be back there soon and you can see me all you want at the crib, the way we used to. But, baby, it's good to hear your voice, but I ain't got much time. See now it's a line here . . ."

"But I haven't talked to you in so long."

"I know. And I been thinking 'bout you. Believe dat. I been thinking about your fine ass."

My insides knotted tight. Heaviness dropped out of my chest and landed between my legs. I squirmed and curled my toes like Aunt Jewel when she talked to the man named Hakim.

"Do you miss me?" I cooed.

"Baby, you know I miss you but I can't get into all that right now. Time is money."

"Well, I miss you."

A coming question filled the silence and I waited for him to ask what I had known he would: "You ain't told nobody, have you?"

"What?"

"You *know* . . . you know what."

"About us?"

"What the hell else?"

"No. I ain't told. I know I can't tell."

"Now I need you to promise me you ain't gone say nothing, baby. I need your word on that."

"Yeah, word is bond baby."

"Word. 'Cause I can't have shit more fucked up now than it already is. How my shorties?"

"They right here. Sleep on the couch. We was watching *The Cosby Show.*"

"Tell them boogers Daddy love 'em."

"Tell me you love *me.*"

Another pause.

"I told you, I can't get into all that right now. I'll call you again."

My good-bye hovered in the hollow of my mouth before I heard a dial tone. And when I put down the phone, I finally knew that man didn't love me.

FIVE

EVENTUALLY, THE SONG ended.

Nakesha and I finally made our way to the New Horizons Family Planning Clinic down on Seventy-first Street. It was a century-old, one-story flat-top once owned by a Black woman with thin, crooked silver locks and six-inch yellow fingernails twining like antlers. From what I knew everyone had called her simply Miss Jones, and she had refused to name the building because she thought names brought bad luck. Folks just knew it was a pharmacy, ice cream shop, town hall, and juke joint all at once—depending on the day and time. With the owner herself refusing to name it and Bell Atlantic omitting it from the phone book as a result, South Siders eventually settled for an address: 632. Say "632" and everyone knew where to go, be it an after-school jukebox jam, retirement party, rap session, or a chicken pox emergency. Miss Jones sold her nameless building to retire after one heat-wave summer when the roof dripped black tar and a crawling, limbless veteran suffered a heat stroke under the awning. She had credited the shop display window's only item—a mammoth King James Bible—as the sole explanation behind five decades without a break-in.

Today, any and all signs of that old-time religion were gone. The place both prevented and got rid of babies from people like us. Chicago University Hospital had swooped in to save it from becoming another redundant currency exchange or high-priced grocery store. Instead of candy and ice cream, New Horizons' draw became birth control and condoms. Everybody from baby-faced preteens to ancient-faced drug addicts could get exams, prenatal care, and birth control—all for free. But any woman, no matter how old or how much she made, had to cough up the money for her own abortion.

Ezekiel's Holy Children Pentecostal Temple had the un-wanted privilege of sharing a parking lot with New Horizons. With no new adults bothering to join in years, Ezekiel's old folks competed to see which member could swell the pews with the most grandchildren. Old, husky, jowled women and their waiflike men made up the congregation. Every Sunday and even Wednesday prayer nights, anybody who passed by could hear the collective humming of raspy voices, and sometimes the music made them want to come inside. As they did on any other busy city street, old men who liked to stand on the corner, they had the time of their lives tiptoe dancing to a gospel jam session, courtesy of New Horizon's musicians with pasts obviously soaked in the blues. You couldn't help but hear them while you waited in New Horizons' hard pink chairs, and I wondered if the women who worked in the registration vestibule simply drowned out God's music while they went about their business.

For the past seven years, ever since Miss Jones had sold 632, one of Ezekiel's own sanctified had stood posted under the awning with the heaven-sent task of dissuading girls like me from going inside—usually a woman with rolled-down stockings holding onto a toddler nagging to be taken home. One stood the day Nakesha and I arrived. A Big Mama who snatched the arm of each and every woman who made her way inside. Most of the girls yanked their arms back and didn't care how hard they pulled, even if Big Mama stumbled while her helpless grandchild watched. I knew I didn't have the heart for that. I would talk to the lady, at least say, "Sorry, I ain't interested, have a good day." Nakesha and I stood at the corner just long enough to be sure we were ready to make our fucking official.

"We might as well," Nakesha said, balking at my reluctance. "I'm getting that shot. I don't care if my hair fall out. I like wearing my braids all the time anyway."

Leroy was locked up. Nobody my age wanted me. Unlike Nakesha, I didn't have a line of homeboys and "play" brothers dying to get a piece of me. One night, I had had a dream about the elevator boy, and when I woke up I was so tense in my panties I couldn't stop thinking about him all day. And he wasn't even cute, so I knew I must be desperate if I was sweating somebody who wasn't sweating me and wasn't worth the sweat in the first place. Something told me birth control wasn't what I needed. And neither did she.

"Let's just go in there and get some rubbers," I told her.

Nakesha's eyes shot open. She started to walk away from me.

"Girl, you know those things don't always work and these niggas don't be trying to wear 'em. You do what you wanna do. I'm handling my business."

"I didn't say I didn't want to go . . ."

"Well, we gotta do something . . ."

Do something. Do *something*.

I wanted to do something. I wanted to do a lot. I wanted to be noticed. I wanted to have fun. I wanted to laugh until tears rolled. I wanted to dance and not feel ashamed that I had too much rhythm, or that my butt flopped to the beat before my mind could catch up to it. I wanted to be the type of student the teachers talked to after school and looked at when they were asking questions. I wanted to make the honor roll and not have to apologize for it, to Patty-Cake or nobody else. I wanted to cut my four inches of broken-off hair and be proud of the knotty curls underneath—like Jewel had been once when she showed up in Chicago "with a head as bald and smooth as a new baby's behind," as my grandma put it with scrunched-up lips. I wanted to join some kind of club that would keep me busy after school and in charge of something. I wanted to do something. I just needed somebody to tell me what.

"I mean, I want to do something too. But girl, maybe it's not this."

"Well, what else is it gonna be?" Nakesha dared me, her eyes suddenly slit like an enemy's.

"I'm just saying, maybe it ain't worth all this . . ."

"Girl, quit acting like you the first person ever walked up in here! What, you ashamed? Ain't nobody gonna see us."

"Fuck what people think!" I screamed, like she really was the enemy this time. I was hurt that she seemed to be turning on me. I cut her a little slack. A little attitude now was no different from how she had always been; it wouldn't make me cut her off as a friend. I knew about Nakesha's mother and father working all the time, leaving her with sassy younger siblings, a key on her neck, and something thawed-out in the fridge. She was braiding hair for a while, but her ma was always borrowing money for bills (without paying back), so she stopped. Boy after boy ran through her house after school, slipping out before either of her parents got home, and when each one tired of whatever it was she was giving, he simply stopped talking to her and she moved on to the next. Most of the boys she seduced at the bottom of the bunk bed she shared with a sister were already tight-lipped and moody by the time they were walking out her front door.

I watched her big ass jiggle away. We had both cut school to go to her house and take scorching hot baths. We knew some doctor was going to be feeling around our privates, and I knew White people thought we all stink. I was here, smelling nice, ready for them to stick their fingers up there. Might as well get it over with.

Big Ma had the bulgy face of a bulldog, but she wasn't fat as her face would have suggested. Across her shoulders was a ladder of bones, and her boptail skirt clung to a stomach cinched inward. She had this white head wrap on top of her head, probably hiding silver hair and smooth, bald patches. A snotty-nosed boy hung on to one of her hands, and she held a Bible in the other. Nakesha shoved past like they both were mannequins, leaving me to catch the sermon. The little boy held out a smudged pink flyer with a message bordered in tiny crosses.

"Now baby," Big Ma said, "why you wanna go in here and do this to yourself?"

"Ma'am, I'm not getting an abortion," I told her, my shoulders flung back in pride.

"Every time you take that pill or get that shot or whatever you plan on doing up in there, you getting an abortion honey. In God's eyes, you killing a living soul and that blood gonna be on your hands."

"I'm sorry, but I gotta go . . ."

"Oh, you gotta go alright. Right into the arms of the Lord, chile."

I was, as I knew I would be, intimidated by this soothsayer drug up from Hades. Her nose hairs stuck out like spider legs waiting to poison me, her brush-thick eyebrows hooded a face wrinkled in sympathy, her long throat divided in two by a man-size Adam's apple. I felt her fingers cutting off my arm's circulation before I pulled it away and rubbed off her fingerprints.

"Fornication is a sin, but Jesus is forgiving. Give up the ways of the world, and them temptations of the flesh gone fall right on away. Chile, you want to end up out here on Seventy-first selling your soul? You young, honey . . . don't fall into the ways of a Jezebel. . . ."

But it was too late for that. I already had.

WE WALKED THROUGH the heavy glass doors of 632, past a lobby packed tight with brown sugar–faced girls, arms folded like they were in the principal's office. We thought we were going to walk out sterilized, or at least on our way to it, the exact same day. But a young Mexican nurse behind bulletproof glass told us to come back in two weeks for an "orientation" session before we had our appointments.

"Orientation on what? Sex?" Nakesha snarled.

"There are some basic things which need to be covered before we treat anyone," the nurse answered in that tough accent all the boys liked, straining her neck to look behind us at the long line before the doors were locked for the night.

"I think we know everything we need to know. That's why we here," I said.

"It's policy, miss. Now can you all please step aside . . ."

"Well, I ain't gonna be here in two weeks," Nakesha lied, leaning to the side so all her stomach fat squeezed out the right hip of her Jordache jeans.

"There's another orientation and appointment session scheduled for a week after that . . ."

"What if we already know what we want?" I asked. They acted like they were dealing with the types of girls who expected a nice mommy-daughter lunch on Michigan Avenue, right before that birds and bees shit, just because they started the rag. That wasn't us.

"When services are government funded, the government requires us to disclose certain information before we administer any treatments or dispense any products. Now if you don't mind—"

"The government needs to understand folks already doin' it and don't need no information from them about it," Nakesha said, her mouth now a stanky lopsided triangle. She was determined to show out until she got her way, but behind us sucked teeth clicked against glossy lips.

"Now look . . ."

"Don't she see all us standin' here?"

"They 'bout to close."

"She need to come on . . ."

"Okay?!?"

The potbellied, weaponless Wilkes security guard standing by the door turned toward us and away from the busy street he had spent all day longing and living for.

"Let's just go ahead and take it for now," I said while staring at Nakesha. I turned to the nurse before her stubborn ass could open her mouth again. "You can put us down."

I gave her our names and dragged Nakesha away by one arm. Although she had made me mad earlier, I would have been the second one (after her) to throw a punch had any of those bitches staring us down so much as dared to lay a hand on my friend.

MRS. CARLY RETURNED. ONCE everybody (even the likes of Patty-Cake) was reminded she had missed the month because her husband passed, we decided to be good. We were immediately calmed by a compassion happily rejuvenated, tired of lying dormant, and watching the "me and mine" mentality rule. The usual jerks decided to shut up and stay dumb alone. Those chronic troublemakers too far lost in sadness and madness did us all a favor and skipped every class. Attendance and homework improved. Disruptions subsided, proving they could be eliminated and controlled if we cared enough to do so. Both eager and indifferent hands feigned out notes as Mrs. Carly droned on excitedly like she was on speed. Who knows? Maybe she was. The yearn for knowledge was buried deep within most of our hardened exteriors, though we were all most comfortable pretending that yearn had faded out of style.

In exchange for our attention and mercy, Mrs. Carly returned most of our work with high grades and stopped talking early each period so we could start. Of course no promises could be made as to how much sympathy a husband's death (sudden and unexpected) could buy, but no one ever questioned heavy, wet clouds threatening to sit a brutal heat wave down; they just sighed "*finally*," set a chair at the nearest entrance, and waited for the wet-wind breeze. So Mrs. Carly, a stout Black woman who wore clown-hair wigs, never cried in our third-period biology class like I heard she did in all her others. We hadn't done a thing with the substitute, so a month after we started it we were still on the reproduction unit. Mrs. Carly told us for the rest of the year we would be taking our time.

I think about now what I didn't have a reason to think about then: how I was almost mechanically obsessed with opening my 543-page *Human Biology* book right to the page where the embryos were pictured. To me, they were plain and hideous. Deformed little aliens really, begging my fingers to trace them out on the page. How I didn't want Jewel slapping my behind no more, like I was suddenly too grown. How I started eating all the expensive fruit Jewel forced down me and Ma's throats in a more hungry way—down to sucking a peach pit or pomegranate seed, pulling it out from my mouth and wondering how such a little thing could make all that sweetness grow around it. Then there was that day I was late to third period, told Nakesha, "Girl, just go on," 'cause I suddenly felt slippery between the legs. I made it to the ugly, pink, shit-scented girls' bathroom to find just two milky smears of rust had showed up when a flood of red should have, and that was the one day in class that I didn't feel like opening that book.

The milky rust smears had followed my sore breasts, my heavy eyes that Ma pointed had suddenly cast gray, my cold that had come at the end of October and wouldn't go away. By the time Nakesha and I came back in two weeks for that orientation and our appointments, I knew *something* was up.

THE TUESDAY TWO weeks later Big Ma was still there, though the frowning grandbaby rocked his butt back and forth, with his head leaning to one side on his hand, on the curb far away from her. This time, I shot past like she wasn't even there. Mamacita was still arguing with attitudes at the front desk, so we just signed in and left her alone altogether. There really wasn't much to do but look, tap our toes, pray nobody who walked in recognized us ('cause they would spread it at school), and wait. Mamacita later called us back to the screening area at the same time. About twenty of us were around the table (I say *us* 'cause it was all Black girls, except one Puerto Rican or mixed one with her man, then one little White girl and a snow-haired, pinch-faced lady right next to her with her arms folded on top of humongous tits). At every place on the table, there was a glass of water, Tootsie Rolls, Hershey's Kisses, and a couple of pamphlets. One each on STDs, tubal ligations, Norplant, and Depo-Provera.

"What if all you want is the pill?" I asked the dark-haired, mahogany-lipped young woman named Rebecca—the "Family Planning" specialist.

"There are some great new methods, more effective than the pill, that I want to discuss with you today," she beamed.

"These girls ain't gonna take no pills," the White mama said. We all looked at her the minute she opened her mouth. She sounded surprisingly nasal, country, and Black. "I already tried *that*."

The White girl rolled her eyes, smacked her lips, and slumped in her seat. The White woman hit her upside the head while we all winced. A thin coat of brown paint and they could have been me and Ma.

"Exactly!" Rebecca laughed, like she hadn't just seen a juvenile get slapped. Or maybe she saw it all the time. Looking at this smiling chick, fingering the tiny gold Crucifix hanging into the V of her pink sweater, I wondered whether we were supposed to be in a preschool and not a clinic.

"So," she continued, "I'll give you all a couple minutes to look over the pamphlets and then we'll get started, 'kay?"

For the next hour or so, Rebecca told us our options, talking so long about *reliability, responsibility,* and *cost-effectiveness* that there was little time left for questions.

"How come it's free to put it in but we gotta pay all this money to take it out?" Nakesha asked about the Norplant—six little miracle sticks inserted in a forearm, pumping out enough hormones so a woman was sterilized for five whole years.

"Well, we're really trying to encourage everyone to use it for the entire term . . ."

"What if we get married or something?" another girl asked.

"Then you would have to visit a certified removal specialist, which we don't have here, but—"

"I don't want my period stopping," another girl complained.

"Me neither," I said, wondering where mine *was.*

A couple of skeptics had roused the entire group.

"Yeah, I don't know about all this . . ."

"I don't like the rag no more than the next, but damn, how else I'm gone feel like I'm a woman . . . ?"

"And what you mean 'bout these hormones might make our hair fall out?"

"Shit, I done worked too hard on my head . . . I ain't losing shit . . ."

"Forget yo' head. What about cancer?"

"And blood clots?"

"And I don't need to gain no more weight . . ."

"Shit, neither do I . . ."

Our impatient calm had disintegrated into a frenzy of chatter.

"Hold on everyone," Rebecca said, with her arms spread out over us and her long, slender white hands sprawled wide to display the ice-blue rock on her wedding ring finger. "You can always go home and think about this. But keep in mind, there are risks with all contraceptives, even the pill."

"Well, I don't care," I muttered as I gathered my backpack and signaled to Nakesha that it was time for us to get back to the lobby. "I'm sticking with what I know."

"Word," Nakesha agreed.

After another half hour of waiting, Nakesha and I finally went into our separate examination rooms. Luckily, my doctor was a woman. I knew all about them sticking their fingers up in you and stuff, I had already been through that one time when I had this nasty infection that was making me smell bad and Ma took me to her doctor. I just closed my eyes, thought about my favorite SWV song, and when I opened them it was over. The whole thing really only took five minutes. I came out and joined the other women in the sedate lobby with its calming salmon-colored walls. A playpen and baby dolls sat in a sunlit corner. A couple Black and brown babies who had just met played peacefully. One couple that looked about my age sat smug holding hands; who knows what they were there for. *Parent, Baby,* and *Working Mother* magazines lingered on the round glass table in front of me; the smooth neatness of the circle they made suggested they had not been read all day. We all sat quiet, save for those screeching babies who couldn't be settled with quick knee thumps. Even the nurses worked in silence—filing rainbow-colored folders, entering data into computer screens, and filling out forms as if we were in a busy bank. I folded my arms, thinking about where I would hide my pills. Ma snooped in my drawers all the time.

Then she got into cleaning moods where she dusted between the mattresses, so my bed was out of the question. For now, it would have to be my locker at school, and I would figure out what to do on the weekends.

Nakesha burst out of the back swing doors with her hands raised, dancing toward me like we weren't somewhere halfway dignified.

"Did you have a man?" was the first thing she said.

"No, it was a woman," I answered.

"Girl, I had a man!" she yelled. "An old White man with gray hair and these long funny eyebrows."

"Ugh!" I shrieked.

We both laughed so loud everybody in the lobby looked at us. Then, we got quiet and read the baby magazines until it was time for us to go back for the "consultation," as they said. They called Nakesha in first for her crinkly brown paper bag of condoms. But me, I didn't get anything but a surprise. Once I was behind the shut door of a bare white office, the blond lady with a name tag reading *Sue* said: "Ms. Golding, I'm sorry but we won't be dispensing any birth control to you today."

I folded my arms and wrinkled my nose, prepared to hear about cutbacks and waiting lists.

"Hah? Why not?" I snorted.

"Well, Shivana, you're already pregnant."

"What?" My heart began to pound. I laughed, expecting Sue to tell me she was joking. But she wasn't.

"I said, you're already pregnant," she continued.

"No I'm not."

"Your urine test came back positive. See."

She showed me a long white cotton stick. I knew I was supposed to be looking for colored lines, but all I could see was white. I shook my head, tried to shake away the tears burning the back of my throat, snaking up my cheeks, and pushing against my eyes. I was too late. I started.

"But I haven't been throwing up . . . I haven't missed my period."

"You wrote here that you couldn't remember when your last period was."

"It wasn't that damn long ago!"

"Please don't curse or raise your voice in here, Ms. Golding. I'm here to help."

Help? Help? What the hell could she do for me? Maybe if I had gotten my pills the first day I came in here, closer to when me and Leroy did it for the last time, this wouldn't have happened. Maybe if every time I had called for an appointment before, and they wouldn't have put me on hold until I hung up, this wouldn't have happened. They couldn't do shit for me now but give me bad news and prenatal care. Who gives a fuck about prenatal care? What about *post*natal care—diapers, clothes, food, money, a roof over our heads? Who was gonna take care of this shit when it was all said and done?

"Would you like to come back with the father, and we can all discuss this?"

"Ain't no father." I shrugged my shoulders and looked away from her.

"Shivana, there must be a father or biologically you couldn't be pregnant. Is it that you don't know?"

What did I look like to her? Some kind of Black hoe? I guess that's what they all thought about us. Bitch.

"Of course I would know," I said, rolling my eyes. "I'm not a slut. I don't open my legs for everybody like that. On that paper I put I had one sexual partner my whole life. So, it's that partner."

"Would he be open to coming in so we could all discuss this? You have some decisions to make and I think you need . . ."

I just cut her off.

"He in jail."

Not that he would have come in anyway.

The woman didn't say anything. I knew she felt sorry for me, even though that wasn't part of her job. I knew she heard this shit every day, all day. I was just ashamed she was hearing it from me. I started crying again, this time hard.

"Shivana, I know right now you're very upset, but it's important for you to try and think of the last time you had sex and your period. We need to determine how far along you are."

"I can't remember," I sobbed.

"Was it around the time of a holiday or an event? Somebody's birthday, a big test at school? Something to give us a reference . . ."

I couldn't take it anymore. Did this bitch not hear me say I couldn't remember? I jumped up so fast the chair fell back. I grabbed my jean jacket up off the floor. I needed to get out of this depressing place.

"Shivana, don't leave!" the woman said. She grabbed me by my arm and wouldn't let go when I yanked it away. I yanked again, but she held on harder. I guess she didn't think I would clock her, but I was at the point where I would.

"Get your motherfuckin' hands off me!" I yelled.

"No," she calmly answered, as if she dealt with this all the time.

"Get your hands off me!"

"No," she said again, this time a little louder, then put both hands on my shoulders. She shook me until I couldn't move because I was dizzy. She picked my chair up off the floor, then sat me down in it. She put another cup of water in my hands even though I didn't want it.

"You cannot run away from this!" she finally shouted to me while I cried. It was clear she wanted us to have an action plan before I left, and she wasn't letting me off easy. I could have run out of her office, but to where? So, it was just as well she sat me down and told me what I had been suspecting in the first place. I sat there for I don't know how long, crying before I started hiccuping. At some point while my hands hid my twisted face, Sue had left the room. She came back with a box of cheap, rough tissues and a plastic cup of water wrapped in a napkin. I wanted to throw that cup of water in her face and leave her behind with those cheap tissues to clean up the mess. No, it looked like a piss cup so I would use it as that before I threw it. I hated her; she had the nerve to drop this shit on me now, just when I was thinking about what I wanted to do with my life. Just when I was realizing my future was in my hands 'cause nobody else cared. Now, I had to worry about my future and a child's? No. Not me. I wanted an abortion. *Today.* I took a sip of water to stop those hiccups, so I could tell her I wasn't having it, but she already knew what I was thinking.

"You do have options."

She was settled in her seat, and couldn't catch me this time when I ran.

"I know I got options and I plan on using 'em," was what I said before running out. This time, Sue didn't try to stop me. I glanced back—just because—and saw her shaking her head in both hands, the way she probably ended most of her days. I turned away well before I hurried past Nakesha without stopping, only shouting, "Let's get the fuck out of here." Like a driver waiting for criminals to finish their job inside, she took off right behind me without first needing any report. She was a true road dog.

From the minute I emerged into the sun, out of New Horizons, past the Big Mama who had seen right through me and rightfully marked me a Jezebel, I was already thinking about ways to get rid of this damned baby.

"WHERE THE HELL you been, Shivana?"

I walked right on past Ma without saying a word. Not even *hey Ma.* I knew better than that. Ma didn't put up with that kind of disrespect. But I didn't know I had done it until she was in the kitchen, damned near on top of me. She still had on her tight black uniform from work. Her shoes were untied, not off. But she had already rolled her hair. I heard Diana Ross pretending to be Billie Holiday coming from the living room. Ma had put that in the VCR for the fifth time that month. The whole house was dark. The glow from the TV lit my way to the kitchen.

"Answer me, Shivana. Where you been?"

"I was hanging out with Nakesha," I lied.

"And you couldn't call nobody?"

"We was out and I didn't have no change to make a call."

"Not even one quarter?"

I didn't say anything.

"Well you could have called me if you wasn't gonna be home 'til six o'clock. It's gettin' dark outside. You know I don't like worrying about where you at."

I couldn't tell her, "Don't worry then." There was some sloppy joe sitting on top of the stove in our black skillet, right next to a cold pot of canned sweet corn. The corn made me nauseous because I imagined punched-out, yellowed teeth. I walked around her to get a plate. I was starving, all the time. Now I knew why. Aunt Jewel was out; she had lain low for the first couple of weeks, but had recently gotten around to making pit stops to the relatives who seemed to have forgotten even me and Ma, and we were still here. Then Ma just stood against the table with her arms folded, like she was expecting me to say something else. I opened the refrigerator to get the bread, but Ma slammed it shut so hard the handle scraped my hand.

"You gonna come up in this house late without no explanation, feed your face, and not even say 'Hi Mama'?"

"Hi Mama," I managed with my hand in my mouth.

Just like I thought her and Jewel could smell the sex panties, I imagined they could smell a baby's breath inside me. I backed away from her. Her nose picked up on the closest thing.

"You ain't messin' around with no boy is you?" she spat, grabbing my arm so my hand cut from between my teeth and stung even more.

"No," I whined, starting to cry again.

"I mean it, Shivana. You better tell me if you are."

"I'm not!" I screamed, yanking away my arm. I knew Jewel was gone. That opened the door for Ma to be free to whack me as long and hard as she felt like. I was hoping she would today. Maybe she would whack the thing loose from my body. But she didn't touch me. She just stared me up and down.

"You ain't lying are you?" she asked me. "Jew Jew told me about some boy you liked."

I wasn't surprised Aunt Jewel had betrayed me. Her and Ma could be thick as thieves when they wanted to be.

"I just liked him, that's all. I'm not messing with no boy."

"And you couldn't tell me you liked somebody?"

"I don't know . . ." was all I could say. Not that I was scared to, just that I didn't think she would understand or care anyway.

When she let my arm loose I just went back to fixing my plate. She didn't like missing too much of her movie, so maybe she would just go away and sing along with Diana like she always did. She didn't know it, but one time I had found an old telephone bill stuffed in top of her panty drawer, when we hadn't done laundry for weeks and I needed to borrow a pair of hers. Ma had spelled out Diana's name like she was a boy she liked: *Diana Determined, Intelligent, A Superstar, Not fat, Attractive.*

"These boys don't mean you no good," she started. "They just wanna get your little butt and move on."

"Whatever . . . ," I muttered, then I felt her fat palm in the middle of my back. I ignored her even more, hoping she would be spurred to hit me again.

"Whatever? Whatever? Oh, you think it's a joke?"

I didn't answer. I scooped a pile of sloppy joe on my plate. She always spiced it real good. I didn't need bread. I hoped being busy would make her stop. It didn't.

"And don't talk to me like that. You don't need to be out here messing with these boys. Go to school and come home. Do your homework. You got any?"

"I already did it," I lied.

"Well, I don't care. Get in there and read one of them books Jewel done brought you back from the library. It's a whole stack of 'em on your bed. I don't want to catch you smoking reefer either, 'cause I know that's what y'all doing these days. I'm trying to tell you something for your own good."

"You already told me. A million times."

"Well heifer, you better listen. You come up pregnant and that's it. You can forget about doing somethin' with your life. 'Cause that man ain't gonna be there. I'm gonna start sending you back to church. Just 'cause Mama ain't here don't mean you can't go . . ."

I grabbed a spoon from the drawer and starting eating my food standing at the counter, my back to her. My tears just fell in my plate.

"I'm serious," she went on behind me. "Jewel is right. You need to keep your head in them books and off them boys. They don't mean you no good."

I chewed for an extra long time, not wanting to move too much because I really wasn't in the mood to argue or fight. Not today. I had some things to figure out. Before I knew it, Ma's hand was on my shoulder. Light this time. I turned around. I didn't want her to see the lies in my eyes so I just looked up at her and stared at her scar. She brushed the tears away from my face.

"Girl, stop crying. Ain't nothin' to be crying about."

A softness crept into her voice that I hadn't heard in a long time.

"Is this the shit you want? You don't want to travel and see the world? Get a good job? Have a nice house? Get married? You don't want to do none of that?"

I didn't know what to say. The problem wasn't that I didn't want to. I just didn't think I could. Or didn't know how to do all that stuff.

"You gettin' to be to that age now where you gotta start thinking about something more than hanging out and babysitting. And bringing whatever grades up in this house. You gotta think about your future and what you gonna do when I'm gone."

"You ain't goin' nowhere," I cried.

"I might," she said, her hand holding on tighter. "I'm getting sick of shit myself. I might just up and leave one day my damn self. Not tell nobody where I'm at for a change."

She let me go real quick and just turned around. On her way out she told me, "And I ain't gonna be here forever anyway so you need to start thinking about what you gonna do when I'm gone."

I waited until I heard our old couch squeak under her weight before I turned back to my food, sniffling and shoving it down my throat. From the living room, I knew the movie had got up to one of her favorite parts, one of her favorite songs. When Billie Holiday had to pee on the tour bus but there were no public bathrooms for miles, so her and the White band pulled over so she could go under the Southern trees and she saw a Black boy hanging from a tree against the hazy white sky. Ma didn't like it 'cause of that part, since it made her cry once. She liked the one Billie sang onstage right after with this big white flower pinned behind her ear. Ma liked to hum that slow, sad song about flowers falling from Southern trees, with only a piano in the background and Diana's voice cracking from the tears. She was humming the end of it when I sulked past her, through the cigarette smoke, with a second helping, and shut my bedroom door for the rest of the night.

I can't remember the number of times Ma told me that the minute I popped out of her, she got old. And I was only fifteen. I wasn't ready to be old. Soon Aunt Jewel would pull off in a bright yellow taxicab, press Hakim's number into my palm, and promise to call me every week. I aged that much more thinking about it, knowing I would have to face Ma and this mess alone.

I wasn't scared of death because I had never been scared of the dirt, the earth, the soil that would smother me for the rest of time. When Daddy was here, he and Ma took me down Lake Shore Drive to Sixty-third, to Rainbow Beach, a couple times before I started school. There were times she was in a good mood, so Ma teased me about how I played in the dirt while they tried to coax me to water. I found a small sand dollar and gave it to her, thinking she could make a necklace out of it. From the knee height of a child's dreams, I remember seeing swarms of Black people—laughing teenagers, playing kids, women with babies on their chests, and men with their babies' legs slung over their shoulders—coming and going in the water. Strong, happy, close families—in spite of it all. Smiling, proud, and free. On our side of town, with our own kind, playing our own music, taking a much needed break—our way. One of the only times I saw my parents kiss each other was standing with the water just past their knees, outlined by that soft, lazy blue that shimmers when water meets sky. They had started the foreplay I knew they would finish much later that night. But for then, I was all that mattered. Daddy's hands reached out and waved to me; Ma hung on his shoulders and nodded her head to let me know it was alright. But I never came; the dry scratch of sand satisfied me, to me a much softer feeling than the grittiness I was daily surrounded by. The water rocked and slid too much for me, like it couldn't make up its mind. I was scared by it because I couldn't control it, couldn't hold or mold or shape it like I could the earth. Finally, Daddy and Ma gave up and joined me back on land—burying me up to my grinning face in the sand. I thought I could have died and gone to meet Jesus right there, under the soft, wet sand that coaxed me into deep sleep, under the brightest sunlight I had ever known, faster than a lullaby ever had.

I was only six when Ma shook me awake (gently, for once) and told me through a slow-motion half dream that Grandma was going to die. She didn't say how, when, or why. In my still dream-sleep, I imagined each of her tears as beads in a necklace that would choke my grandma—stealing her away from me forever. After I washed my face and hands, we three ate cheese grits and bacon in silence. An hour later Grandma came out of the bathroom with weightless balls of her long, always-pressed hair in her hands. I remember the shower of golden dust falling from the purple velvet hatbox she pulled from top of Ma's closet, a hatbox she filled with the brittle dried-out strands. She said she was going to sew a wig of her own hair after it all fell out, and she had started on it when she died.

Later on that night, Ma was snoring on the couch and Jewel had stomped downtown in thigh-high boots to "practice on how I'm gonna spend Hakim's money." I slipped into Ma's bedroom, stood tiptoe on a step stool she kept in her closet, and eased the purple hatbox down by the dingy cream ribbon choking its brim. The black hair was still furled deep inside, a tight knot of coarse strands filling the bottom of the box like a lost baby animal fighting the cold.

Some people leave behind clothes. Some people leave jewelry too old-fashioned to wear. Others leave their loved ones money. A house was too much to expect in my neighborhood, although relatives would fight over a dead one's money and argue it was a real house all their own—and not the money—that they were after.

Grandma, needing few clothes, having no jewels but a wedding band, earning no money and certainly no house, left us her hair when it still had shine. Each and every time I had no one to talk to, I pulled down that hatbox to talk to her; each time, I half expected to open it to a puff of gray—as if she were still alive and resting underneath it. That day, I pulled out a couple of strands and twisted them around the middle fingers of both my hands. I tested the elasticity of a dead woman's hair, pulled it taut and dared it to break, and from the other side Grandma called my bluff.

We had snapped off her hair in bits and pieces when she was going down fast before our eyes, but in the five years she had been gone I had never been able to snap apart the same hairs that leaped for joy off her sad, miserable head. Was she laughing that I was even trying? Was she trying to tell us she was better off over there, stronger, healthier, with a full, young head of hair so resilient she had no need to claim or destroy these? I had seen her suffer and watched her go, and made up my own mind at that time that I would never beg God to let me stay in this world when my closest friends became pain and suffering. And with me knowing I had gotten myself into a big mess with Leroy, my pain and suffering had already showed up. I knew the story of girls and women like me well—abandoned, forever struggling, forever explaining where Daddy was, pained that they didn't know, suffering in silence, pretending not to care, getting old before their time. And why should I pass all that on to another little Black baby when I could save it and myself from all trouble? Besides, if I get rid of it—who will know, who will see, and most of all, who in *this* world will care?

SIX

"GIRL, YOU AIN'T got *no* money?" Nakesha asked me that next night. It was Wednesday, November 18. I was one more day pregnant. About six weeks if I had it right. Soon I would be seven. Each passing week meant I would have to pay more money for the abortion.

We were sitting Indian style with our backs leaning against the black leather couch. I had thrown the kids in Leroy and Renelle's room with the remote control. Nakesha leaned forward to slick Wet n Wild's Glamorous Red nail polish on her crooked toenails. I was trying to brush capfuls of pink lotion through my dried-out hair, but I had to stop sobbing long enough to be able to do it. We had BET blasting way louder than we would have dared to at home, and JoJo and Devonte's fine asses were gyrating in front of us singing "Freakin' You." There was no point in me wiping my nose or my tears anymore; neither were going to let up anytime soon.

"Girl, nope," I told her. "This the only job I got, and you know they don't pay me nothing . . . I spend it on lunch and stuff."

I saw her eyes slant to ask me, "Yo' mama don't give you lunch money?" But then, she shook her head like I didn't even have to explain.

"I bet Leroy got some dough hid in this house," she said instead. "If we could find it, girl . . ."

"I already looked. He keep it under this tile in the kitchen. Or in this hole back in the linen closet. But it's all gone. I checked. The popos got that shit."

"Damn! Mothafuckas . . ."

"I need five hundred dollars."

"You know not to even look over here."

"That or two heavy ass feet."

"For what?"

"Jump on my stomach and make me lose this shit."

"Girl, no! That shit don't work. 'Member Tonya Gray tried that when we was in eighth grade? Broke her pelvis but didn't lose that baby. His head just shaped funny."

"Well Nakesha, what else I'm gone do? I don't have no money. My baby don't have no daddy. I don't have no daddy either. I can't do this, Nakesha."

"See, I told you to quit letting him hit it raw. I told you . . ."

"Yeah, you told me. Don't matter now."

"Girl, you just need a spliff. Shoot, I need one."

"Nakesha, I'm pregnant, remember?"

"So! That's even more reason. You stressed. When I was doing it with Darnell he told me two pulls off a blunt and every single muscle in your body relax. Instantly! Even your eyelids."

"Girl, quit talkin' 'bout it 'cause you gonna make me knock on apartment three-oh-one and cop a nick . . ."

"Shit, do it for me if you ain't gonna do it for yourself. Ain't no tweak in the world like that. Ain't *nothin'* like that tweak . . ."

"I'm not doin' it, and your ass don't need to be doin' it either.

You seen the commercials. You know what your brain look like on drugs. So imagine my baby's brain. He ain't even got a brain yet."

"How you know it's a he? Shivana, I want you to have a she!"

"Don't matter. I ain't havin' a he or a she. Only thing I'm havin' is an abortion. I just gotta figure out how to get the money . . ."

"See, you gettin' rid of it anyway so what the hell you care what its brain look like? I don't do it all the time no more, so one more time shouldn't hurt. My mama smoked weed all when she had me and I came out alright."

"You sure 'bout that?"

"Don't play with me bitch . . ."

"How you know what your mama did when you were in her stomach?"

"Look, I know she smoked it with Darion and Joy. So why wouldn't she have done it with me?"

I had too much respect for Mrs. Murray to picture her so dependent on reefer for a clear head that she couldn't put it down for the nine months it took to grow a baby. So I left that alone. I wish I hadn't though. Because I don't know why I moved on to this next. Before I knew it, I just asked: "Why don't you do it?"

She finished off the last pinky and wiggled her toes like she had new strappy sandals rather than old jellies waiting. She swirled a fingertip of pink lotion into the ashy gray callus on back of one big toe.

"Do what?"

"Help me. Get rid of it."

"What you mean, Shivana?"

"Girl, just jump on me . . ."

"Uh-uh! *Noooo.* Don't even ask. I ain't tryna kill no baby . . ."

"Come on, Nakesha . . . please. It ain't been that long so maybe—"

"Shivana, hell naw I ain't jumping on your damn stomach! You can forget it. I'm not doing that. Uh-uh. God ain't striking me down."

"He won't strike you down. He'll strike *me* down."

"I can't do that to you, Shivana. I can't. I just can't."

"Nakesha!"

"No, Shivana!"

Jesse came out of the room.

"Shivana, can we have some—?"

"No!" I spit at her. "Y'all can't have nothin' so don't even ask! Get back in there."

"Shivana, why you crying?"

"I *said* get back in there. And don't come out 'til your mama get home! Matter fact, just go to bed. I ain't got time for this shit tonight . . ."

"But it's not eight o'clock."

I glared at her. "*What* did I say?"

Jesse stomped off. I turned back to Nakesha. She was crying.

"I'm not doing that, girl, so don't ask again," she said, right before the phone rang. We let it go to the answering machine.

"You have a collect call from the Cook County Correctional Facility from Leroy. Will you accept . . . ?"

Nakesha jumped up before I did.

"Hell yeah," she said to the operator after she snatched up the phone. "Put that nigga on the phone."

I knew what she was about to do, and when Nakesha's mind was set to something she did it. She ran away from me, around the couch, then into the kitchen with the cordless phone, ignoring my pleas to hand it over. I heard Leroy's deep, dry voice crack in over the phone.

"This ain't yo' baby!" Nakesha shouted. "She at work trying to take care of yo' damn kids."

"Nakesha, no. *Don't* . . . lemme talk to him."

"Don't worry about who this is," she just continued. "Worry about how you gonna take care of Shivana baby . . ."

"Nakesha, *no* . . ."

"I said *Shivana baby*. What you think I'm talking about? You stupid? . . . I'll stay on your phone if I want to stay on your phone! You ain't payin' the bill no more you jailbird . . . you heard me . . . I called you a jailbird 'cause that's exactly what you are . . . This bitch is Nakesha Murray, asshole, and you got my friend pregnant! Now what the hell you gonna do about it?"

She did her damage, then threw the phone at me.

"Leroy . . . it's Shivana. Don't listen—"

"Vana! This you? Who the fuck you got in my house? Who the fuck she think she talking to? I'm gonna break her neck . . . And what the fuck she mean yo' ass is pregnant?"

"She was just playing . . ."

"No I wasn't!"

"She better be. You bet not be pregnant . . . I don't need this shit right now. I don't need . . ."

"I know. I know . . . She was lying. I mean, I thought I was, but I'm not."

"See, this what I'm talking about. Little silly young girls. That's why I ain't never take you nowhere. Don't you know what I'm going through in here? I'm dying, Vana. I'm dying. Y'all gotta help me get out of here . . ."

"What he sayin', girl?"

I ignored her.

"I know. I know you going through a lot. I'm not pregnant. She was just playing a joke."

"Well I'm gonna make sure Renelle don't pay you tonight 'cause y'all joking just cost me money."

The phone went dead.

Red. All I saw was red. The black leather couch faded into the wall like blood oozing out onto a clean white floor. In my head I peeled Nakesha's skin away to the meat. I charged her like I was a bull. Slammed her against the glass end table with its cheap, hollow, scratched, gold tin legs. The plastic black table lamp flew to the side. The table's legs bent like spitty toothpicks under her weight, and the glass crashed against her back. She was screaming and crying, but not swinging. I put my hands around her neck and squeezed. She struggled, but she wouldn't kick or swing. She wouldn't even raise her voice. Softly, she begged.

"Let me go, Shivana . . . *Stop it.*"

I hit her head against the wall as glass crunched under my feet. The back of her head seemed as tough as the rubber soles of my shoes, because she wouldn't even make the closemouthed hiss that usually followed a newly registered pain.

"Kick me!" I shouted. "I'll let you go if you kick me."

"No!"

"I said kick me, bitch! Do it . . . you owe me now . . ."

"No . . . I'm not doing it," she sobbed.

"Well I'm not lettin' you go then . . ."

We had reached a standstill where the only movements were our hearts pumping heavy and hard. I knew if I just held her there long enough, pressed her hard enough into that glass until it started to cut through her thick Chicago Bulls sweatshirt, she wouldn't have a choice. That sharp fire-hot pain would make her force me off, with her feet or her knees. I thought about strangling her, but God changed my mind. I stared into her eyes before I sat on her chest with my knees crushing her breasts. She had just gotten that shot, so I knew they were sore. That did it.

"Oooohhh," she finally moaned. Her pain invigorated me and I pressed harder.

"Okay! Okay," she said with her eyes scrunched and her face frowned in pain.

"You better do it," I mumbled through tears, then closed my

eyes tight because I could see she was getting to the point where she had no choice, Like I had eyes in the back of my head, I saw Junior and Jesse standing in their parents' bedroom doorway, holding each other and crying. But I couldn't hold Nakesha tight and stiffen myself for her blow at the same time. I squeezed my eyes so tight I gave myself a headache. Then, I howled—a high-pitched scream that rang my ears like noon church bells for the seconds it lasted. The seconds it took Nakesha to slap my face. The seconds it took me to loosen and focus back on crushing her.

"Shivana . . . no . . . stop . . ." I heard one of them kids cry through snotty hiccups. I didn't hear keys jingling in the lock, the front door opening, Renelle's brown paper Aldi bag full of groceries falling to the floor, the swish of her Mickey Mouse nursing scrubs as she ran toward me to dig her fingernails into my shoulders.

"Shivana, what the hell . . . ?"

Renelle shook me backward and held me up while I flailed. Nakesha jumped up, coughing and unable to catch her breath. Once she sucked in one entire breath, I saw her eyes flame. She charged Renelle and me, slapping me in the face over and over again.

"You better get out of my house!" Renelle shouted. "Shivana, who—?"

"I hate you, Shivana!" Nakesha screamed so loud I came to and stopped. "I hate you! You bet not ever speak to me again! I hate you!"

"Just stop it!" Renelle shouted, holding her arms out straight so that Nakesha couldn't get to me and I couldn't get to her. I had stopped moving, stopped breathing, stopped seeing. Jesse and Junior had run to their mother, clutching her legs and hoping the madwomen didn't turn on them. I saw their fear, and was ashamed. I dropped my arms loose and felt ready to take whatever Nakesha had to give me, but she wasn't interested in kicking my ass anymore. She was ready to leave a deeper wound.

"Don't be mad at me just 'cause Leroy got your stupid ass pregnant!" she said, with a grin on her face, running around me to grab her Detroit Pistons Starter coat from the end of the couch. All the blood drained from Renelle's face, decayed into an astonished gray. She opened her mouth in a perfect circle, but no sound escaped.

"Yeah . . . she fucked yo' nasty ass ugly husband and now she pregnant," Nakesha said as she stuffed her feet into raggedy jellies. Then she started on her way out the door. The last thing I heard before a slam that rattled a couple oranging pictures off the wall was: "Find a new girl, *bitch*."

When I turned back toward Renelle, shock had captured her. Her mouth, frozen; her breath, trembling; her eyes, two black tombs waiting; her hands, trembling and holding the wild, knotted, uncombed hair on top of her babies' heads. Before she could ask her question, scaled back to simply whispering my name, I had run out the door behind Nakesha.

AND JUST LIKE *that, I felt myself suddenly jolted inside her.*

Visions of storms invade my growing mind always, frequently, and unexpectedly. Living and growing inside my mothers is always much like that, waking up to a daily storm whose nuisance offers only the excuse to stay inside all day. The commotion of outside life fades to background music after a while, like the soon silence of a blizzard whose screeching wind and combative snow are searching for conquests—simple destinations to invade for their short lives. Or a rainstorm with its threatening prelude of thunder and lightning finally giving way to the calming, hypnotic onslaught of an all-night torrent. Both are greeted by early-morning disdain and curses spit out between hands peeling back curtains, but all their possibilities are soon forgotten by people caged inside warm rooms and sturdy houses. The irony is that I could forget them, let life outside slide into background music; but my mothers could never, ever forget the life inside no matter how hard they tried.

To know Shivana did not want me, to know this would be the first time one of them had had the choice, but did not want *me*, injured my fragile heart though it had not even fully formed yet. Not being wanted was a new revelation to me, a condition I could not comprehend so I could not tolerate—at least not from the one who created me in the first place. I had to make her change her mind. Not because of my own selfishness, vanity, or greed. Not because of an elusive joie de vivre that I could not have felt yet, because I had never lived. And certainly not because I craved the life that awaited if Shivana Golding was going to be my mother: an uncomfortable future of tension, misery, obstacles, and want. Very little satisfaction or resolution. Forget relaxation. To be born into a world like hers was to hit the ground running in a marathon with no thin white finish line to stretch your heart out wide to.

What I wished was that she could see and know where I had been before I had found her. She needed to know the power of options, what the availability of choice signified, the freedom of making a mistake and correcting it yourself, rather than having others decide the proper remedy for you. But we could not communicate. The most obvious approach was to attack her conscience; I hadn't yet thought about giving her love. So without the ability to put sound to thought to create a voice, my only weapon was our dreams. But my thoughts were not as pronounced yet, not as potent to persist, to reach the depth necessary to tell a full tale. I was restricted to the bits and pieces, the surface details too searing in a mind to ever evaporate, no matter how much time passed.

The shallow depth of Mississippi swamp water and the taste of nut caramel. Rope burn. The unforgettable pinch of a dying loved one's hand wound tight about another's wrist, like an expensive bracelet impossible to part with once its tightness cuts the circulation.

One night these memories brought me back to the second one—Darlene.

She was hung above a Mississippi swamp in 1892. A group of them were, on sturdy branches of magnolias originally rooted for shade, all with Civil War artillery holes still buried deep in their trunks. Many trees fringed this shallow body of water ornamented year round by soft, white, droopy magnolia flowers. From way above (and I know because I slipped out of Darlene when it was all over and floated far above the water I left behind), the shallow depth of green with its luminescent white flowers could have been a Christmas tree year round. But shallow water is certainly no place for souls to rest easy, with not nearly enough weight to hold their bodies down; they could always rise above and wonder why they couldn't get up and walk against the horizon. So the plan was not to drop the guilty into the swamp but only to suspend them above it. That way, a bargeman could just float up, cut the ropes, and carefully slide the bodies down into a twisted pile. Less mess when the mayhem wore off and it was time to get rid of the result.

Darlene's morning had started off like most of her others. Around dawn, she had carefully squirmed loose from the limbs of her two little sisters. They all shared a twin bed and left their mother alone on the full one; the thirty-something widow fought people in her sleep and the girls had gotten tired of waking up with bruises. The family was lucky to have two rooms in their near-hut, one of many thrown up in a maze of streets and alleys the recently emancipated inhabitants had christened "New Africa." The family had walked and hitched wagon rides from their native Georgia to this promised land, and this new place wasn't any closer to paradise but at least it was farther from hell.

Darlene had put on the pair of man's felt slippers left in the kitchen—the only memento of a father whose whereabouts had been unknown—and shuffled into the kitchen to heat a black coal stove. She had rewarmed a standing cauldron of water and dipped a rough rag in it before she ran it over her bucked and jagged teeth. She would then soak the same rag with castile soap. She always dipped it back into the pot to rinse. She had stood naked in the middle of the room, glowing in the brilliant Southern sun, and vigorously scrubbed her underarms and privates. Careful not to infect the water her mother and sisters would use behind her, she would dip a brand-new torn rag in the pot to rinse before throwing them all in a pile to be washed. She had then slipped a shift over her head and started another pot for German Mills oats. She had roasted cured bacon fat directly over the flame. Minutes after both aromas started drifting through the hut and out of windows, other neighbors' lamps were lit and the beds began to creak in the other room. She had left the food heaped on one stoneware plate on top of the stove and patted down her hair. She had then grabbed a knapsack full of coins, oatmeal cookies, apples, and a school ledger with the alphabet notes from what her sisters were learning in school. She hadn't locked the door behind her when she left for her stocking and cleaning job at Miss Mailley's General Store. She had forgotten the hushed chatter of her mother and several other women from African Episcopal Holy Communion Church as they had congregated the night before at her kitchen table, a popular meeting spot for gossip after the women retired from their jobs at the nearby sugar cane refinery or sweet potato fields, not because they especially liked her mother but mostly because she had two rooms. Darlene hadn't worried about the women's whispered words, hushed whenever the girls came near, telling of the search for a robber on the loose, because something else was on her mind.

Her adolescent sisters went to school while she and her mother went to work. She was comfortably illiterate at eighteen. Darlene had no need to complain about missing out on education but she was funky about missing out on the socialization that came with it. She didn't have the nerve or permission to speak to her boss, Miss Mailley herself, or the White customers who zipped in and out throughout the day. She only nodded at the other Black maids and nannies who crept in with their minds dead set on getting what they needed and quickly getting back; long errands aroused unwelcome suspicions and accusations. The only excitement she anticipated with near-Pavlovian instinct was every other Friday in back of the store. Inventory days they were called, whenever Miss Mailley's sons and a gang of carefully selected Black New Africa boys scurried around the back stockrooms to put away goods and items to be sold over the next couple of weeks. In between breaks that sometimes allowed Darlene to try to decipher her younger sisters' ledgers, she would sneak a peak at the boys out back.

Though the boys proved it was possible to get a job done without ever looking up, Darlene still thought they were tough though they were too scared to look anybody White in the eye. She loved to watch them during quiet moments of rest, when they would lean barefoot against the tight oak logs that made up the store. They would swirl their sweaty feet in the cool dust until their toes disappeared, and the boys themselves appeared as walking ghosts. They pulled their tight suspenders from their chests and spit curse words under their breaths. Sometimes, she would catch one of their pant flies quietly unzipped, not to their knowledge. It was the one they called Tuck who intrigued Darlene the most.

It had been several weeks since she had been spoiled by him. Over months, his smile had turned to hello, then to conversation and finally laughter, then little gifts like a piece of nut caramel or peanuts from the farm where his father worked nearby. She told him she was learning to read and he told her he was learning to farm. Tea was his hope one day. Until one Friday afternoon she followed him behind Miss Mailley's shed, nearly forty feet from the back door, across land Miss Mailley couldn't make up her mind what to do with so the weeds just overran, facing a road where wagon wheels could announce themselves from a quarter of a mile away. His compadres always stood watch in the other directions on their breaks—when the White boys were served supper at a table and the Black boys only opened wax paper, standing and without first washing their hands. They avoided her eyes whenever she came back from behind the shed with Tuck, blank stares at an endless distance went a long way toward numbing her guilt. Perhaps Tuck had warned them, since shame would most certainly be dissuasion against a next time. It had been several weeks since Darlene had seen the boys again, and she only assumed Miss Mailley must be cutting back in time for summer when folks traveled more and brought back as much as they could from their excursions.

That last time she and Tuck's passion had reached such a frenzy that she let him convince her to enter her, when he had pushed her tight against hard wooden heat, their legs itching from the witch hazel and spice bushes surrounding the shed, through which they cut through for the balance the shed walls provided. With pleading in his eyes he had told her, "I can't go back like this," referring to the bulge in his pants that seemed much larger than it had ever been. She did it not because she wanted to but because she felt sorry for him, knew he could be laughed at or worst of all found out. So she allowed him to go where she had always said no one but a husband could, and had felt like a bride ever since. She knew she was spoiled, but did not know she was pregnant. In her world, it was a near-sin to admit, announce, or question fatigue. Her mother had blamed a recent morning vomit on rancid lard; in the absence of a suitor's visits she had no reason to suspect otherwise. Neither did Darlene, even though she noticed a light-headed feeling during her morning walk, while she wondered if Tuck had been called in for a Friday inventory day.

At the end of each of those days, when the boys were musty

*and worn out from a dawn till dusk assignment, Miss Mailley
(depending on her mood) would carefully check to see if the
shelves were overflowing, see if there was so much as a button
missing, and once she was satisfied of their honesty, then she
would offer each Black boy a choice. They could have candy,
spices, tobacco, fabric, canned goods, cake, and around Christmas
maybe a toy—a model train or a doll for a younger sister. That was
how it was, congenial not friendly. Until that last Friday, the end
of the work week as families prepared for Saturday activities and
Sunday church. But that day, Tuck was uncharacteristically
grouchy when Darlene snuck away from the counter to take her
own break, when she sauntered past the rest of the boys with a
tall mason jar of cool water, ready for whatever could happen this
time behind the shed. She glided toward him.*

    "Hey," she said, holding out the jar.

    *"Hey you," Tuck said, his eyes distant like his compadres. He
grabbed the water without saying thank you, then drank most of
it in a couple of gulps.*

    *"Y'all had a lot to do this mo'nin'?" she asked, wanting so
badly to reach for one of his hands. But they were both locked
behind his back.*

    *"Same old same old," he said, curiously unsmiling, like he
had never seen her before. Behind them, she heard the crackle of
wax paper unwrapping and light chuckles as one of the boys finished a joke. A yellow swallowtail butterfly flew in between her
and Tuck, and she ached for him to have an impulse of romance
that might push him to catch it for her. It swirled in the empty
space between them for seconds, before fluttering away. He
looked past her, as if aching only for his hoghead cheese and liv-
erwurst sandwich. She had brought an apple for him, but suddenly remembered she had left it inside.*

    *"You gone eat?" she asked, her head tilted in fear that what
her mother had told her was true: a man don't love nothing after
he spoils it.*

"Pretty soon, yeah . . ." Sweat ran down from his dark choco-late face, from his forehead to the top of his fat, nearly black lips. She half expected a drop to lodge in the cleft of his chin, but he always licked it away before it reached that far. He rocked back and forth, made no move to touch her let alone lead her behind the shed. She turned around, wondering if maybe Miss Mailley or one of the White boys was watching. There was no one behind them but the other Black boys.

"Well, when?" She giggled nervously, thinking maybe it was time to offer the apple. He was through with the water but made no move to give her back the glass. The sun was hotter than it had been in days, and she ached for the shade of the shed.

"When you leave," was all he said to her. There was no smile, no playful grin to relieve the shock on her face, no gentle reach for her quivering lip. She was too embarrassed for words. Her eyes misted over, and she stared at him for several seconds. There would be no more playful walks behind the shed, no more conversation or laughter. The love affair had ended before it be-gan. His coldness toward her spoke it even if he didn't say it. But like the rest, she had been proud; she kept the hurt inside and in secret where it belonged.

"Well then," she said softly, *"lemme not hold you up."* She snatched the jar out of his hand, walked past him fast with a stiff back and high head, stared down his compadres so hard they couldn't help but meet her eyes this time, and not a tear fell from them until she was inside the back door of the store.

What she did not know at that time and would not know un-til it was too late was that the boys had discovered they weren't necessarily called in for work that Friday. Couple days before, Miss Mailley had strangely noticed something missing, and only noticed it after a customer had driven over thirty miles with his son in search of a prized toy she was sure she had: the brand-new 1891 Maerklin model train set, only one year in the making, powered by steam and the first model to run on tinplates.

Puzzled after a thorough search, she realized she had been robbed. She didn't think to question her sons, their friends, or even Darlene for any strange faces that might have come into the shop and made their way out with a conspicuous package stuffed under their arms. Her first thought had been to the New Africa boys, though she couldn't imagine how they could have gotten into the special locked glass cabinet where she kept the high-ticket items. After all, they were unintelligent, colored, poor, ugly, regularly unemployed, really only good for lifting her boxes, certainly not to be totally trusted. She kept her suspicions quiet until the thought wouldn't leave her mind and she told her husband, who spread the news in less hours than it took her to think to tell him. Suddenly, their neighbors complained of missing silver, remembering one of the New Africa boys had delivered milk last week. An antique urn was out of sight at another home, although the lady of the house couldn't remember seeing any Black boys around lately. One family's dog had run off, at least that's what the family had thought until this new explanation presented itself.

By the time a town meeting was held Thursday at the Baptist church where the Mailleys attended every Sunday, all the town Whites had scoured their homes in search of things they suddenly remembered they couldn't find: fancy pipes, brass watches, special china, gold cuff links, inherited cameos, rare coins, handguns, silk ties, and of course hundreds of dollars. By Friday morning, Miss Mailley had reluctantly come to a conclusion as to how they could have gotten into her special cabinet. Or better yet, who could have gone in for them and just passed the box along. Later, after Darlene had returned to work and dried her eyes, blaming their redness on dust energized by an especially hot, dry day, Miss Mailley cornered her.

"I seen you make friendly with them boys come by here to help me," she said.

"Yes ma'am, sometimes, but just on my break," Darlene replied,

sorting buttons by color on the counter and afraid to look her boss in the eyes.

"How friendly are you?" Miss Mailley wanted to know, coldly.

What goes on in the dark always come to light. *Her mother's words entered her head like an infection and she couldn't answer, wondering what had given her away. Had she forgotten to fix a button? Had her skirt been wrinkled? Had she had the Jezebel look in her eyes? Who could have seen? Miss Mailley was usually the one who minded the counter during her breaks and no one else ever paid her much mind. But she knew better than to confess. It was smarter to just let her accuser tell her what the trespass had been.*

"We's friends, we talk," Darlene said softly.

"Talk? Is that all you do?"

Darlene didn't say one word.

"Now, Darlene, I know'd your grandmama and your mama, that's why I let you come work here at my store . . ."

"Yes'm . . ."

". . . I thought you'd treat my store like your own. Respect my business. I even let you handle money . . ."

Darlene could only cry for the second time that day, still unsure of what she had done. Her tears were further confirmation of guilt. Disappointed but vindicated, Miss Mailley was going to be sure to have her say.

". . . I thought you was a good girl. Thought you was different from all the other niggers. Never 'spected I'd have to question you 'bout nothin'."

To Miss Mailley, they were all pitiful. Sometimes able to act like people but really only savages at heart. She could forgive any one of them who was smart enough to ask for mercy.

"I'm sorry," Darlene wailed, and Miss Mailley didn't even offer her a handkerchief to wipe the snot from her nose.

"Now, Darlene, I kin help you, but you got to tell me the truth. Now was you pressured to do it?"

When Darlene didn't answer, only cried harder, Miss Mailley was patient. Hoping for something that might get at least the girl off the hook. But despite how he had treated her this afternoon, Darlene still cared for Tuck. Believed there had to be some explanation for his behavior other than he had just used her and then thrown her away. Though nobody cared about preserving a Black woman's innocence, she couldn't bear to think about what the consequences could be if she told on him. After all, a White woman was involved now, at least a little bit. That involvement could step up Tuck's infraction, even if it was just against a little Black girl.

"No, ma'am," Darlene finally said. "It was my choice."

Miss Mailley sighed, long and hard, shed one tear of her own.

"You gone tell my mother?" Darlene finally whimpered, a veiled confession to the wrong crime.

Miss Mailey just shook her head. "Why, I don't know, Darlene. I just don't know."

After seconds of silence, her mind was made up.

"You can take off your apron and go on home now. Git on."

Only a couple of people had been in the store, and only one within earshot of the trial with no jury: Missus Baxter, one of Darlene's mother's friends, on a mission for nutmeg for the lady she worked for. Darlene was so broken up that she totally walked by Missus Baxter, a sympathetic Black face under a tiny white head scarf, hoping the girl's gaze would meet her and offer even momentary reassurance. The bells above the front door that announced customers were jingling when Missus Baxter uttered, "You ain't gotsta worry 'bout me tellin' yo' mama," but the chimes were too loud for Darlene to hear what she had said.

So it started on a Thursday with a simple model train gone missing, and it would end on a Saturday dawn with an odd constellation of bodies hanging from a massive oak bordering a massive Mississippi swamp. Friday night, each and every shack on the jagged, crooked streets of New Africa was ambushed by the mob of men defending their property, pride, and honor. The women were left out of the violence and instead tarried at the Baptist church, not asking God to forgive them but rather to forgive those who had trespassed against them. They could have let it go, surely, but then no statement would have been made. The looting could have continued, the robbers could go unpunished, the order of things could be upset, the world as they knew it would end. Some walked and some rode high on stallions, holding the Black fathers and mothers at bay with rifles as they snatched up the New Africa boys. There was no father in Darlene's home, and not even a mother holding on to a captor's ankle could get them to turn loose her daughter. There hadn't been the proper warning for escape, though one boy was found several miles away, days later, shivering in a cluster of pussy willows, and he was given the blessing of being shot on the spot. A group of men arrived afterward, most of them wearing ties as if they were on their way to church or the office, to stare at the boy and his empty eyes and mouth locked tight. One of them got the idea to burn the body, and the charred sculpture that resulted lay there for days before his family mustered the courage to claim him. A photographer had been among those who witnessed the burning, promising photos to all who wanted to forever preserve their glorious moment of upholding justice.

Inside, I heard the women wailing although a circle of rifles around the swamp kept the Black folks away. Some of the men had the privilege of owning guns they had hidden for such an occasion, but their attempts at defending what they had brought into the world resulted in their own captivity. There was no law to turn to, no separate justice to protect them, and even the church stayed empty though the minister of African Episcopal opened the doors so they could pray. Nobody showed up, however,

*fearing they could be shot, burned, or carried away with the rest.
By the wee hours of the morning ten bodies hung from ropes tied
to the crook of limbs from the tallest, sturdiest cottonwoods and
dogwoods along the swamp. Darlene and Tuck were side by side.*

*I felt my mother's heart race so fast and furious that her heart
almost stopped beating before the rope was slipped around her
neck. But it held out until even after. Like the rest of them, she
fought underneath the trees, so much so that some of the ropes
became tangled and wound so that they eventually hung at the
oddest angles. The expression on Tuck's face stayed the same as
when he had been captured, the sad downcast look of a boy
about to be whipped by his daddy. Once her life began slipping
away, I could no longer sense her. I would hope they would have
talked to each other with their eyes, and held hands though they
couldn't touch. I can only imagine whether he and my mother
said anything to each other, made any promises to keep in the
next life, tasted just a little bit of rain before they died, rain that
finally washed over the town for the first time in weeks.*

*The overnight was quiet, with only the occasional hiss of a
rattlesnake or laughter of mockingbirds or scurry of a possum or
hare to interrupt the silence. There may have been alligators
snapping their jaws, lurking for prey to drop, though they
wouldn't have made a sound anyway. The blackened silhouettes
swayed against a night sky made blue by electricity precipitat-
ing thunder and lightning. Most of the boys had had no time to
put on shoes, so many of their toes peeked out from holes in their
socks. One of Darlene's daddy's felt slippers had fallen off, floating away among the flowers.*

*There were limits to the mob's artwork. The rain unstiffened
the bodies and warped the ropes, so that what once was an interesting constellation, a display as intriguing as a mobile above
a newborn's hungry eyes, by morning looked saggy, soggy, improvised, and limp. Those who showed up to bear witness were not
only shocked but disappointed, because by then the victims*

were waterlogged and relaxed, so it looked like no one had actually suffered. I knew they had, so much so that the one woman among them had bled from her womb the entire night. Inside that blood was me, dropped into bright green swamp water adorned with magnolia blossoms, so when I looked down at where I had just come from, my people only looked like ornaments that were a part of a Christmas tree.

SEVEN

AS IF GOD himself had called it for me, there was a cab waiting outside the building when I flew out. As if I really had somewhere to go. My coat and purse were still upstairs at Renelle's.
Like there was money to pay for a cab in either one. Shivering,
I looked down the street and saw a fire truck and a couple of police cars had backed up traffic on King Drive. I was in back of
the cab before the driver even noticed I was coming.

"I'm off darlin'," the older gentleman said. It was dark and
he barely turned, so I couldn't see his face. Soft blue coils covered his head and ended along the edge of his ears; stiff gray
hairs like light pencil marks peeked out from inside them. I
thought about Ma playing with Daddy while she sat in the back
of his cab, and I almost touched the old man's soft puff of hair.

He glanced back at me. Whatever he saw in my face got him
back on the clock.

"Where you goin' darlin'?" he sighed.

"Nowhere," I said.

"Hah?" he asked. "Pretty young gal like you gotsta be goin'
somewhere."

Traffic began to move again, so he couldn't look back at me
anymore as he spoke.

"Maybe so," I told him, "but I don't know where somewhere
is."

"Well, you gotta tell me something. Soon as we get past this
here commotion King Drive gonna be movin' too fast to be going nowhere."

He looked back at me again. I just hunched up my shoulders
as if to say, *What you expect me to do about it?*

" 'Bout how old is you? Twelve, thirteen?"

"I'm twenty." I had to make him think I maybe had some
money so he would just keep on driving. Being polite couldn't
hurt.

"Whew." He laughed out loud as his cab came to a jerking
halt again. If we didn't get too far, then maybe I wouldn't have
to walk too long once he put me out for not having any money.
He kept talking and chuckling.

"I wouldn't a never thought you was no twenty. But you
know, these girls look so old nowadays that I done forgot what
a thirteen-year-old one supposed to look like in the first place."

How come every time somebody just wants to be quiet and
cry, there's somebody around who won't shut up so they can do
it? But I guess it *was* his cab . . .

"You comin' from your boyfriend's?"

"No."

"You gotta boyfriend?"

"Yeah, I got one." So old ass Negro old enough to be my
granddaddy don't even start.

"You goin' to him then?"

"Yep. He waitin' on me right now."

"Well, where he stay?"

"Up on Halsted . . ." I could feel the salty snot clumping in back of my throat while my eyes ran. I didn't have any tissues so I just used my wrist and let whatever came on dry.

"Where at on Halsted? See, I'm off . . . you gone be my last fare so I ain't trying to go too far from the depot. I been working since eight o'clock this morning. Been up to O'Hare, took a fare to Harvey . . ."

I was shuddering, staring out of the window, squeezing myself tight, and just now feeling Nakesha's hard pinch on both my arms through my own fingers that grasped my arms tight.

". . . I dropped some folks off at the United Center for the Bulls game. Matter fact, let me turn on the game 'cause it should be 'bout over by now. You been to the United Center? Boy, that traffic was somethin' else. Cars backed up all down Washington. Wasn't nothing but headlights and Negroes wearing red and black for blocks. Been back out down south since 'bout seven though. Gotta couple calls came through on the radio. See, that's what I like. Old folks or women going shopping call you up on the South Side just to take 'em 'round the South Side. Now see, I likes that. Point A to point B without all the confusion and a long ride home. You go downtown and you got stress, traffic. White folks either running late and acting like it's yo' fault, or keep changing they mind about where they wanna go in the first damn place. Just itching for a reason to gyp you by claiming you gypping them. Oh, we movin' again now, miss. You 'bout ready to tell me where you goin'? Miss? *Miss?* Hey, you alright, miss . . . ?"

I guess the middle of a crying fit was as good a time as ever to confess I was broke.

"Sir," I heaved, "no, I ain't alright. I'm not." I couldn't even tell him all the reasons why. Hell, I didn't know. All I could do was sit in the back of that cab, wish I was five smelling Ma's cigarette-smell jeans, wish my baby would bleed out onto this man's nice gray leather seats. And if that couldn't happen at least somebody would come along to help me make it happen some other way.

"I ain't got no money, and I ain't got nowhere to go."

Old man didn't answer me for a while. He just drove on and let me cry. He only spoke when my chest stopped jumping up with sobs.

"Well . . . it be like that sometimes," he finally said. "Shit, I'm fifty-seven years old. If I was to tell you 'bout all the times in my life I was broke and I ain't have nowhere to go, we liable to run out of gas and road. Fight with your boyfriend?"

"Kinda," I managed. "Somethin' like that."

"Pretty gal like you don't need nobody giving you grief. It ain't worth it. That defeat the purpose of calling yourself in love."

"Yeah, I'm finding that out now . . ."

"When you got love you always got somewhere to go. Should, at least."

"Yeah, I guess."

He kept on driving, just turned up the radio. It wasn't yet time for the Quiet Storm. Kool and the Gang's "This Is Your Night" was on. That was Aunt Jewel's jam. If I was at home, in the kitchen with them, we would all be listening to it together, maybe dancing and laughing, sliding across the sticky linoleum and pretending kitchen chairs were our partners. I wondered if Renelle had gone upstairs looking for me. There was no doubt in my mind I had a fight on my hands if I caught her in the hallway, alone. I wondered if Ma and Aunt Jewel knew now. There was no way I could go home. Is this how good people wound up homeless? I thought about my daddy's people who lived in South Shore. Just young cousins and middle-aged aunts who were always happy to see me if I came by, but would never see me otherwise because they wouldn't make the effort. It wasn't that late. I could just pop up. Once opened, they wouldn't shut a door in my face. I *was* family, after all.

"Can you take me to South Shore, by the Seventy-first Metra stop?"

"Yes, ma'am. I sure can. I can do that for you."

"I ain't got no money. Maybe my aunt might . . ."

"Don't even worry. I'm off the clock anyway. This my time. It's my pleasure." He looked back at me. "No, my privilege."

How old were they before they stopped getting that look in their eyes? Did it ever stop? That look I had come to recognize so well. Just a couple steps before that *must* which instantly made it as hard as old wood, which always started out as a tight kernel of lust. That *look*. Shiny eyes couldn't look straight at curled eyelashes no matter how much they concentrated. Shiny eyes fighting curled eyelashes so hard they had no choice but to sit the round out and turn down. Rest themselves on loose shoelaces, lint in hair, a button come loose in the middle of breasts, a single curved eyelash fallen on a plump cheek—anything to give them a reason or a right to touch us. Somewhere between boyish charm and mannish mischief, right before that turned-on twinge we women could smell before we even knew it was there, they always gave themselves away with *the look*. Cabbie had it, and it was only after I saw it in his eyes that I sniffed the air just to find out the scent of Old Spice had gotten stronger. Twice, in one night, I asked a question I knew I shouldn't have.

"Mister?"

He jumped so hard at the sound of my voice his hands lifted off the steering wheel for a second. I saw his thick gold wedding ring catch the lights from King Drive.

"Huh?"

I didn't know if I would be able to get it out.

"Miss, you want something?"

"Maybe."

"Maybe?"

"Yeah, maybe I do."

The whites of his eyes suddenly took up more space in the rearview mirror I was watching him through.

"Lord . . . don't tell me I done picked up another one of these hypes. You in your right mind tonight? Matter fact, where your coat? Why you ain't cold? You ain't on that stuff, is you?"

I needed to get on with it quick. He looked like the type of old Black man who shuffled down Sixty-third at two in the morning with a pistol packed tight against his narrow hips, who could forget about arthritis long enough to aim a slim barrel fast as a switchblade unfolds, and wouldn't hesitate to snap back the trigger if need be.

"Do I look like I'm on that stuff?" I pouted. "Shoot, I know I don't. I see you looking at me. I know I look good."

In the rearview mirror I saw his eyebrows arch in a new, unexpected confusion.

"Don't I look good?" I asked him before he could start to even care if he was attracted to a hype. He didn't answer, so I figured the best thing I could do was to get him talking again.

"My daddy used to drive a cab. How long you been driving a cab?"

Nervous now, he talked fast.

"Shoot, 'bout twenty-five years now. Since 'bout 'sixty-seven, when my last daughter was born. Shit . . . the money I made! And I put half of it on the horses and made even more."

He laughed out loud.

"You talkin' 'bout hundreds of dollars a day. And this was the sixties, seventies. So you didn't even have to work five days a week. I mean, you could have, but who wanna do that? You couldn't get no better job than this back then. Not in the factories, not on the roads, not on the buses, the trains, nowhere. Wasn't no job as good as driving a cab. Maybe drivin' a truck. But that was it. 'Specially once you bought your own car. If you had your city car you used that for work and your *big* city car you used for play. I mean, what more you need?"

I thought of change in my pocket as we drifted past a second Kentucky Fried Chicken in a couple of minutes. I hadn't eaten since school lunch. A couple of oatmeal cookies and a Sweet Valley cream soda at Renelle's didn't count. I doubted if I had enough for a KFC two-piece with mashed potatoes and my favorite coleslaw in the whole world. Cabbie kept on talking while my stomach talked back.

"But you see, back then, it was way different you know. Lot more going on. Lot more happening. Chicago was happening more than it is now. You know, these gangs and thangs done changed everything. We had them, hell I was in one myself, but not like now. Not like today 'cause folks wasn't never scared to go out they house for no reason back then. Maybe for White folks, but that was about it. Even that wasn't no problem 'cause for the most part they done always left the South Side alone. I didn't drive nowhere but south in those days. You didn't have to go downtown or to the airports to make the good money. Sixty-ninth Street all by itself paid my bills for a couple years, back when all the clubs was 'round on Halsted, 'fore they started tearing down the shopping on Sixty-third . . ."

I let him drone on. Cabbie had been as far north as O'Hare and as far south as Harvey, out here since eight o'clock this morning. He had dropped off people just itching to tip because they were in a good mood, anticipating the once in a lifetime chance to see Jordan fly. His nails were manicured, clipped, and buffed to a new money shine, made so just so they could flicker when he handed a young girl like me a piss-colored drink in a smoky lounge. If he was smart like my daddy had been, he would have dropped his half day's take off somewhere earlier in the day. He would have pulled out just enough cash to be able to make change, but left the real money somewhere besides his pockets or the console of his cab. He had probably dropped it off to a wife about his age, whose homemade buttermilk corn bread and day-long beans couldn't get him home right at twilight like they used to. But that still left half the day. He was too young to be incapable and too old to be in crisis. He could get it up to do it to me if he wanted to, and it would be exactly what he wanted to do.

"You want to go somewhere, just me and you?" I suddenly asked him, and I imagined my ears sealing shut so they didn't have to hear what was coming from my mouth. He chuckled, and I let him continue until he turned again, and I saw the *look* reappear.

"I mean, you said you off work," I said sweet. "What you do for fun? Maybe we could go somewhere and have some."

Fueled by desperation, I didn't want him to get a word in edgewise—yet. Aunt Jewel had taught me that to get what you want from a man, you have to fool him into believing that what you want was his idea in the first place. And I wanted every single dollar he had in this damn cab.

He chuckled again, but didn't say a word. He glanced back a couple times in a couple seconds, but this time that other look was gone. There was another one in its place and that's when I knew I had him. I knew this other look because I felt it had crept across my own face before, though I couldn't actually see it. Didn't matter. I knew it had been there. The first time Leroy clasped my waist real quick while I moved past him to reach a Lucky Charms cereal box sitting on top of the refrigerator, when his touch lasted way longer than an accidental brush. I had looked back at him and grinned in spite of myself, knowing what his offer was though he hadn't yet officially put it on the table. A stupid, clumsy look—frozen by the disbelief I could be desired.

"What kinda fun you talkin' about?" the cab man said, his interest betrayed by an adolescent crack on the question mark. Then, of course, he cleared his throat.

"I don't know, just fun. Whatever that mean to you."

"Naw, you tell *me* what it mean to you."

It had to be *his* idea.

The speedometer jerked down from thirty-five to twenty and we were crisscrossing the street's white lane boundary lines. I didn't say a word even to correct him or to protect us. I just sat quiet and smiled out the window, catching real quick a star that was shooting or falling; I couldn't tell which. Didn't matter in the sky hovering over this part of town, so there was nothing to tell him he should see. A shooting star with nowhere to go aroused less excitement than a falling one.

"I don't know what fun is anymore." And that wasn't a lie.

"Oh, you know." He let the chuckle loose first so a stomach-filled laugh could slide into its place. "You know. *I* know."

I just laughed right along with him, hoping he was thinking about head or a hand job. I thought about how the gray hairs on his chest would most certainly scratch. I wondered if he would be as hard, sturdy, energetic as Leroy. His age should get me off the hook with that, although it might not since it probably had been ages since he had been with a young thing like me. He retreated back to the chuckle before I knew it. Against Aunt Jewel's instruction, I intervened.

"I guess my idea of fun is the same as everybody else's. Me and a man I like doing the things we like to do."

He faltered for a moment. I knew to lean forward and hang on to the back of his headrest like we were about to crash, like I had seen women on television and in the movies do. I let him feel my sour breath so it could make him think of a morning after. He had hardened into a blank face, much too stiff and strained to not give way.

"How old is you, girl?" he asked softly, the shame already evident in his eyes.

"Old enough," I answered. "You ain't gotta worry. I do this all the time. It's no big deal. You ain't gotta worry."

He was thinking about it.

"Shit . . . What you want? From me? *With* me . . . ?"

"Whatever you want."

"I don't know what I want. I mean, I do, but . . ."

"But what?"

"I mean, I'm married. I'm a deacon . . . I gotta wife."

"I know. But that don't make it impossible."

"Yeah, but it don't make it right either."

I wasn't going to beg, so I let the headrest go. Aunt Jewel had always cautioned me to exercise restraint with any man, that the best way to keep them interested was to act as if you weren't. Falling back was just what I needed to do for him to come to me.

"Well, I mean . . . what you *want*? What I gotta give you?"

I didn't have to think twice about it.

"Shit, you can gimme all you got."

I don't know why I followed him and started laughing until my stomach convulsed. Maybe so my tears of shame could flow again in disguise. When I finished laughing and flicking them away, he had already pulled into a vacant, rubbish-strewn lot in back of an abandoned Laundromat. I didn't know exactly where we were, but I could hear a coming Metra train sound its bells. So we were in South Shore, probably within walking distance of my aunt's just in case I changed my mind or things got out of hand. He parked the car but didn't turn it off. It was cold. He swallowed hard and I finally was able to hear his breath even though the volume on the radio hadn't been touched. I didn't exactly notice how he maneuvered his way upon me, slithering over the Lincoln Town Car's middle console with an ease that made me suddenly think he did this all the time. I had no reason to be, but I was disappointed anyway. I could feel the decades-old cracks in his lips slicing a pattern into my own. The hairs I had known would scratch my chest instead stabbed at my chin. Then he held me tight against him for a whole verse of Luther, which song I couldn't make out because I had lost my focus. But he was my mama's favorite so I could make out that voice underwater if I had to. The old man squeezed me into him and ran his lips and chin over the top of my hair. He massaged my back, let me taste his heart beating on my face so strong I felt the need to open my mouth and swallow. I inhaled too many breaths of Old Spice and felt the tart beginning to throw-up cascade down the back of my throat. *Mind over matter,* I convinced my pregnant self, knowing he might be too disgusted to continue—even if I wiped every last speck of vomit off his nice leather seats. I needed to push him off me to concentrate on keeping it down. I held out my arms tight as my eyes watered from nausea.

"What's wrong there, sugar?" he whispered, holding my face in both his hands and looking into my eyes with a new rage of want. "What's wrong, darling? Huh? I ain't scare you, did I?"

"No," I managed. "No. I ain't scared of shit."

He started to fall back into me but I wasn't ready yet.

"How much you gonna pay me?" I shouted, turning away and bending forward from my stomach.

"Huh?"

"I *sa-id,* how much is you gonna *pay me?*"

It was an unfair question at this time, and that's exactly how I liked it. His mind was too gone to expect any other response than the one he gave.

"Whatever you want. I got money. I mean, this ain't all I do. I do more than drive a cab. I got a house. I got money. I could take you out, anytime, wherever you want to go . . . I got money."

"Well give it to me." I shut my eyes tight, and the rising vomit sunk down once more. I opened my eyes long enough to see his hips jerked forward as he lifted himself off the seat to reach into his left pants pocket. I had been right—a slick black pistol slid out right along with countless bills. He bent down to collect them before I could ask, and when I opened my eyes again his hands were outstretched and in them he held a pile of cash that looked like a fat, giant spider in the moonlight.

I grabbed a fistful of bills and stuffed them down my shirt, then grabbed more before those were secure in place. The more I stuffed the money, the more it seemed to fall, until I simply gave up and started to cry. Caught off guard by my reaction and change, the old man wouldn't touch me or let down his hands. I guessed he wanted me to keep on grabbing the money, but my hands were fisted over my eyes by now. He suddenly threw the money on the seat in between us and started to neatly fold the bills. He was quick about it, but still very, very neat—like he was wrapping a present two minutes before the party. He only stopped when a police car squealed off in the distance, and he grabbed the back of the passenger's headrest as he looked around wildly. Except for the police car, there hadn't been any signs that we weren't alone for a while. But when I opened my eyes, I saw a group of rowdy boys freestyling rhymes over a garbage can. There were people collecting at a bus shelter a block down. A light suddenly went on in the Laundromat, and the windows glowed a dirty gold. We both looked around, then at each other, and then all of a sudden I was in his arms. The bills smashed and crackled between us as he held on to me tight, and I cried. Not just a stream of snot or little pearls of silent tears, but that hard, long, stomach-hurting and eye-scorching kind of cry, for I don't know how long. But at some point in the middle of the outburst he had eased back into the front seat, leaving a pile of bills stacked on the backseat as neatly as a new deck of cards.

"Seventy-first Street, by the Metra?" he asked as soon as I slowed down. But the crying with this stranger had cleared my mind. In minutes, it had demolished the wall standing between me and a new courage, a new maturity, a new acceptance of the bullshit I had gotten myself into.

"Naw." I sniffled. "Take me on back. Just take me back home. Back where you picked me up."

"Yes, ma'am," he answered, and for fifteen minutes of stoplights never stopped so it seemed like we were on open road, neither one of us said a word.

I hadn't planned on saying anything to him when I opened the door to get out, not even good-bye. I left the money where it was because I hadn't earned it. But with just one of my legs out the cab, the old man grabbed my shoulder before I could ease out another.

"Take the money," he told me. "Go on. You can have it."

"But . . ."

"Naw, just go on, take it." He nodded his head sure. He nodded with his hand on my shoulder until I turned to grab the stack, held it in my hands like it was a baby I wanted. Then like I couldn't before, I stuffed it all down into my bra and this time not a single dollar escaped. I wasn't sophisticated enough for a corny response, a thank-you full of sarcasm or wit. I was more grateful than he or I could have ever known, but I was also alone, scared, about to get my ass kicked by Renelle, my mama, or both. I really couldn't think of one thing to say so I just shut the door of the cab real light and promised to say something right if I ever saw him again.

When I walked up to my stoop, that boy—with the funny white cheeks and knotty hair—was sitting on the stoop, lighting a Newport and nodding his head in between earphones. Despite my nappy hair from the fight, eyes bloodshot from the crying, my ridiculously bare arms despite November, my chest deformed from the mound of cash, I smiled at him. Instinctively, almost. I felt my own dimples pinching my cheeks, my eye creases touching. I smiled for no reason, just because—as wide as I could. He didn't smile back as wide. Just kind of grinned a tiny bit, lopsided with one side of his mouth. I stood in front of him and we looked at each other for a couple of seconds, both waiting. Anticipating for one or the other one to say something. I don't remember who spoke first. Didn't matter anyway. We would be together from there on out.

THE TIME HAD *come for me to intervene.*

By the time I got to her—*October 11, 1992—I was ready. And it was time.*

Shivana.

To me her name sounded first like flooding water, then ended with the strong huff of a sudden strong wind. Cool water that begged to be waded in and touched, hot wind that spanked cheeks so unexpectedly it was impossible to tell from which direction it had come. I shouted, but she couldn't hear me. She couldn't hear me calling her name.

Shivana. Fifteen. Black girl. Mine. And I have to make her keep me.

THE FIRST TIME *I saw her, through her own dark brown eyes in the cracked glass of an elevator's mirror walls, I knew she could make me a pretty baby if only it got that far. I knew it was*

1992; family life had lost its lure. Broken homes, dreams, and promises spun awry, tragically centrifugal from a desirable past of quiet, stable domesticity; selfishness, arrogance, hopelessness, and irresponsibility was instead on the loose.

But those weren't her *reasons. She, I couldn't judge. I fell in love with her because deep down inside, I knew exactly what she wanted. I just had to figure out a way to give it to her.*

She wanted all the things I did: comfort, security, affection. In the safety of the spirit world, I'd imagined sleeping in a labored-over, palely colorful, fresh nursery, ripe with the smell of a crib's dark finished wood, decorated with a fairy-tale motif. In a diagonal corner of a high ceiling, someone has affixed a net to hold up soft playthings, silent decoration to everyone else but joyously alive friends to me—the stuffed bears, rabbits, lions, monsters, and baby dolls that I will talk to with eyes wide open while everyone else sleeps. My brand-new eyes, eager to look even if it is at nothing, could stare into the endlessness of carefully painted, smooth white or cream walls, their infinity broken only by the right straight grandeur of a bookshelf filled with the bright, parallel, slim spines of my bedtime stories. The many gifts for my coming—some practical but most just frivolous—have been neatly put away in a closet with golden knobs. My young ears, with clarity sharp as a cub's, will find the jumbled, sappy songs of nursery rhyme albums annoying and dull. With the skill of a jungle cat waiting for sounds of the slightest disturbance— parted leaves or a blade of glass quietly wounded by the prey's paw steps—I will instead strain for the dawn and night sounds chambered in tricky silence: dew landing, crows calling, train tracks rumbling, insects mating, exhausted night wind practicing for the next busy day. A rocking chair will rest near my bed for my mother and our visitors, and in that chair is where I will get to play the new role best: whining, crying, nursing, cooing, twisting for attention, and smiling in my sleep. New life never rests easy; only recently mortal, we remain cynosures of a jealous spirit world eager to steal us back. So we sleep in short stints and wake often to keep the searching spirits at bay, at least until we make up our minds about the new world and decide if we want to stay. In the middle of the night, I'll wait for the friends I had on the other side to appear, or not—though I'll know they're there when the rocking chair tips and sways to music in my head, remembered from a past begun many moons before birth.

But none of that is usually waiting for us, the children conceived of carelessness and slipups. Maybe a bassinet has been placed at the foot of a lonely bed, at best. A tensely divided one, at worst. Two people found out somebody else was coming and decided to take up because somebody older told them it was the right thing to do. Or maybe they had already taken up. To the woman, an "accident" suddenly became a brilliant idea; his waning interest could possibly be ignited with the new responsibility of the something she will make, for him and by him, created in his own image. Wonder how it happens in true love . . .

The universe should rule that we can go back when we know we're not wanted. Or needed. Eliminate this disappointing journey of travel so long and hard to get into this world, just to realize no one cares you have arrived. When no one wants you, no announcements are sent, no celebrations planned, no preparations or adjustments made. It's a coming greeted as a nuisance, like a wisdom tooth reemerged. Like that relative who talks too much and always stops by unannounced in the middle of somebody's favorite TV show. Like that child some startled mother put on a bus to nowhere before she disappeared to prospect for a life, and it just happened to arrive at the doorstep of distant relatives. A thorn in everyone's side, a sty in everyone's eye, a paper cut bleeding on overdue bills, a helpless victim of those who relish every opportunity to point out the burden of its presence, he is constantly chastised in hurtful conversation overheard from his mismatched chair at the dining table or his sleeping pallet on the floor:

"The child just showed up?"

"Just showed up honey."

"With nothing?"

"Can't count the lunch box empty 'cept for some potato chip crumbs, dried-out bread, and sucked-clean chicken bones."

"No clothes, no nothing?"

"Two bags, no money, and no note."

"Out of nowhere?"

"You *heard* what I said."

"And nobody bothered to tell you the child was coming?"

"Ain't nobody told me *nothing*. Still ain't! This child been here for two weeks and that phone still ain't rung."

"Honey, shut yo' mouth . . ."

"Chile . . ."

"You gone let him stay?"

"I ain't got no choice now. It's here. What can I do?"

"You can always put him back on the bus."

"Yeah, but to where?"

"Don't know. Gotta be somewhere . . ."

"No. I already checked. *Ain't nowhere.* The mama's gone . . . nowhere to be found. Nobody know the daddy name."

"Who is this child?"

"I barely know. That's the killin' part."

"Well, he got Uncle Simon's eyes, Aunt Linda's nose . . ."

"Oh yeah, he's definitely one of us. I know we related. But these girls done had so many of these babies it's hard to keep up . . ."

"What's his name?"

"Don't know. I done told you there wasn't no note."

"The child don't know its own name?"

"If it don't know the mama or daddy name, what make you think it know its own?"

"You gone name him?"

"First, let me decide if I'm gone *keep* him."

"This a crying shame . . ."

"*You* telling *me*? I'm the one gotta feed him. Showed up on *my* doorstep, not yours. I mean, if he was just a little older and not growing like a weed, maybe I wouldn't mind. Now, all he want to do is eat me out of house and home. Grow out of his clothes quicker than he put him on. Wasn't nothing in them bags but a couple of pants and a few shirts. No socks. No night-clothes. What he had on, I couldn't remove the stains, so I just washed it best I could and he been sleeping in that. Done come to me already complaining about his shoes was tight, say his feet hurt. I ain't got no money, so I just said, "So do mine—take 'em off.""

"How you gonna afford all this?"

"Who you asking? I've raised my kids. I don't need no more. Now I gotta deal with a child dumped in my lap and I don't know when somebody gonna come get it. This don't make no goddamned sense. The mama's lucky I'm a Christian."

"Well, he can't be too hungry."

"Better not be. I just fed him."

"That's what I'm saying. He outside now and left that whole plate of spaghetti and salad on the table."

"Where?"

"Right there."

"See. This what I'm talking about. He ain't asked me if he could go nowhere! I'm too old for this . . ."

"And look like he just messed over it."

"He ain't ate nothing! Just mixed it up on the plate. And gone be hungry again before the sun set. Well, I ain't cookin' no more tonight . . ."

"Chile, it seem like you done got yo'self into a mess . . ."

"Who you tellin'? But I ain't staying in it. I can tell already, he gone wear out his welcome real soon . . ."

"So what you gonna do?"

"Don't know, girl. I don't know . . ."

. . .

OF COURSE, ELEVEN-YEAR-OLD *David Rasul Evans knew his name though he pretended to forget when his mother, sick and tired of being sick and tired, gave up on it all and decided in 1984 to ship him off to her mother's people up North. She was fed up with drifting through scorching Missouri one-rooms and efficiencies, not being able to catch another job before one lay her off, not being able to depend on the circle of girlfriends whose predicaments were not much better than hers, certainly not being able to depend on the daddy who loved get-rich-quick schemes more than his son. She had had the number of a cousin who was supposed to alert the brood spread out on Chicago's South Side that one of theirs was on his way. For how long, she couldn't say.* Just put up with him until I get on my feet, *was all she asked.*

Of course, that proved to be too much when no one wanted to put up with their own. He would have wanted them to call him Davey, just like his mother had, but the problem was nobody would listen to the child long enough to find that out. He, however, was always within earshot of the latest boarder's self-aggrandizing tirades about his new mouth and how it was too big to feed. He never failed to notice how he got the smallest portions, the last and shortest turn in recycled bathwater, the narrowest sliver of the shared bed or the end of the couch nobody else wanted to sleep on. He never failed to hear the other cousins crack on him for his ten-dollar jeans or his twenty-dollar shoes. Not to mention the ivory-colored splotches all over his face, body, and hands. No teachers at the eight schools he transferred to in less than eight years bothered to pay him much mind either. He woke up every day in whatever temporary place he was staying, went to school, wilded out with the few other strays in between and after classes, dreamed about nothing, planned for no future because no one took the time to tell him to.

His real mother barely called and she never wrote since she never managed to get on her feet; even though she no longer had the boy tying her down, she was still an uneducated Black woman with no looks and no skills. So by the time David was twelve, he associated both woman and manhood with neglect. By the time he arrived at an aunt and uncle's in a dilapidated building on King Drive, where he was sent because the couple's own son had joined the army and left his room vacant, David had packed and repacked his two little bags (he lost the lunchbox at the first distant aunt's house) eleven times in eight years.

In the close of 1992, two children were searching for one place to call home and I took it upon myself to help them find it. And home is not always just a place. Since he was necessarily numbed in order to protect his emotions and his sanity, not much could catch David's attention. He was nineteen, so I knew the right girl just might. Just like I knew the right boy was what she needed. David had finally found a name he could insist on being called, noticed on the birth certificate he refused to lose and perfect because Africa had come back into style: Rasul. It was the name he finally shared with the rude, feisty chocolate Black girl he kept running into around the building, although she wouldn't reciprocate and tell him hers until he suggested a trip to the movies.

So before they knew it, I had started them on the journey to love. For me, it was a matter of simply waiting for the night he would hold her in his arms and convince her that everything was going to be alright. Their relatively quick, innocent journey to closeness was started by me, but I needed them to want to close the deal. So as the Midwest winter became official, I took advantage of the passing time to think ahead, to see where I wanted them to be, which was lying in each other's arms in a dark motel room along the Indiana Interstate near Christmas, and hear them speak the promises I knew it was just a matter of time before they made:

"I been through a lot of shit in my life," *she would say.* "I been through nights, weeks, months where I didn't have nobody to talk to at night. No friends, no money."

"Shit, me too," *he would confess.*

"Not bad as me."

"How you know?"

"Well, guess I don't. I mean, we really don't know each other that well yet."

"Yeah, but we gettin' there."

"You sure you wanna go?"

"With your loud ass, I don't know . . ."

"Go then. I don't care. I don't need anybody. I can make it by myself."

"You really want me to go?"

"Ummmm . . . yeah."

"Too bad. I'm here to stay."

"Yeah, right. That's what you say now."

"What I gotta do to make you believe me?"

"A hell of a lot more than this."

"I'm listening . . ."

"Well, all this is nice. I guess. But I'm not talking about this play brother, we play house and go to the movies shit. I'm talking about some real shit. Really being there for each other, no matter what else going on. No matter what, we know we can depend on each other, can call each other. Be friends. We can talk, say what's on our minds, say how we feel. Deal with it. Just be real, not fake and phony. And shit, I guess we gotta have some fun. And a lot of sex."

"You like sex?"

"Ha ha! . . . I think you already saw."

"Can I see some more?"

"Rasul, stop! There's more to a relationship than sex."

"I know. I know . . . you think I'm like all these other guys out here."

"All of y'all claim you're different but then—"

"There ain't no then. This is *me*. This is who I am. I like you, a lot. I'm not gonna change."

"Okay. Alright . . . I'll believe you then. As much as I can with everything else I got on my mind."

"What else is on your mind?"

"You gotta ask? Shit, this baby."

"Which one?"

"Don't play with me, boy."

"This one?"

"Yeah. This one . . . my baby . . ."

"Yeah . . . your baby . . ."

"My baby . . ."

"*My* baby . . ."

"Shut up . . ."

"No . . . yeah, my baby. Our baby."

"For real? For real? *Rasul?*"

"Yeah, Shivana . . . yeah. For real. . . ."

PART TWO

EIGHT

HE LIVED ON the fourth floor. We had talked about the building and the block, out in the cold, for about ten minutes because he couldn't smoke in the house even though nobody else was home. He had offered his hand and said, "I'm Rasul." All I had done was shake it and say, "Hi Rasul." When he had finished his Newport, he offered to walk me to my door but I had told him I wasn't ready to go home yet. I wanted to walk up because I knew Ma and Renelle would only take the elevator. Turned out we would have had to do that anyway since the elevator was out of order. I wondered what Renelle had done after I ran out. She couldn't call Leroy, and he had already had his one call for the day so she wouldn't be screaming any questions into the phone tonight. Maybe she didn't believe Nakesha. I'm sure my girl had looked pretty crazy and the whole thing was a blur to Renelle. About the most she had probably done was knock on my door for me without explaining why. Maybe. I hoped. Then Ma would have gone off and Aunt Jewel would have panicked because I wasn't where I said I was going to be. Then Ma would have started going off about me being with that boy I supposedly liked but wouldn't tell her about. Well tonight, she would be right.

Here I was, alone, in the apartment of some strange dude I had only seen a couple of times. Grandma would have said I didn't have a fool's sense. I told myself that I was taking a chance, having an adventure, broadening my horizons, "stepping out on faith" as the preacher would have said at Grandma's church. But I thought back to the feeling he had given me the very first time I saw him. It had been like a bubble bursting, a wave crashing into me, or even the shock of that first raindrop falling on my forehead when a storm was coming. It had felt good, in a way that had nothing to do with sex like it did with Leroy. I knew I had nothing to be afraid of.

Rasul's apartment was the same style as mine. Large living room, small kitchen, tiny bathroom, and two bedrooms arranged in an L-shape. But this one was hooked up. There was a three-piece velvet living-room set and nice dark wood breakfront to match. Tall speakers stood in the corners of the living room, and an entertainment center held a thirty-six-inch television and *serious* stereo with a record player on top. What seemed like a thousand albums were encased behind glass at the bottom of the entertainment center. Strange art decorated all four walls—real painted pictures, not Jew Town posters in cheap gold-tone frames. The raised paint scratched when I ran my fingers along the colorful shapes. Pouch-faced African masks were all over the walls, and their few family photos were all in wooden frames. An older couple with gray hair smiled in one eight-by-ten picture as they held on to each other. They were both dressed nicely, in dark suits. The woman even had a red flower on her lapel. Candles were burning and the air felt calm.

"This your place?" I asked, astonished that someone so young could afford all this. I wasn't trying to get hooked up with another pusher.

"Yep," he grinned. Then after my eyes got wider and my mouth opened, he confessed.

"Naw girl," he finally said. "This ain't mine. I live here with my uncle and his wife."

"Oh. I was 'bout to say . . ."

" 'Bout to say what?" He playfully slapped my shoulder.

"I was 'bout to say you slanging and I'm not into that."

"Naw . . . that ain't me. I just go to school and come home."

He hadn't invited me to sit down yet, but I did anyway. My feet hurt and I suddenly realized how much I ached. My arms, my feet, and the fronts of my thighs were all pulsing with a dull pain. I wished I could soak in a hot bath with Epsom salts and menthol alcohol, but I wasn't trying to get naked with some brand-new Negro fantasizing outside the bathroom door.

"Where you go to school?" I asked him, sinking into the pile of pillows on the couch.

"Well, I had kind of dropped out for a while. So now I'm just down at Olive Harvey trying to get my GED."

Great. Another stupid.

"Why you drop out?" I asked him while he lit a stick of incense. I hoped he wasn't setting the mood for something. Had just let me come and chill at his place because he thought he was about to be getting some.

"I'm not fucking you," I announced before I knew it.

He didn't even answer, just bucked his eyes and ran his hands through his knotty Afro. He shook his head back and forth and started to open his mouth, but then just grinned again.

"You want something to drink?"

Hell, why not?

"You got some Kool-Aid or somethin'?"

"Naw . . . wish we did though. They don't even buy it. We got some pop though."

"Okay. That's fine."

"What kind you want?"

"Orange," I said. He walked away.

For the few minutes he was gone I took the time to look around some more. Right next to the entertainment center was a tall bookshelf. I walked to it just to see what it held. I didn't recognize anything, not that I expected to. I really didn't read other than in school, and Ma didn't read much besides the *Sun-Times* occasionally and *The Enquirer*. My eyes slowly ran along the titles because they all seemed long as hell: *The Crisis of the Negro Intellectual, The Souls of Black Folk, Sent for You Yesterday, Their Eyes Were Watching God, Song of Solomon, I Wonder as I Wander, Tell Me How Long the Train's Been Gone*. They all sounded interesting, but were way too big for me to even think about reading. I saw *Roots* and *The Color Purple* way down at the bottom. I had seen those movies a thousand times, but didn't know they were books too. Maybe I would ask him if I could borrow them one day since at least I knew the stories; I could skip through if I needed to. *Roots* was about slavery and *The Color Purple* was about Celie and Shug. And Nettie and Sofia. And I guess Mr.'s stanky ass too. But I had to get my head on straight before I even thought about reading anything.

Rasul scared me when he appeared suddenly behind me with a can of Sunkist (not Aldi's Sweet Valley like I expected) and a cold glass clinking with ice cubes.

"Thanks," I said, and went back to the couch. I cracked my pop open and poured it into the glass, listening to the fizz and watching the bubbles burst one by one. Usually, I drank pop straight out of the can. Rasul was staring at me, I'm sure wondering why I was so fascinated with a glass of pop. I was thirsty as hell, but didn't guzzle it down because I didn't want him wondering about that too. I took a few ladylike sips.

"So why you drop out?" I asked him again.

"Oh. Yeah." He leaned back into the couch and slipped his

hands toward his crotch. Then he wiggled his big feet out of 1990s Air Jordan's. All I was thinking was I'd crack this Negro upside his head with this glass if he didn't understand I had meant what I said. But he didn't make a move. I guess that was his way, like every man's, of getting relaxed.

"Well, I had kind of went to a buncha different schools and my credits kept getting messed up, so I just stopped going for a while. 'Fore I moved here. But my uncle made me go back. His wife work at Olive Harvey so I just signed up for the morning classes so I could go with her. Then I work in her office for a couple of hours filing and stuff. Just to have some change in my pocket."

"Oh," I said, satisfied.

"I'm about to be through in December though."

"Good for you," I said. "I wish I could drop out and get my GED." I finished the glass in one long gulp. That might be what I would have to do if I had this baby. I wondered how much time I had left for the abortion . . .

"You want some more?" he asked me.

"Naw, that's alright." I wasn't trying to look too hungry. Plus I had enough home training to know not to show up at some-body's house and be greedy.

"Where your uncle and his wife at?" I wanted to know. I couldn't trust him all that much yet. And I didn't want some mad Black woman coming out of the bedroom accusing me of being a "fass hussy."

"They in Kentucky for Thanksgiving vacation," he said. "They go down there every year to visit her people."

"So they just leave you here all by yourself?"

"I'm nineteen," he said. "Shit, I'm a grown man."

"Grown men got they own house and they ain't got to live in nobody else's."

"True that," he said. "I'm working on that. I do music."

Goddamnit, that's what they *all* said. He must have seen it in my eyes because he kept on trying to explain himself.

"For real. I know these cats got a studio in they house up on Champlain. We go down there and make beats and record our rhymes."

"You know Cognac?"

"The rapper?"

"Yeah."

"Hell yeah! 'We Likes It Ruff.'" He started to juke on the couch like the music was playing. I busted out laughing because he didn't have any rhythm. Dancing like that, he obviously was trying to impress me (and wasn't). But I was about to impress him.

"Well, I know the girl who sung on that song."

"Quit playin'!"

"I do. She go to my school. We used to eat lunch together every day."

"Damn . . ." He stared at me. "Can you give her my tape?"

"Why should I?"

"Shit, 'cause it's the bomb."

"Maybe. I'll think about it. I gotta hear it first though." He didn't need to know I hated Patty-Cake's guts.

"You seen *Juice* yet?"

"No, but I want to." So take me.

"Man, I seen that shit five times already. Auntie Linda got me these sneak preview tickets plus I got it on bootleg. That shit is raw! Everybody in it—Queen, Big Daddy Kane, Eric B., Rakim. Man, Tupac go straight ballistic at the end. You wanna watch it?"

"No, I don't wanna see no bootleg. I was gonna see it at the movies," I said, wondering if I had the skills to coerce two men in one night. Apparently I did.

"Well, I'll go again if you wanna go."

"You payin'?"

I was expecting him to say some bullshit, like "Hell naw" or "Why should I pay for you?" or "You ain't my woman." But he surprised me, as he had been doing all night.

"I guess I could. Seein' as though you homeless."

"I ain't homeless!" I screamed louder than I had meant to. He looked shocked and leaned away.

"I was just jokin'," he said.

"Well, don't play with me like that," I pouted. "You know I live in the building. I got somewhere to go. I just ain't trying to go there tonight."

"Why not?"

"I don't know. I just don't feel like dealin' with some shit."

"Well, you can stay here. They ain't comin' back 'til next week."

"Alright now. I ain't trying to beat your girl down when she come up in here asking questions."

He just grinned lopsided again, but made no reply. I didn't push the issue because I didn't want him to think I was sweating him. He wasn't cute anyway, only kind of nice. I wondered why he had white splotches on his face and neck, but I didn't want to embarrass him so I didn't ask.

"So I'm taking you to the movies, now you stayin' at my crib. And you still ain't told me your name."

I thought I had, and hoped I wasn't so ugly that he didn't even bother to remember it.

"My name Shivana."

He just nodded and didn't say a word. Talking about home made me remember I should call it.

"I need to use your phone," I told him.

"It's right next to you," he said, and I saw a gleaming silver cordless on the end table next to the couch.

"In private."

"Oh."

He got up and I followed. He took me to what was most likely the grown folk's bedroom. It was almost nicer than the living room. Everything—the comforter, curtains, even the carpet—was white and cream. I wondered why the carpet at our house was a nasty, spotted-up gray. I wondered why his uncle and aunt were still living here if they had money for all this. There was a fancy, old-fashioned cream-and-gold phone on the glass nightstand. Without saying a word, he walked out and shut the door. Right when I picked up the receiver to get ready and dial, he came back in.

"Don't call long distance," he said.

"Don't worry," I snapped back, and held my breath to make my call. It was 10:17. Ma should be knocked out cold. I exhaled as soon as I heard Aunt Jewel's voice.

"Golding residence," she said, most likely expecting her man.

"Aunt Jewel?"

"Shivana?"

"Hey," I said sheepishly, waiting for a cuss-out. Even Aunt Jewel had the potential to flip over this.

"Hey! When are you coming home?"

Just from that, I could tell Renelle hadn't been there. At least not yet.

"Well, I wanna stay the night at Nakesha's," I lied, stalling for time to figure out what to say after Renelle talked to Ma. Because deep down, I knew she was going to.

"On a school night? Shivana, I don't think that's a good idea . . ."

"I know, but she broke up with her boyfriend so she came over to help me babysit 'cause she upset."

"Nakesha doesn't live that close. How you all gonna get there? You're not taking the bus this late."

"Her daddy comin' to get us."

"Well, I don't know . . . you need to ask your mother."

"No! I don't want you to wake her up. I know she sleep by now. Just put her a note on the refrigerator. She ain't gonna see me anyway before she go to work."

"Hold on. Lemme get a pen to take down their number and address."

Damn Aunt Jewel always trying to do shit the right way!

"Oh, you need her daddy to call you?"

"No. Shivana, I trust you. You're a young adult. I just want to know in case anything happens and we need to reach you."

When she came back I gave her everything she needed to know and said good night. Relieved, I came from the bedroom with a smile on my face. I made a short detour to use the bathroom (which had this purple and green bird thing going on). Thank God I hadn't had much to eat today and didn't have to shit. I couldn't blow up the spot on the first night. There wouldn't be a second then. But I did need to sit for as long as it would take to do just that. Needed to clear my head. Suddenly I remembered the money—the mound in my shirt that Rasul hadn't bothered to ask about. I pulled it out of my shirt and piled it on top of the toilet seat. I ran the water so he would think I was washing up for bed and not shitting. I got on my knees and counted it as quickly as I could. Just 227 dollars. Not nearly the five or six hundred dollars I needed to get rid of this baby. I didn't know how much it would cost, but I knew it was more than that. I decided to divide the money stack between my two pockets, which he probably wouldn't bother to open just in case he surprised me and was a thief. Then I lifted the toilet seat and sat my ass down.

For the first time since I had run out of Renelle's with nowhere to go, Nakesha's face popped into my head. The look in her eyes as her face darkened with hate for me, the snarl on her face when she called me a bitch. Ma always said pregnant women get on her nerves. She hated to be in the same room with them, because all they do is cry or laugh over the least little thing. At least I had plenty of big things to cry about so I didn't feel too guilty about sitting on Rasul's squeaky clean toilet with my face in both hands and tears running down my cheeks. I rocked back and forth with my pants around my ankles, thinking about my girl. *My girl.* My friend, my partner, the only chick in school I said more than ten words to in a given day. The one who would have had my back no matter how many bitches we had to face, then come to find out the one she would end up swinging at was me. Our bond broken by bullshit, the friendship severed by temporary insanity not to mention stupidity, I was scared I might not ever have her back. *Ever.*

I pulled up my pants, washed my hands, and splashed my face with the cool running water, then came back into the living room. I saw Rasul had already closed the blinds and put a sheet and blanket on the couch. He was lying on the opposite love seat staring at an old Freddie Jackson video on *Midnight Love.* I assumed the covers were for me, and flopped right down on the couch. I was so tired, so drained, so needing a good night's sleep, that I closed my eyes almost as soon as I lay down.

"Aw, that ain't for you," he said, his hands still slyly stuffed into his Karl Kani jeans.

"Who it's for then?"

"I was gonna sleep out here. You can sleep in my room if you want to."

I knew enough about niggas my age to know you can't trust what goes on between their sheets, whether they were alone or with somebody. Especially when they were alone. I decided I was fine right where I was.

"No, I don't want to take your bed away from you. I'll sleep out here."

He looked disappointed. He grabbed the remote control to turn the volume down.

"That don't bother me," I said. Then, "I like it."

"Oh, alright."

I felt myself slipping away, in this strange apartment with its strange books and this strange boy. But as I sank deeper into the couch with the blanket up to my chin, nothing at all felt strange about being there. I rubbed my navel and wondered what the fight had done to what was inside. I wondered if it was still in one piece, or if it was even one piece yet to begin with. I couldn't remember from the Reproduction unit in school. But right then, I didn't care. I would look in my book whenever I went back to school.

"I ain't goin' to school tomorrow," I whispered, but he heard me anyway.

"Shit, I might not go myself. It's almost over anyway."

"Let's not go," I giggled.

"Cool with me," he said, not looking my way, only staring at the TV. Freddie Jackson sang on to that light-skinned, green-eyed model that was in almost all the videos. *You are my lady, you're everything I need and more, you're all I'm living for . . .* Before I could imagine what Rasul might be thinking, I was asleep.

NINE

WE DIDN'T GO to school and we didn't go to the movies, but
we did watch the bootleg *Juice* tape the next afternoon after
Rasul made me some fried sausage and real French fries,
butchered from fat Idaho potatoes. I took a twenty-minute
shower and didn't worry about him walking in on me. I could
already tell he wasn't that type. I washed out my sweatshirt,
socks, and even panties in his bathtub and hung them over the
shower rail to dry. I used whatever lotion and deodorant I could
find under the bathroom sink, and started to think about stealing a pair of his aunt's panties before I thought that he might
think wearing another woman's panties was more nasty than
not wearing any at all. I dried myself well down there. Just
thinking about what might happen if he started touching me
without my panties made the bells go off in that tiny spot, and I
was moist. I was embarrassed at myself for even thinking about
that, considering that's why I was in the place I was in now. I
slipped on the baggy Chicago Bulls sweats and triple x Nike

T-shirt he gave me. I didn't have a curling iron so I just slicked Ultra Sheen through my hair, and brushed it all back. To my surprise, I looked kind of cute that way—my eyes popped out more. He took a shower right after me, changed into an Adidas wind suit, and came out of the bathroom smelling like Speed Stick deodorant and cocoa butter.

I was confused about like, not to mention love, until that night with him. We talked for hours—about our mothers and fathers, the scar on my mother's face, the white spots all over his body, the best friends we were both claiming to have. I told him I had never been to the carnival and he said we could go one day. I told him my daddy had let me have a kitten once, but I found it weeks later dead and stiff on our kitchen floor with no explanation. I had concluded it got a hold of some of our rat poison, though Ma just said he was sick. He told me that when he was little in Missouri he had seen a dog having babies in the middle of a dusty road, and no one thought to try to move her or the puppies. A truck came along and killed the puppies just as the mother was having the last one, and when the dust settled he had seen their tiny pink bodies smashed flat into the road. His mother wouldn't let him keep the last one. So he told me we could find a kitten and a puppy to adopt. I couldn't help but start loving him after that.

Most guys I knew just ran away from women with drama, and most of us had it. Didn't care about anybody but themselves. So many of Ma's friends and chicks I knew from school were trying to collect child support, but couldn't find their babies' daddies in order to serve the papers. And if you were the type of woman who got out and worked rather than collect a welfare check, the child support authorities really didn't care about you; nothing was coming out of their pockets, so they didn't care to track down the deadbeat. And even when they finally did find the deadbeats, the guilty offenders only had to pay ten dollars a month or something ridiculous like that—not even worth the effort when you really thought about it. The rest of them were doing or selling drugs, skipping school, and getting us pregnant. The rest of them didn't love nobody but their mamas. The rest of them probably wouldn't love me.

But Rasul was different. He was at least trying to do something with himself, trying to stay out of the game. He wasn't in the streets; he was legit. He was nineteen, and looking for a way to get into computers. He was finishing a GED course. That first day, we just talked, for hours and hours—about everything from school, to the block, to memories I thought I had forgotten. That night, I didn't bother to call home. As dusk descended long after I was supposed to be home from school, I knew panic had set in up at my apartment. I knew Aunt Jewel was scrambling to find the piece of paper where she had written down Nakesha's information, but as scatter-brained as she was I knew she wouldn't find it. Her imagination had gone wild, filled with all the fates that were quite possible for a fifteen-year-old girl walking alone on any street in America, let alone one on the South Side of Chi: some nigger had snatched me up after school, raped me, then thrown me through the window of some abandoned building on the South Side where the twenty-degree temperatures would ward off the telling scent of my rot; a group of boys had made fun of me and I had decided to talk back, so they took turns stomping on my head under the shadow of El tracks and left me there to be found by someone who could not have identified my smashed-in face even if they knew me; a pusher who had been jabbing at me every day after school finally convinced me to give it a try, and I had decided to follow him into a new world; a pimp had thought I was cute and given me a hundred-dollar bill to turn my first trick; or maybe the pusher and the pimp were one and the same, pointing a penis as tall as the Sears Tower and shooting heat into my arm to catapult my mind to the tower's peak. Aunt Jewel would shove past Ma on her way out the door to the police, and they might have gotten into their first fistfight since they were teenagers. Ma was too callous to imagine the same things Jewel had, so callous that Jewel's dead-on view of our world was one she had forced herself to forget. *Shivana just fass don't what to do what I say and she done called herself running away well she bet not bring her ass back* . . . is all Ma would think, or say. She didn't have a car; would she drive on past everybody at her stops and spend the day looking for me?

"Won't they call the police?" Rasul asked me as I lay on the couch again that night, this time in his arms as I leaned against him. I felt dizzy and intoxicated as our tongues swirled around each other's, as he was careful to keep his hands above the line I had told him not to cross. In my mind, I thought about the first day I had ever seen him, the night I had gotten pregnant, and how I wished he had been the one. This must be the way the marriage love started, and I knew I just had to get rid of this baby if it was ever gonna start again. Nobody like him was gonna want me after this—with baggage and another mouth to feed. Fuck that. Being waited on, being talked to, being held, being slow with it all—this felt too damn good. A dream I had had for a long time was finally coming true—that a boy I liked finally liked me back, wanted me, if only for one night.

"Maybe," I answered, and we started kissing again until we fell asleep hazed by the glow of love songs on BET.

The next morning, our second together, I made him wake and find me a piece of paper and an envelope. He ripped out a sheet from the Mead notebook where he did his math home-work. I wouldn't let him see what I wrote in the note to my mother, and made him promise not to open the Commonwealth Edison payment envelope after I had sealed it shut with saliva I had to muster from deep inside, since my throat had gone dry with terror as I pondered what Ma was thinking—and what would be done to me when I got home. There was no need to confess my predicament now. I still hadn't decided what I was going to do.

Friday November 20, 1992

Ma,

I wanna ask you to not be mad at me but I know you gonna be mad anyway so I gotta tell you why I can't come home. I'm okay. I'm staying with one of my friends you don't know. But I got something to tell you and I'm just gonna have to go ahead and say it. I know Renelle done came and talked to you. I know you probably know so I'm gonna tell you that what Nakesha said to her ain't true. Don't believe her. But I am in a little bit of trouble right now, with Renelle, and I can't let her find me. I think she might kill me cause Nakesha told her something that ain't true. So I can't come home right now cause I can't have Renelle find me. And I can't go to school either cause she might find me there too. Just don't believe what she say, don't be mad at me, and I'm going to come home soon. I'll call you first.

Love, your daughter Shivana

"Slip it under there real quiet, so they won't hear," I told him.

"Shivana, I don't know. What if they got the police there or something?"

"They ain't got no police there. You just gotta put it under there and run or something."

"They gonna see the paper come up under the door and open it and see my black ass. Next thing you know I'm down at the station. Naw, hell naw . . ."

For the first time since I had met him, Rasul rolled his eyes and the gesture made my own sting.

"So you got me up here in your place, having me kissing and grinding all on you, thinking you 'bout to get some, but you can't do me this one little favor?"

"I ain't trying to get none. Don't act like you didn't start it."

I remembered I had started it.

"Don't matter if I started it or not," I shot back. "You went along. Now if you can't do me a favor then you ain't really trying to be my friend."

"Maybe you should go on home," he said. "Whatever the fuck is going on gonna be right there when you get back. Fuck it and get it on over with. Running away ain't gonna solve nothin'."

I exploded, raising my voice like he was my child and not somebody I wanted to be my man.

"You don't *know* me. You don't fucking know me! You don't know shit about what's going on in my life. You ain't got a mothafuckin' clue so don't be telling me about what I can and can't run away from."

"If I don't know you what the fuck I'm doing letting you in my crib?"

"Fine, I'll get the fuck out of your crib. I don't need you or your funky ass crib."

He grabbed my arm as I started toward the bedroom to change back into my own clothes.

"Fine," he agreed. "Fine, I'll do it, but I'm not doin' it till later on. When everybody sleep."

"But she lookin' for me now . . ."

"You want me to do it don't you? That's the only way."

With my back against the wall in more ways than one, I couldn't argue with his offer. And for the first time since we had met, I let him see me break. There was no way to determine whether or not someone would stay. That was a decision they made on their own, with or without your help. Men were scared off without anything significant happening to do the scaring. In his eyes, the pressure of his grip, I felt what couldn't yet be called love. I preferred to at least think it was the beginning of caring, an act I had seen taken advantage of too many times and by too many people. Including me, who had betrayed a woman who had put pocket change in my pockets for almost a year. I decided to tell him before things went any further between us.

"Look Rasul, I'm pregnant."

He didn't release me quickly as I thought he would, though I felt him softening right after I spoke. My hold on him was already slipping away. I wiped my face on his shirt.

"Before you start thinkin' I'm a hoe, I'm not," I shouted in defense of an accusation I was sure he was waging in his mind. He must have been replaying the previous night, mistaking my affection for simple lust, and wondering how many other strange men's apartments I had slept in.

"I only been with one person but I wasn't careful about it," I explained further. "And he was married but I thought he loved me and I didn't think I was doing nothing wrong at the time but now his wife wanna kill me and I just can't go home 'cause I know she told my ma and that mean now my ma wanna kill me too and my aunt gonna be disappointed and I just really don't know what to do . . ."

He shushed me, either not wanting to hear any more or needing time to take it all in.

"Damn, Shivana," was all he said while I shut up and cried. "Damn . . ."

He led me to the couch and we sat down. I started crying, began to hiccup, and was officially a hot mess. He got up and went to the kitchen, returning with a cool glass of water. Did people think water was some type of abortion juice, because it seemed like the only thing they had to offer whenever I had a meltdown. I drank half of the glass and then we just sat still.

"What you gon' do?" he finally asked.

"I'm gettin' an abortion," I said without hesitation.

"You got the money?" The thought crossed my mind that he would offer it to me if I said no.

"No."

He didn't offer.

"I got 'bout half of it now. I gotta save up for the other half. Problem is my job was keepin' this woman's kids, and now that's over."

"I'm strapped," he said. He could have been lying, but it meant a lot to me that he had known he should at least try to offer or explain. "Maybe you *should* tell your ma. She might give you the money."

"Ma ain't gon' let me get no abortion. She don't believe in that. She ain't gon' let me kill her grandbaby."

"But if it's gonna be this big problem . . ."

"Still. She don't care. She ain't gon' let me kill it. She just gon' kick my ass or cuss me out every day to remind me I fucked up. But she ain't gonna let me kill it."

Rasul leaned back against the plush pillows and pulled me into him. I felt his heart beating against my back. He said nothing for a while. Then he spoke, so suddenly I was startled by his words.

"She right . . . don't kill it."

WE WERE STILL on the couch, dozing off against each other when Ma knocked on his front door. Rasul rubbed his eyes and stretched while I simply stared straight through the door, as if Ma's eyes already had a hold on me I couldn't break if I wanted to. I knew it was her though she hadn't said a word.

"Who the fuck . . ." Rasul began, stretching one arm out and rubbing his eyeballs with his fists.

"It's her."

There was something to be said for children's intuition as well as mothers'. It was a curious bond, where two beating hearts still seemed to be connected to the thoughts, activities, and well-being of another. Ma always said she knew Grandma was sick long before Grandma broke down and told us, toward the end when she knew she really had no choice but to explain she was leaving. Ma looked her straight in the eye, defiant almost, like she had won a prize, and said "Well Mama, I already knew *that*."

This time, the knock was much harder. Rasul looked agitated and began to whisper.

"I ain't gettin' it. What if that's the popo's?"

"No, it's Ma," I said. I just knew it, as if I had been on my way to dreaming it and someone suddenly woke me up before I got to the good part. I threw him off of me and carefully paced toward the back of the apartment, as if she could hear my footsteps on carpet through several feet and a heavy wood door. I feared if I could sense her, she could sense me too, sniff me out. I remembered watching a show about lionesses protecting their young in the jungle. Cats can't count, so they keep up with each and every newborn by scent. I was sweating before I reached my hiding place, and knew Ma could smell the sin between my legs if she was that determined to find me.

"Who is it?" Rasul shouted deeply, trying to sound in charge and grown up. By the time Ma answered, I was already on the other side of the bathroom door, shutting it so quietly it barely clicked. I pressed my ear against the door trying to hear, hoping Rasul would be smart enough not to let her barge in, although a Black woman on a mission was a force he might not be able to reckon with. I couldn't hear her voice, only his.

"Yes. Uhh huh . . . man, I'm sorry to hear that. Unh huh . . . oh, okay."

I giggled in spite of myself, trying to hold back from bursting through the door and letting my mama know I was okay. I knew she really loved me, despite. I heard another voice that I couldn't make out. It sounded like a man's. I thought Rasul had been right about the police. I thought about perjury, and how I had pulled Rasul into my mess of lies and he had only known me for a couple of days. He wasn't going to want a thing to do with me once he got me out of his apartment, was probably only being nice now just because he had too much heart to tell me to get the fuck on.

"Sir, I really don't pay attention to people in this building . . . you know I just go to school and work and go home . . . Well, it really ain't no point 'cause I'm sure I ain't never seen her . . . I mean, I'm pretty sure I wouldn't remember 'cause I kinda be in my own world . . . Well, okay, I guess I could take a look . . . I guess she look kind of familiar, but I don't know. Like I said, I really don't pay that much attention . . . okay, alright. No, no, ma'am. I ain't never seen her before."

I saw my ma crying in front of two strangers, although it was something she had never let me see. I saw her in uniform. It was cold. She had on her long, scratchy, gray cotton trench. It was open because she never buttoned it all the way up, only held it tight across her every morning when she walked out of the house for work. Her long, fat, out-of-style shoelaces were frayed and dangling at the ends but somehow she never stepped on them. She had her black knit cap pulled down over her scar.

"I'm for real, sir . . . I mean, I woulda remembered if I had seen her in the last couple of days. She kinda cute . . . Oh sir, I'm sorry I'm not trying to be funny . . . I'm just trying to help . . . But you know I guess I gotta get back to my home-work . . ."

My ma . . .

"Oh, ma'am, my name Rasul . . . umm my aunt and uncle live here but they out of town now . . . naw I don't go to high school I go to Olive Harvey . . . umm I'm nineteen, ma'am . . . you tell me your apartment and I can let you know . . ."

My ma . . .

"Well, she probably alright. She probably just at her friend's house or something . . . oh, you already been there . . . you been back? Oh, you been everywhere . . . Man, she ain't been to school . . . she got a boyfriend?"

My ma . . .

"Ma'am, I'm really sorry for your situation right now but I'm pretty sure she okay . . . uhn huh . . . uhn huh . . . I don't think you should be all upset 'cause you know girls do this all the time . . . run off somewhere for a couple days . . . I know she gone come back but she just got to get ready I guess . . . uhn huh . . . uhn huh . . ."

My *ma* . . .

"I mean you might just be overreacting . . . I'm sure it ain't nothin' . . . you should calm down . . . she gone be back in a couple of days . . . Ma'am . . . Ma'am . . . I think you should just go home and quit worrying and calm down . . ."

I was in her arms like I had sailed over water without once having to look down. I burst out of the bathroom crying, with my arms folded and my head down in shame. I was ready for whatever Ma had to give me when I opened the door—a beatdown right in front of Rasul, an ass-whooping to beat all, a tongue-lashing using street language I thought she didn't even know. I had nothing to say and wouldn't have even been able to get the words out if I had. I had been found out, now it was time to take my punishment like a woman. I was carrying a baby now, a real woman, officially grown. I was hurting the person who put clothes on my back and whose food I ate every night after. I was hurting the woman who had kept a roof over my head my whole life. I was a rebellious, ungrateful, fass, disgusting, immature harlot—everything I thought she was getting ready to call me.

But Ma shocked me and pulled me into her arms as soon as she saw me standing behind Rasul. She ripped the door away from his hands as she rushed in, wearing exactly what I had thought she would be. Behind her, I saw a tall brown man with a full beard and mustache standing with his hands in the pockets of shiny black slacks. He wasn't wearing a uniform so I assumed he was a detective. He and Rasul stood helpless at the door as Ma wept, clenching me tighter than I had ever remembered, seemingly pulling me up until I realized I was the one holding her up.

"Shivana, I thought you was dead . . . I thought you was dead . . ."

From the corner of my running eyes I met Rasul's gaze. He looked embarrassed for his part in the ruse, a part that the stranger behind him now reminded him of with the disapproving look of one brow lodged higher than the other. Rasul just hunched up his shoulders and hung his head. Ma cried on, and we held each other. Soon, I was weeping right along with her, not caring how much she knew, only needing her to know I was sorry.

"Young man, do you realize what we been through over the past couple of days looking for this child?" the man bellowed. Rasul didn't answer him.

We?

"You nineteen, eh?" he continued. "You a grown man. You ought to be ashamed of yourself. I should make a civil arrest, right heah right now . . ."

I heard the heavy, clipped voice of the man who called every night for Aunt Jewel. This was Hakim.

"Having sex with this *bebe* and keeping her away . . ."

"Man, I ain't touched this girl," Rasul said, suddenly catching on.

". . . If I was ya' fatha I'd beat you myself. You lucky you in ya' own home, otherwise . . ."

"Man, I don't even know her!"

"Oh, you don't know huh, eh man? You don't *know* huh? She holed away in ya' apartment while ya' aunt and uncle is away, yet you don't know huh? Man, *c'mon.* Who you think you talking to, eh?"

"Shivana, would you tell this fool I don't know you!"

"*Oh?* Now I a fool? We shall see who will be de fool . . ."

"It's not his fault!" I shouted from nearly inside Ma's coat. Her grip hadn't tightened since she had gotten her hands on me. "I'm not having sex with nobody."

Ma continued to sigh, almost whispering to herself. "I thought you was dead. Lord thank you Jesus. Thank you, heavenly father."

"Well, something is going on and I don't like it," Hakim continued. "Annette, let's take Shivana back to ya' home and get to the bottom of this. Sir, you shall see me again. C'mon ladies."

He pushed past Rasul and grabbed me and Ma, who was still shuddering and unable to speak. She looked terrible—bloated, darker, worn-down, older. Hakim, unsatisfied and unconvinced, nudged Rasul out of the way with a push to his shoulder as we made our way out. Still dressed in his clothes and with my money in the jeans in his bedroom, I didn't even get a chance to look at Rasul and mouth that I was sorry.

TEN

THE NIGHT WAS long and hard, but ultimately successful. Until nearly midnight, through a haze of chain smoke and with Diana as our background music, I was fired questions from Ma and Aunt Jewel. Hakim patiently stood far away to seem out of it but close enough to intervene if necessary. Had I known this stranger was here, I might have come home long ago. Ma wouldn't even hit me in front of Aunt Jewel, let alone someone else who had no reason to believe she wasn't respectable. When we three had walked to my front door, Aunt Jewel had said into the phone, "Thank you, ma'am . . . she just walked through the door," and left it dangling while she ran to hug me. After holding me away for inspection, like I was one of the garments she tossed and turned carefully before deciding to buy, she began a tirade I had feared worse than Ma's hands.

"Shivana, where the hell have you been for the last two days? We've been sitting up here thinking you were murdered! We've been up to the precinct demanding they do something. We've been running around the building and the neighborhood. You've lied to us. You've hurt your mother. You've hurt Renelle. You owe us an explanation little girl!"

They received an explanation, just not the correct one. Jewel did most of the talking while Ma recuperated physically and emotionally from her earlier breakdown.

"The woman from upstairs, Renelle, came by to see us yesterday . . . ," Jewel started.

I just looked out the window at the concrete wall outside it. Being in Rasul's home had enlightened me to our standard of living. The fact that I hadn't chosen where I live made no difference in the disdain I experienced upon my return to my own apartment. Not a home, barely an apartment, just a place where emotions grew restless before they fled. Had it been a person I was passing on the street, I would have thought it was deformed. Ma's diligence alone had spared us the curse of rodents—though simply glancing at roach motels and mice traps on the counters, under the sink, and behind the toilet stung because they were reminders of the possibilities. No effort had been put into creative motifs and color schemes for our rooms. Instead, I lived among an odd assortment of cheap, unoriginal dollar-store finds and forgotten hand-me-downs. The wall above our stove was dotted with years of cooking grease. Our sorry curtains were dingy and in need of washing as they hung from cheap, bent, rusty rods. Patches of paint peeled from our ceiling. Our floors were scuffed with everything from the wheels of my first bright red ten-speed to skid marks made when Ma and I had to push the dining table we found in an abandoned apartment across the kitchen floor ourselves. Cigarette burns marred the carpet in every room and the stale odor of smoke hovered like a toxic fog. Our paper-thin lamp shades were crooked. We had no books except my schoolbooks and plastic-bound ones Jewel had brought from the library. We only had plenty of old, crinkled, even yellowing copies of *Jet, TV*

Guide, and *The Enquirer.* The rugs were worn thin in patches and the metal stand our television rolled on was leaning. Black mold had collected in large circles along the bathroom window-pane where shower water daily pelted. Even our bath towels were hideous—hard, holey, and cheap. I had felt repelled just walking through the front door.

To Jewel's question, I hunched up my shoulders and mumbled, "So."

Jewel leaned in quicker than I could have predicted and shocked me by slapping me—hard—against my face. Hakim had stayed close for a reason. He grabbed her arm to prevent her from slapping me again.

"Let me go, Hakim!" she yelled at him. "Stay out of this. It has nothing to do with you."

"It do now," he proclaimed. "Now we need to be civil about this . . ."

"Civil? Civil? When you bring a child into this world and don't know where it's at for days, then you come back and talk to us about being civil."

"I may not have ever given birth but I do have tree children, do you remembah?"

"Of course I remember. I'm about to be their stepmother. But I won't tell you what to do with them so you don't tell me what to do with this one."

"I will tell you!" he shouted to her, and she cowered in front of him. He was much taller than he could have ever looked in his pictures, with a voice to match his stature. "And I want you to tell me when I'm wrong. Hitting the chile will not get to de bottom of what is going on."

"What *is* going on, Shivana?" Ma suddenly asked, coming alive for the first time in what seemed like hours. "You got Renelle coming down here ready to fight me, sayin' you been sleepin' with her husband and now you pregnant? Shivana, please tell me you wouldn't do nothin' like that. I raised you better than that. I know I ain't been the best, but I raised you better than that . . . you know better than that."

She started crying again, and this time Jewel reached for the bottle of rum previously guarded by Hakim. She poured three shots, and finished one first before pouring a fourth.

"Shivana, you have to tell us the truth. Is this true? Are you pregnant? Were you sleeping with Leroy?"

I couldn't answer, I could only look away and let the tears stream. I was gonna be hard, I wasn't going to break. I was going to go back down to Rasul's apartment, get my money, rob another cabdriver, maybe start turning tricks, and go somewhere to be on my own. Alone, with no baby holding me back. No dirty, ashy kids that made the men want to leave me. No other mouth to feed but mine. I wasn't going to be one of the chicks at school arguing with the baby daddies against the lockers, or one of the women at the clinics and grocery stores managing a bunch of bebe's kids alone. I wasn't going to be a lonely heart sitting at the bar of the dark lounges I peeked into, wondering where he run off and when he gonna return. And I felt perfectly justified in my decision; years and years of overhearing Ma and her friends talk about the sorry Black man had confirmed my decision. I was going to be by myself with no kids—forever young, pretty, and free.

"Now she get quiet," Ma said, smirking and lighting another cigarette. "See, this what I'm talkin' about. I'm tired. Just tired. I can't do no more . . . I done my job. I'll be glad when she's on her own. I can't do no more."

"You might as well just tell the truth because we're going to find it out with or without you. I can take you into that place . . . New Horizons or whatever it's called. Were you sleeping with this man and are you pregnant?"

"No," I said, rolling my eyes.

"What was that, no?" Jewel asked.

"No," I repeated.

"No you're not pregnant or no you weren't sleeping with this man?"

"Both."

"Because, Shivana, if the answer to either one of those questions is yes, you need to be honest. There are things that need to be done either way. Things you can't understand because you're too young."

"I'm not pregnant 'cause I ain't never slept with nobody." I glared at Jewel.

"Well then why would that woman come down here ranting and raving like that? Getting all this mess started. I almost had to kick *her* ass."

Hakim chuckled.

"I'm serious, Hakim! She came up in here like she caught 'em in the act! Spreading lies and telling stories. I'm gonna tell you what I think. I think that man of hers is a dog and she's one of them crazy bitches and looking to blame anybody she can for his hoeing. That's what I think."

"That's what you tink, *bebe*?" Hakim asked. "That's what you tink?" He grinned at her, and she grinned back, playfully slapping his arm.

"Hell yeah, that's what I think." She rolled her neck straight South Side of Chicago style.

"Well, only Shivana know de answer." Hakim stared straight at me. "Is Jewel correct?"

I couldn't look anyone in the eye and so I just stared at my shoes.

"Nakesha was mad at me about something else, so she just started telling lies," I said. "I was scared to come home because Renelle told me she was gonna kill me."

I held my breath, waiting for their reactions, waiting to see if I was as good as I thought I was. They all started chattering at once.

"Well, deh it is . . ."

"Shivana, why would you run away rather than just tell us what was going on?"

"Renelle bet not never bring her ass back down here again and you ain't babysittin' no damned more . . ."

I exhaled.

"But that seems like an awful big lie for someone who's supposed to be your best friend to tell," Jewel pointed out skeptically.

"Leroy just like me. He had tried to talk to me once."

"Talk to you, like how?!"

"Lord Jesus . . . ," Ma sighed with her head in her hands.

I went on to make Leroy the bad guy. He was locked up anyway, so he could be made to look guilty of anything anybody wanted him to look guilty of. So I told them about his "propositions": more money if I did what he asked, little gifts if I would let him touch me, frequent calls even when they didn't need me. I told them how I continued to spurn his advances until I threatened to tell Renelle. I explained that I didn't want to lose my job because I knew Ma had it hard and couldn't afford to give me money, so I just put up with it hoping he would stop. Nakesha was mad at me because of an argument over a boy and she wanted to get back at me, so she lied and told Renelle I was sleeping with her husband. To take the weight off of Rasul, I assured them he was just a friend whom I occasionally talked to in the building, and he had let me stay over since I had nowhere else to go. He had a girlfriend, and hadn't even been there when I was because he was with her or at work. I had told him to lie about everything and he only did what I asked. When it was all over, the Quiet Storm had been playing for hours, the adults were tipsy, and I looked innocent, unstained, and honest.

"We're pressing charges," Jewel slurred.

"Jewel, let's just let it go," Ma sighed.

"We can *not* let this go. This man is a predator, Annette. He has a daughter of his own. What if he's touching her?"

"Leroy wouldn't do nothin' like that," I said before I knew it.

"How do you know?" Aunt Jewel shouted. "If he was trying to get your little butt how do you know he wouldn't try his own daughter's? You're a baby yourself. Men like him are sick and need to be put behind bars."

"Well, he's already there," Ma said.

"Well we need to make sure the key is thrown far away. The police wouldn't do a thing to help us when she was missing but shuffle paper. The least they can do now is intervene before this man really hurts someone."

"Jewel, you 'bout to start some mess and carry yo' ass off to New York leaving me to clean it up," Ma said.

"I'll support you every step of the way," Jewel said. "We can delay our trip back, can't we baby?"

Hakim held up his hands. "Jewel, I have a business to run and I can't just—"

"Well go run it," she spat. "I'm staying here handling some more important business."

Ma raised herself up from the table, swooping up all three glasses in one gesture, signaling the conversation was over.

"You heard what I said Jewel. Get on to New York. I'll handle this situation here."

"What's your way of handling it?" Jewel asked, standing to confront Ma while Hakim braced for possible blows between them.

"*My* way," was all Ma answered before saying, "Good night," and retreating to her bedroom with Hakim's bottle of Caribbean rum she snatched off the table.

I DIDN'T NOTICE Aunt Jewel's packed suitcases and bags until I lay alone in the dark on the living-room couch. I was furious at her, for leaving I supposed, and decided not to speak to her in the morning. Ma had set her and her soon-to-be husband up in my bedroom while I was gone. The boiler had been overset and the radiators were rebelling—hissing, clanging, shooting out spit from their rusty valves. I couldn't sleep because the window was cracked, and though it was the bitter start of a winter the hypes, drunks, and other vagrants weren't dissuaded from acting up all along King Drive. I listened to the honking horns, laughter, frequent whoops, and arguments rise from the street. A pool of sweat dampened the space between my breasts. I wouldn't remove my sweatpants because Hakim might rise in the middle of the night and have to use the bathroom. Instead, I threw off the scratchy throw Jewel had bunched around me after she washed up for bed and I pretended to be asleep. She used cocoa butter all over her body every night before she went to sleep, and the scent from her hands wafted down from my forehead, making me imagine chocolate or something else sweet. Like the butterscotch we made, the perfume she wore, the comfort she gave me. Then I knew why I loved her. She gave me the taste of sweetness I could never seem to find on my own.

Apparently, Hakim thought so too. Though they tried to be quiet in the beginning, I heard him and Aunt Jewel making love. At first, I thought the light knocking was another complaint from the radiators. But soon, I detected short, faint pants that went along with it. The knocking and the panting always stopped as soon as my old, thin mattress began to slightly squeak. But within minutes, it always resumed. I would have never thought anything or anyone could make Jewel purr; she sounded so young. If Hakim made any noise at all, it was too low for me to hear. I wasn't embarrassed, for them or myself, but only interested in what could make grown folks all of a sudden sound like children. My bedroom had always been directly across from my parents', who kept even their kissing as discreet as possible before I'm sure they stopped doing even that. Lovemaking was something I had never heard outside of TV. It

sounded patient and strange in real life. When I was still close
to my father's family, I used to stay with an older female cousin
when both my parents happened to be at work. She had a
never-ending cycle of man-friends who would come by while all
the adults were away. Though my cousins and I always strained
against the bedroom door we were locked behind, we never
heard anything but the stereo she blasted. Whenever I had been
with Leroy, I was unaware of my own sounds. I often forgot I
had ever made any once it was all over.

I imagined them in my bed, in the corner of my room, with its
posters of teenaged singers torn from *Fresh* magazine and my
teddy bears piled everywhere. Jewel often walked around half-
naked, and the black around her breasts was darker and wider
than any other woman I had seen. She was thin, lithe, and always moved with purpose though sometimes it seemed the
wind could blow her over. Hakim was overwhelming, not at all
boyish like Leroy and Rasul. I wondered how he didn't crush
her, how large men had sex with small women. It was then that
I noticed his waist-length tweed coat peeking out from the open
coat closet near the front door.

I moved outside of myself, got up, and began to walk toward
the closet with my eyes seeing only the bulging pockets. So
trusting was Hakim, so naïve that Chicago couldn't possibly be
as treacherous as New York City, that he would leave his wallet
unattended in the closet of his fiancée's sister's home. I reached
inside quietly, keeping one ear toward my bedroom door should
one of them decide to run to the bathroom like I always did after sex. They were probably hugged up and asleep. Inside, as I
had hoped, was a slinky wallet. In the dark, I opened it and
stuck my fingers between the slivers in its crease. The radiator
clang once more, and I jumped, momentarily frozen that I
would be found near the front door once more, with Hakim's
wallet in my hands, and beaten for trying to escape just when
everyone thought they had talked some sense into me. I felt

what I was looking for: the dry, smooth surface of money. Without seeing, I calmly pulled out all the bills and divided the stack in half. I stuffed the other half back into the wallet as neatly as I could. I tiptoed back to the couch, curling toward the back of it where I counted out the money by the bluish glow of the lights from King Drive. There were two fifties in back of the pile, and the rest was twenties. I prayed he didn't organize his money by numbers, or that I had started in the middle of the stack with twenties and left most of his largest bills behind. I didn't have the nerve to go back, so I only counted out what I had gotten on the first try. $260. I stuffed the money underneath the middle couch pillows among loose change, crumbs, and lost barrettes. Satisfied, I focused back onto the sounds I had just heard.

I had thought they were finished, hearing their laughter and mumbling for a while before silence. But then as suddenly as they had started, Aunt Jewel, Hakim, and my bed began making the love music again. It was much later, well after two, so they were probably confident I was deep in sleep and even the weeks-awaited release of their passion couldn't wake me. They exercised little restraint this time, as the knocking and squeaking were fast and loud though their own noises remained tame compared to the bed. As Hakim finally allowed himself to groan and Aunt Jewel made high-pitched sighs, they were unaware I was taking mental notes, searching for clues to their love within the music, naïvely thinking I would be able to use them to determine when I was just fucking and when I was making love. They now drowned out Ma's snoring in the other bedroom. I could hear they were talking to each other sometimes, in between the heaves of my mattress springs when I could tell they were changing around. She was probably telling him she loved him, and he was probably speaking to her in his different language. The "oohs" and "ahhs" were no longer muffled as they had been, so much so that I had almost gotten up and pressed my ear to the door. I imagined them tumbling and turning, moving against each other in a dark room that fooled them into thinking they were totally alone. Aunt Jewel moaned and panted for what seemed like hours as I rubbed my tiny spot the way Leroy never did. Finally, after Hakim began to suddenly moan in perfect time with her, and after she called his name several times, so high and fast each call began to sound like one word, all the noise stopped. I wondered if they had made a baby, the right way this time. Let down that I hadn't been able to listen to the love music until morning, I settled for the hiss of the radiators until I finally fell asleep.

I WASN'T SURPRISED the recently reunited, already honeymooning Jewel and Hakim were the only ones in a good mood over Saturday breakfast. For Jewel's going-away meal, Ma had pulled out all the stops. She had bought bacon still on the rind instead of the usual thin, crispy strips we bought at Aldi's. She scrambled an entire skillet of fluffy brown eggs, whipped and seasoned perfectly. Her pancakes came out thin, light, golden, and exceptionally round. Not one lump interrupted the smoothness of her grits. We poured honey on wheat toast from a jar where the honeycomb stood stuck in time. She had made sausage patties from a pack of round meat that she further seasoned with Lawry's and crushed red pepper. A gleaming pitcher of orange juice sat in the middle of our small table. The adults sipped coffee while I gulped milk.

Remembering the sounds of last night and feeling guilty I had overheard, I could barely look Aunt Jewel in the eye as she tried to be cheery about her parting.

"Shivana, when are you coming to visit us?" she asked. "I think Easter would be perfect." She knew better than to ask Ma, who always used the excuse of work to never fly anywhere and see her.

"Brooklyn is beautiful in de spring," Hakim chimed in. "So much to do and see. You would have fun."

I looked at Ma for my answer. Her silence gave me the go-ahead to reply.

"I could come," I finally said, wondering how far along I would be by April if, for some reason, I changed my mind about the abortion. "How I'm gone get there?"

"A plane!" Jewel shouted. "It's about time you got on one."

"By myself?"

"You're old enough," Jewel said. "We'll send you the ticket."

"When I come from Bermuda I come alone," Hakim said. "I was just ten years old de first time."

"We could get somebody on your daddy side to drop you off at O'Hare," Ma surprisingly said. I smiled, hopeful, knowing I really had to get rid of this baby now otherwise Jewel wouldn't think I was worthy to come. The promise lightened the mood, as at least now there was a definitive time I would see her again. Jewel started telling Hakim about me when I was a baby, about how cute I was and how they shouldn't have been surprised I was missing for two days because I had loved to go hide when I was little. A "chubby little prankster," she called me, which made even Ma laugh and remember. Everyone had second helpings, no doubt to delay their departure. But around ten, Hakim began to look at his watch. He mentioned traffic and suggested it was time for them to get going. I stayed in my seat after everyone else got up to collect the bags and take them downstairs. Ma returned to the kitchen to get me.

"Shivana, you ain't gonna come say bye?"

My back was to her, and I was afraid to turn around. I must have thought I could make Jewel stay by not saying good-bye. People who didn't want to leave would often linger, in everything from relationships to hospital wards, waiting for the other person to say good-bye because they couldn't find the strength to do it. A little immature stubbornness could lengthen Jewel's stay. I was no longer mad at her. She had morphed into something more than my daring, colorful, and bewitching Aunt Jewel. She had never been mine or anyone else's, otherwise she would have stayed right here on the South Side of Chicago with the rest of the Goldings.

"Look, Shivana, they got to go," Ma said. "Now get on up from there and come say bye. Don't be disrespectful."

Reluctantly, I slipped out of my seat and followed Ma to the living room. Aunt Jewel and Hakim were already at the elevator, laughing and holding hands, looking forward to hitting Interstate 80, crisscrossing Indiana, Ohio, Pennsylvania, and New Jersey with no other passengers but the radio. They would snack on things Jewel would never have admitted to eating around us—potato chips, beef jerky, and McDonald's. They would read a map or stop for directions together if they had to. It seemed like such an adventure. I wanted to hop in for the ride.

"You gone call me when you get there?" Ma asked once we emerged onto the stoop. Hakim's car—a glistening burgundy Buick—was parked a couple feet from the building. Sensing the true parting was not his, he had already hugged us, said, "I can't wait to see you again," and gone ahead to load the trunk.

"Of course," Aunt Jewel said, her voice cracking slightly. "Probably won't be 'til tomorrow night though. We're going to get through Indiana and Ohio and sleep over in Pennsylvania. You know, due to the late start."

"You gone let him drive the whole way?" Ma asked.

"Yes honey," Jewel said. "Why should I drive if I have him?" She laughed, and that's when I broke down. I already missed the sound of her laughter. She only hugged me like I was a child missing a toy that she knew where to find.

"Oh, grow up girl," she said. "You're gonna see me again in April. That's right around the corner."

I couldn't say anything. Ma, forever stoic, just stood beside me and shook her head.

"Just think about April," Jewel said. "Annette gonna take care of you. Don't worry."

Hakim pulled up so Jewel wouldn't have to be bothered with walking just a few feet. He waited patiently while cars honked and drove around him. He didn't even respond through the open window where he smoked after one teenaged boy in a green hoopty yelled, "Move out the fuckin' way old man." That was Jewel's final cue, and she squeezed me hard once before letting me go.

"April," she said while walking away. "Call me or write . . . you got Hakim's address and phone number. Just call me!"

She seemed to skip to the passenger side of the Buick, and the picture of her smiling with her flashy leather bag was only missing a "Just Married" sign and empty aluminum cans dangling from the back bumper. We watched the car speed down King Drive before I sat down on the stoop alone and Ma went back inside without one word.

FOR TWO DAYS, we were peaceful. Neither one of us left the apartment. Ma was probably too worn-out from worrying, and I didn't want to chance running into Renelle. Matter fact, I was certain she had told Leroy by now and I had nothing left—no job and no chance in hell for a father for my baby. I wanted to try to go down and talk to Rasul. But after everything I wasn't trying to start something by asking so much as to go to the Laundromat, though we needed to. Ma and I mostly watched TV in silence, on opposite ends of the couch with bags of junk food separating us. We left the beds unmade, and I washed the dishes without being asked. No hits, no lectures, no spiteful words. I waited for the phone to ring, anticipating Jewel's voice on the other side, telling Ma about the missing money. She and Hakim had to have discovered it by now, especially when it came time for him to pay for the motel they would stay in in Pennsylvania. I could hear him saying, "Jewel, I know what I had," and her telling him to get over it. As I had hoped, she would defend me until the end—ultimately blaming it on the entire male species' carelessness before admitting to him or herself that her runaway niece was a thief as well. As Saturday night droned into yet another weekend of a mediocre, lukewarm Amateur Hour on *Showtime at the Apollo,* I felt surprisingly calm.

When the show ended and Ma found one of her other favorite old movies, *Imitation of Life,* I laughed and shook my head along with her all while formulating different plans in my head. By the time the large Black lady was belting out that last funeral song in her dry, throaty voice, I had come up with dozens of scenarios. My couple days' take had eased my mind, sedated me even, so much so that I had reached under the couch as everyone stirred awake the next morning. I casually walked into my room once both Jewel and Hakim emerged, placing the money under my mattress without even bothering to close my door first. At some point, I had to get up to Rasul's and collect my things before he figured out I had money in my jean pockets. I knew I would call New Horizons first thing Monday morning to schedule the solution. I would go back and talk to Sue, who was sure to remember me because of how I had run out. I had counted back to the exact day I got pregnant, and I knew that at just six weeks pregnant they would have no problem getting rid of it. I would request the first appointment available and skip school for it. I wasn't proud of how I had gotten the money, but was too relieved it would all be over before it began now that I had the means to end it. By the end of next week, I would no longer be carrying this baby and Ma wouldn't have known a thing.

On Sunday night, the last thing Ma said to me was, "What

you wanna eat tomorrow?" I thought about it for a while, my eyes glued to the last tense, revelatory minutes of *Columbo*.

"I don't know. Spaghetti maybe."

"Okay," Ma said, lighting her last cigarette before bed.

ELEVEN

EVERY TIME I ran out of clean panties and needed to borrow
Ma's, it seemed like I found something she had never meant for
me to see. I was running late for school Monday morning, and
couldn't risk the consequences that would accompany a tardy
when I already had to explain three unexcused absences. I had
found everything from dime bags to seizure notices from Rent-
A-Center in that drawer. Today was no exception as I scrambled to get out of the door at the exact minute I needed to in
order to be firmly in my algebra seat when the first-period bell
rang. On paper ripped from one of my notebooks, Ma had written me a letter. The papers were folded into a tight roll that immediately curled out as soon as I opened the drawer. I saw my
name at the top in Ma's writing, and didn't bother to read any
farther than the first couple of lines before grabbing a pair of
black granny drawers. I stuffed the letter in my backpack,
knowing I would get home before she did and be able to put it
back. My heart pounded and my mind fixated on what it could

say during the entire walk to the nearby El station. Stuffed between an elderly woman and a middle-aged factory worker wearing heavy steel-toed boots, I buried my concentration in Ma's words like I was reading a love letter. Well away from the tail end of the car where other kids my age collected and cursed, I didn't notice anyone's entrance or exit, nor did I feel the car's sudden, screeching stops and starts as it rumbled along wooden tracks. I heard my ma whispering in my ears.

> *Shivana,*
> *I don't know how to get this letter to you but I'm*
> *your ma and I want you to come home. I don't*
> *know why you run away but we gone talk about*
> *all that when you get back. Cause I run away too*
> *but I was way older than you and I wanted to*
> *marry your daddy but didn't nobody want me to*
> *marry him. They said he was a bum and I guess*
> *he was but for long time he was more than that.*
> *But you really just need to come on home. I*
> *won't hit you no more and we ain't got to argue*
> *no more. We can get along. Cause I know why*
> *you ran away. I know we ain't got no nice things*
> *and I can't buy you the nice things the other kids*
> *had. But that ain't my fault. I know it's hard for*
> *you to live with somebody like me. But I'm gonna*
> *try to do better. I'm gonna try to get better. I been*
> *talking to Jewel. Or I gess I should say Jewel*
> *been talkin to me. She told me I gotta get a*
> *boyfriend and I just laugh at my little sister*
> *'cause its hard for me to imajin a boyfriend now.*
> *She told me I gotta do something with my life.*
> *Something I like to do and something I like that*
> *make me feel good. So I guess when she said all*
> *that was first time I knew I must feel bad then.*

*And I told her Jewel don't nothing make me feel
good no more I just want to go to work come
home. I be so tired. I get tired of sittin on that
bus all the time. My behind and back hurt in that
seat and my legs get stiff but when I stop just to
smoke or take a look outside or strech or talk to
somebody folks get mad wanna know when the
bus gone move. So I just get back on. Sometime
somebody talk to me but is hard to talk and
consintrate at the same time so most of time I
just listen and I can't member what we talked
about when they get off. I look at the same streets
all day long so I just get sleepy cause it ain't
nothing new but I gotta stay up cause I can't
crash no bus with all them people on it. She told
me that mean my mind got to get some exersize
but I don't know how to exersize my mind. I ain't
never been smart like Jewel. I couldn't never
figure stuff out like her. And I ain't never been
pretty like her. Seem like I used to think I was. I
used to feel good when you was little. When I left
mama house and went on my own. Cause when I
met your daddy that's what he wanted us to be
was on our own. You know I met him on the bus
so sometimes when I'm on the bus I see the little
kids with they own boyfriends so I think about
us. When I met your daddy he had on some
overalls and he had this red bandana on his head
and I had on a scarf to so he strike up a
convasashun with me when he told me we match.
We match. We match so good we make you. And
when you was born that's when Stevie Wonder
used to have his song called isn't she lovely playin
on the radio all the time. So that's what your*

*daddy used to sing about you but he ain't never
sing it about me. So that's kind of when I stop
lovin you just a little bit. Not a lot. And not no
more. Just a little love lost then cause I wanted
your daddy to sing about me sometimes. I
couldn't wear no makeup on my scar cause its too
deep. All the makeup just sink right in like quick
sand. I started to think it might fall out like sand
and I ain't never wanna get my shirt dirty.
Spechully when I really want to wear makeup is
when I got on something nice, when I get dress
up. So I just let it be and I forgot all about it. You
don't know I been through terribul things cause
when I fell out that ride I thought I was gonna
die. Everybody thought I was gonna die. I fooled
them. I always been mad at Jewel cause she was
in there with me. Right next to me she was. We
was in the same one and she was even littler than
I was so I don't understand why I slip out and
she didn't. I just leaned down just a little bit to
wave at everybody and try and smile for a picture
and then I was just falling. I reached out but
wasn't nothing to grab on. It all happened so
quick. I was in there one minute. I was gone the
next. I couldn't see nothing cause it was all white.
It was cold to. And I reached out and I just
thought I was falling and somebody gonna catch
me cause thas what sposed to happen when a
child fall. But ain't nobody catch me and I hit the
ground so hard. I can't never forget that when I
hit that ground. I have bad dreams bout that hit.
It was like somebody threw my head against the
sidewalk like it was a basketball. And I couldn't
see nothing in this world no more but I didn't*

know I wasn't dead. So they say I was lucky we
was turned around on the ride. I was lucky we was
coming down and not going up. So Ma and daddy
was happy I wasn't dead but then thas when
everybody start saying I was slow. Folks start
whispring about me like I couldnt hear. Sometimes
they got quiet when I walk in a room but
everybody smile when Jew Jew walk in. So all I
could do was be mad at her all the time. I know I
ain't stupid. When I was little I did everything
everybody else did so how can all of a suddin I be
stupid just cause I hit my head hard one time?
And I know you might think I stupid but Im not
stupid. Cause I passed my driver test and I been at
my job way longer than some of those other folks
get fired cause they can't do it right. But folks
think just cause you ain't got no good job or no
school after high school that mean you ain't smart.
So Jewel right you got to go to college Shivana
otherwize folks gone look down on you. I know
you miss your daddy and I don't know where he
at. I talked to Till and she say he doin alright. She
say he in California. You got some other brothers
and sisters. She say soon as he get back to Chicago
she gonna make him come see you. But that been a
long time ago now. That been years and ain't
nobody still seen him so maybe he ain't gonna come
back. But you got to forget about that girl. You got
to get over that cause I had to get over it for you if
not for me. But don't you leave me and not come
back. That ain't right. Women ain't sposed to leave
and if they do they always come back. Like Jewel. I
just want you to come back home soon as posibul.
I'm not mad no more. Love, Mommy

I didn't remember getting off the train, sifting through the jumble of down jackets squeezing through a metal-detector entrance, nor did I understand how I turned my locker's combination when it seemed like I had never been in the building before. Ma's words were still in my head as Mrs. Carly contained me in the now-emptied hallway. She had pulled my jacket as I entered the classroom. I had noticed her standing watch outside her door because I was too busy looking out for Nakesha. I didn't know if seeing her would result in the fight that led to my permanent unexcused absence—expulsion. Mrs. Carly already had her grip on me by the time Nakesha showed up, looking shocked to see me but then wiping the emotion from her face just to reinforce her new hatred of me.

"Shivana, where you been?" Mrs. Carly demanded. She had a new wig—red with boxy, looped curls—and her eyes appeared larger behind the thick lenses of her glasses.

"I had to help my ma with some stuff," I told her.

"Shivana, you missed the unit exam on Thursday," she said. "Without an excused absence, I can't let you make it up. You were already on shaky ground."

I guessed she was telling me I was going to flunk. I didn't know what the hell she expected me to say. She was going to do what she was going to do. Maybe it was for the best. I wasn't going to have time for this shit once I was living on my own and trying to pay for my own apartment. I would just have to be like Rasul and get my GED.

"Well?" she said.

"Well what?" I asked her, rolling my eyes and hunching my shoulders.

"Your mother needs to get your absence excused or else you gonna flunk my class," she said. I didn't respond and she just stared at me. I twisted my lips until she sighed and shook her head, walking into the classroom with me following her inside.

She slammed the door hard and loud enough to crash the party her students daily started without her.

Nakesha and I locked eyes as I made my way to the empty seat right next to her. After that she refused to meet my gaze, instead drawing circles on the "do-now" worksheet Mrs. Carly had handed to every student who entered the classroom. She didn't even look my way as I raised my hand to get a worksheet from Mrs. Carly. There was the figure of the human body, with blank lines to be filled out from head to toe.

"We've finished Reproduction and we are now starting on Vital Organs," she said, handing me a sheet, her authority dangling over the class and keeping closed all the mouths who dared to open with nonsense.

"What's Vital Organs?" Patty-Cake asked right before Mrs. Carly snatched a red lollipop out of her mouth.

"Lungs, heart, kidneys, brain," Mrs. Carly said. "All the things we need to keep us running and alive."

"What about that other stuff?" my old crush Tavares asked.

"What other stuff, Tavares?"

"That other vital stuff, down below the belt?"

His comments did little to shake Mrs. Carly or any would-be rioters.

"We will be looking below the belt—at waste systems and the like," Mrs. Carly snarled. "Anything else you're thinking about we probably already covered in Reproduction."

"Well he ain't never reproduced so he wouldn't know that . . . ," Patty-Cake started, and the insurrection began.

In the midst of it, I decided the best way to break the ice would be to write Nakesha a note. I turned over my worksheet, pulled out a pen, wrote down, *I'm getting my abortion girl,* and held it at my side until Nakesha begrudgingly snatched it. I was waging that sympathy could settle our feud.

Well get it then bitch.

I was not amused by her stubbornness. Undaunted, I wrote back, fanning the last embers of our friendship, restarting the familiar rhythm we had shared in countless classes, where only our words scratched hurriedly in pen behind a teacher's back could make the hour drone by.

You still mad at me?

Hell yeah.

I'm sorry. I feel like I'm losing my mind for real.

You lost it already.

You feel alright from that shot?

No. Couldn't fuck nobody if I wanted to. Been through three boxes of pads already.

Damn. You on the rag now?

Hell yeah. Started that day and ain't stopped since. Plus my stomach hurt.

See I told you you shoulda got the pill. Least your face coulda cleared up.

I wish I would have.

Least you got something. You don't want to be like me.

I WAITED TEN minutes for her to pass back to me, but she didn't. When the bell finally rang, she grabbed her things quickly and walked on ahead of me without waiting like she used to.

WINTER HAD TURNED Chicago into a pencil sketch on a misty gray canvas—thin dead branches, dozens of dull buildings blending into the same outline, the occasional bird cloaked in a dull, gruff coat, the steel El cars bellowing on tracks glazed with ice, stray animals with the jutting ribs that made them appear almost see-through. On my school's corner, I caught sight of a tiny beige cat balanced on the edge of a garbage can; she ran away with jaws locked tight around her take—a chicken wing covered in red sauce. A couple weeks ago the sight would have made me nauseous, but the bitter cold probably froze the liquids inside me before I lost feeling in the solid. Achromatic valley of sky seemed to stretch on for miles without leaves to break it. I saw only one tree shivering with stiff hard leaves hanging on for dear life, refusing to give up and blow away. Missing the lush fullness of milder seasons, the city looked like the practice of a novice who had nonchalantly flicked their wrists to simply get an idea off their mind. Transparent and undefined, playful wisps of smoke and breath were more animated than the people and cars who generated them. Cloudy billows flew out from bus and car mufflers, building smokestacks, opening business doors. Open mouths mocked chimney stacks, especially those of the hypes with no teeth. Puffs of air flew often from in between the lips of old-timers smoking and talking at the same time. These kinds of temperatures scared both the color out of the world and the get-up-and-go out of everybody. The Windy City went to work and school, then came home and shut the curtains. About the brightest vision you could catch on our cracked, rocky streets was a neon-green Newport ad on the door of a corner store.

As usual, Big Mama decorated the entrance of New Horizons, only she had added a red cap to the top of her head this time—no doubt thinking she would attract more listeners to her sermon. I had decided to come in rather than call. This situation was too urgent to accept an appointment weeks away—I needed to get it over with before I changed my mind. I strolled on past casually this time, used to her now and knowing how I would handle it.

"Good day, ma'am," was all I said. She took me off guard by not responding, only staring down the quiet street. I noticed she was alone today, and wondered if the young boy who usually accompanied her had run off.

"Something wrong?" I then asked, spinning her around by the shoulder until we faced each other. One of her eyes—just one—had turned into an icy blue-gray. A cataract had closed over it. I waited for her rant, but she stayed silent.

"You lookin' for that little boy?" I asked her, but again she just stared at me quiet. Guess the cold had frozen her mouth shut. She probably was just one of those old people who needed to get out of the house every day just to feel alive, so she came here even when she didn't feel like heckling. She was obviously nuts, standing out in this cold for nothing. If she was going to be out here, she may as well bother folks like we expected her to.

Just as I let her shoulder go and was about to go about my business, I saw a mangy white mutt wavering at the curb. Among the empty cigarette packs and pop cans, it looked ready to run. But right after school and work Seventy-first was busy as ever, and there would be no breaks in traffic before the nearest streetlight turned red. The mutt darted anyway, and because cars had backed up it almost made it—until a bright green Chevy rolled over its hindquarters. The mutt's howls echoed for blocks and pierced my ears—quick, short screams that sounded like a whooping cough. A sloppy fat guy with a curl cap on his head put the car in park and leaned over the driver's door to view his victim. The stopped vehicle prevented another car from running over the dog again and ending its life for good, though from its screams death might have been the best thing for it. Everybody on the street had stopped walking to find out where the screams were coming from, but not one man, woman, or child made a move to do anything. I wanted to move forward and at least nudge it to the curb, but I was afraid it could be in shock and try to bite my leg off.

"Somebody need to at least get 'em out the street," one of the fur-covered hoes yelled from across the street. The men outside the store on the corner shuffled and ignored her, then when she wouldn't shut up they started cursing her out and telling her she should do it herself. The driver of the car made no move to do anything, and Big Mama just stared at him and shook her head. The kids walking home from school were now chuckling at the sight, moving on to the excitement of waiting in empty apartments before their parents got home. I wanted to make a move, but I had never seen anything close to dead before. Right before I turned away from the scene, a bony dark man in a plaid parka walked toward the mutt with a paper bag and outstretched arms.

"Just stay right on there," I heard him say to the car driver with a deep Southern accent. He probably handled injured animals all the time. I felt less guilty about turning my back on the scene, right before Big Mama broke her silence and belted into song, sounding nothing like the large Black woman in the movie who I had already heard sing the song.

Soon we'll be done, with the troubles of the world . . .

I cut her voice off as soon as I shut the second glass door that led into the lobby, scowled at the long line before me, and headed straight to the first window without caring who I was cutting. The abortions took place in a large, separate facility way in back of the clinic and I was ready to bypass this line to get in the one back there. My money was secured tight in a zipped pocket of my backpack.

"Young lady there's a line . . . ," the same old Mexican girl explained.

"I got an appointment," I told her.

"Well you're supposed to arrive twenty minutes before your appointment so you can wait in line."

"I had a detention after school."

"What is your name?" she hissed while I heard the girls behind me running their mouths about how long they had been waiting and how much nerve I had.

"Shivana Golding."

Mamacita sighed and rolled her eyes.

"I don't see your name down here . . ."

"I got a private appointment with Sue," I lied. "She told me to come back and see her today."

"Sue doesn't make appointments with anyone," Mamacita groaned. "Now if you'll excuse me."

I saw Sue's unmistakable blond, Carol Brady hair suddenly swish through the hallway behind the mountain of colored folders in the office vestibule. I leaned my small head into the narrow window cut out of bulletproof glass and shouted her name. "Oh no she didn't," I heard behind me. Mamacita stood up to try and shut the window, but she wasn't fast enough. Sue had already backtracked.

"Remember me?" I yelled while Sue walked forward to the window. Mamacita had her hands on her hips. Sue looked at her face and immediately grimaced, no doubt remembering the mess I had left in her office.

"You told me to come back and talk to you," I said to her, my eyes pleading.

"Well, I meant with an appointment . . . ," Sue started.

"I got all the information I ain't have before. I'm ready to talk about it now. I don't have that much time because I have to be home at a certain time."

I wasn't lying. Ma wasn't going to tolerate me coming in a minute late after the stunt I had pulled last week.

"Come to the side door," Sue said, shaking her head. She walked away and opened the locked wooden door that girls who had appointments spent what seemed like hours staring at, hoping their names would be called next. I walked in behind her and started talking as we walked through the hallways.

"I got the money for the abortion," I proudly announced.

"Oh, that's right," she suddenly remembered. "You were pregnant and needed to decide what to do. Shivana, right?"

"Yeah, it's Shivana and I know what I want to do," I said. "I ain't got no doubt."

We reached her office and she shut the door. I expected her to pull out a pamphlet, explain to me the different types of abortions I could get, and send me to the front with an appointment. Nobody took the time to talk to us—only to grudgingly give us stuff: pills, appointments, procedures, and bullshit.

"Shivana, an abortion is a very serious decision," she said, taking me off guard.

"I know, and I'm serious about getting one. I think I'm about two months."

"You're going to have to live with this for the rest of your life," she continued.

"I would have to live with a baby for the rest of my life. I would rather live with the thought of a kid than the kid itself."

"Well, that's what you say," she sighed. Then she started talking to me in this sappy therapist tone. "I just see so many girls come in here all the time, getting abortions and then pregnant again within months. Shivana, this is not birth control."

"Well whatever it is, it's my business. I don't need your advice," I spat.

"Obviously you do or you wouldn't be here," she said. I guess my South Side attitude couldn't shake her because she was used to it. I began a different approach.

"I want to do this now so I don't ever have to come back and talk to people like you later," I said, rolling my neck Aunt Jewel style.

"People like *me?*" Sue's eyes bucked.

"Yes, *you*," I explained. "All the folks that give you public aid and WIC and food stamps and doctors' appointments where you ain't got no choice in what you get. Telling me what to do and how to do it. I got to fill out forms telling my business just to get a gallon of milk, just 'cause I got kids. You know who I'm talking about. Mr. Welfare."

I stole that name from this other movie Ma made me watch a couple of times—*Claudine,* where this pretty Black woman back in the day couldn't even let her man buy her a toaster because the welfare social worker considered that income. They wouldn't even let her marry a damn garbage man without losing the benefits she needed to raise the kids, and at least she was lucky to find a daddy for hers.

"Shivana, I think you might have a skewed idea of what social services are."

"Service I ain't gonna want or need. I'm gonna take care of myself. Me and me alone. Nobody else."

She could see after this tirade that I was not going to budge with the abortion.

"I can certainly help you get it done, but you have to see a doctor first."

"Damn, why the fuck is this so complicated!" I growled, stomping my foot and leaning back with my arms folded. "Why can't I just get it?"

"It's not that simple. There are things that have to be known about your health before we actually complete the procedure, like we need to know exactly how far along you are."

"I told you, almost two months by now."

"Well, a doctor will make sure of that."

"I don't want to wait," I whined. "I want to do this now, while it's on my mind and I'm sure it's what I want to do."

"Well, if you're really sure, then waiting a little while longer shouldn't change your decision," Sue said definitively. "Now, let's see . . . we've had to fit a lot of people in due to our closing over Thanksgiving weekend. The soonest you can come is the Monday after Thanksgiving. About two weeks from now. I can make sure you have the appointment. How does soon as you get out of school sound?"

"Then how long will it take for me to get the abortion?"

"We should be able to fit you in a couple days after that, no later than a week."

"How much is it gonna cost?"

"Around four hundred dollars. A little more if you opt for any anesthesia."

Damn. That meant I definitely had to go face Rasul and try to get the rest of that money.

"Y'all ain't got no payment plans?"

"Are your guardians receiving Medicaid?"

"My ma don't know nothing about this," I confessed.

"Well, if you or she were on Medicaid, you could get almost anything you wanted subsidized," Sue said. "You could even get your tubes tied if you wanted to."

"So I gotta already have a bunch of kids before somebody will pay for me not to have no more?" I shook my head and folded my arms.

"Not exactly, but something like that," Sue said. "We're actually not supposed to dispense advice, but I just hate to see people do something they might regret so I felt the need to explain all your options. Maybe in between now and Tuesday, you'll have thought about it a little more so you can be one hundred percent sure."

She didn't understand I didn't have shit to think about. In my own family and others, I had seen too many kids running around hopelessly spotted linoleum kitchen floors with messy faces and soiled diapers, crashing into stained walls that landlords refused to paint. I had pictures of myself bathing cousins in a stained tub with tiles missing from the walls in the background. I knew my hair would be fuller and longer if only I could get my hair done every week like the popular girls. Ma made just enough that I didn't have to suffer the shame of getting free lunch, only reduced, but that still wasn't as good as being able to walk up to the front of the line and buy the more glamorous junk food. Once the men ran off, my aunts and cousins—and even my own ma—became old and cranky before their times. Kids weren't the problem, but not having money was. So until I had money, I wasn't having no kids. There was nothing to think about. My kids were going to grow up in a *Cosby Show* house.

Even though I knew I didn't want the thing inside me, I put my hands under my coat to warm them once I came back outside. The commotion from the mutt's accident had calmed down, and Big Mama had disappeared. I walked all the way to the El with my hands on top of my belly, which was still soft and loose, jiggly with my own stubborn baby fat, not yet hard and taut. I circled my fingers around my navel as I waited for my stop, well aware that something was attached to the other side. I had been so busy being mad about my situation that I hadn't really thought about what was going on. I was just one person, one life, one soul, walking through this world by myself. Yet, something I hadn't even realized was there at my side. Just like that silly "Footprints" story Grandma had kept on this plaque above her bed before she died and her room was mine, where Jesus was walking alongside a man all along and he didn't even realize it. There were now two of me, one familiar and one foreign, but both strange as I finally realized what and who I had become. I still had that plaque on the wall in the middle of my *Fresh* magazine posters.

"Damn," I whispered to myself, muffling my cold lips inside my jacket. "Damn . . . I got a baby. *I'm a mother*."

The tears flowed freely from this revelation, and I wasn't even ashamed at all the people who stared without one parting their lips to ask me what was wrong.

I HAD DONE *it. She had felt me, heard me, sensed me—
and now loved me without being able to help it. I was closer to
winning the debate she didn't even know she was having. A
small nudge of doubt had burrowed inside her head and, more
importantly, her heart. It had taken three tries and almost 150
years, but the odds were in my favor that I was about to finally
get my chance. And I was ready, no matter what shortcomings
or misgivings or circumstances were waiting for me. I had seen
enough to know that there was no such thing as the rose-colored
life for me, but acceptance had come and now I was ready to face
whatever waited. To be ripped and bled out of her this time
would be just as bad as what last happened to me.*

*The last time before this time, it was Harlem, somewhere around
1942. It was Tawana, the first to have a husband and the only one to
have the real freedom that gave me hope my birth day would finally
arrive.*

Before the two small kids she already had, Tawana's favorite thing to do had been to mount Billy and whisper the things she was supposed to. After the kids, Tawana's favorite thing to do became taking a bath with her newest baby on top of her breasts. The water added a lightness that motherhood had taken away, and she imagined herself sailing far beyond where she was. A vacation, a sojourn, a holiday with a respite from a cleaning job that gave her little pleasure and even less money. The night before, her husband, my daddy, Billy, was shot in mistaken identity by NYPD looking for an armed liquor store robber. He had come home uncharacteristically early. The sounds of his wife's strange ritual greeted him: water splashing, slow singing, and occasional bursts of amateur laughter. This vision of his child and its mother in the water excited him; the vision of her husband hovering over her silently startled Tawana.

"Baby—I didn't even hear you come in," she said as went to cover herself with her baby's slick, jelly roll flesh.

"You left the door unlocked, woman," he told her. "You should know better than that. This Harlem, not Hollywood."

"I'm sorry."

"Don't be sorry," Billy said as he moved in and put his heavy hands on his son's back. "Just be more careful." He loosened the top buttons of his garbageman uniform.

"How was it today?" she asked him.

"Same old trash. Different day." He did not have the heart to tell her he had quit showing up and the uniform was only for her benefit.

He moved the baby from his wife's breast and kissed the black nipple that had wrinkled into a soft, sweet raisin.

"When he gonna get away from these so I can come back?"

"When he gets teeth," Tawana said as her moisture began to mix with the bathwater.

"Isn't it about that time?"

"My God, he's not even four months Billy!"

"*How long I gotta wait then? When my son gonna get some teeth?*"

"*I don't know. You can't never tell.*"

"*I thought women automatically know these things,*" he said with his mouth almost completely over hers.

"*You tryin' to say I ain't a woman?*"

"*I don't know—why don't you get out of that tub so we can find out?*"

He removed his son, now fast asleep, from Tawana's breast, dried him, then wrapped him in a fresh nightshirt. He surrounded him with Tawana's crocheted blankets in the crib at the foot of the child's five-year-old sister's bed. Then he returned to the bathroom to pull his wife from the tub, dripping wet and with soap suds still clinging to her back. She pointed to the kitchen, wanting him to know that with a little extra money she had made his favorite that night—candied sweet potatoes and chicken baked to a perfectly seasoned crisp.

She protested momentarily, then surrendered and allowed her body to loosen up for him. She was surprised by his affection, and found she missed it. Usually, his conversations with her were not at all flirtatious or marked by curiosity of the babies' firsts. He could burden Tawana's ears for hours with grisly details of the differences between babies' and adults' bullet-ridden flesh, or of the similar appearance of yellow, brown, and white skin peeling with third-degree burns. A war veteran at twenty-four, his idea of pillow talk was describing how he had learned how to aim a shell just right, perfectly, patiently, so that its fuse could detonate just by passing near his target. Sometimes foreplay was hours talking about all the blurry, watermarked pictures he had saved of the stone-faced men he had befriended overseas—most of whom met their demise over there, and the rest of which never spoke again once they disbanded after the war. In her attempts to understand and connect with him and relieve his anguish, Tawana would

*just follow his lead and chuckle or cry at these disgusting sto-
ries. She never joined him and shared any of her pain—her
loneliness, her uncertainties, her desire for adventure, her
wish for a real kitchen to cook in.*

*But that last night, there were no stories or pictures. There
was only music as Ella Fitzgerald serenaded them from a radio
that had finally become clear. Billy used the clothes he was peeling off himself to dry Tawana's body. By the time she was naked,
they were both weeping—Billy for having his innocence stolen
and no idea how to get it back, Tawana for feeling helpless she
couldn't help him find it. Then, Billy pulled his hopeful wife into
bed with him in order to make love to her like they were Harlem
newlyweds again, when the discovery of their passion was still
fresh. They ravished one another like they had done before they
really knew each other, before either of their imperfections or
haunted memories had revealed themselves like fingerprints pur-
posely left behind as a confession. Their lovemaking—at once
hungry, violent, and necessary—played out like the battles they
had begun to fight long before they met, when they were both
searching for love, good jobs, and a sunny place to call home.*

*His last night on this earth, Billy lay on his wife's stomach
and started to have a dream—it began about his babies, what the
future held, the life he and his woman could make once the right
chances came along. He couldn't have known he was lying on top
of me—newly conceived, already a spirit planting the good life in
his mind. Most of the memories he had of his first nineteen years
had been squeezed out of his brain by two short but long years of
being tossed around Europe. He had been seeking honor, purpose, earnings, and skills—the promises that lured him and over
a million other Blacks to fight in yet another war they had nothing to do with. Away from all that he knew, he had felt like he
was chained in a movie theater and forced to watch a story that
was not his own. During the day, there was vision, but no sound.
At night, horrible sounds that spared the permanence of vision.*

With his first violent introduction to the highly mechanical war-fare that paralyzed even the most well-trained American soldiers, he had witnessed his closest comrade's lips moving in prayer even after he was nearly decapitated by shrapnel. Billy decided then to no longer believe in God or any reliability of relation-ships. Yet he had returned to the States and fallen back in love with the girl he had married and gotten pregnant before it all, a Southern enigma recently migrated with her family from Missis-sippi. The dream turned into a nightmare when scissors held by a blue-eyed soldier were cutting open Tawana's stomach, and he woke up screaming with his hands still across her navel.

In the aftermath of this dream and all the others, she asked him with wet eyes, How can you still love me?

He answered her only with a frightened embrace that an-swered, I need someone to hold after the dreams . . .

She was the angel he had remembered and prayed to in for-eign darkness, only she came much, much too late.

All she could think in the weeks following that last night was, what had been God's point of sparing her a telegram for three years just for the police to knock on her door when she thought the worst was behind them? She and the children had arrived home from the house she cleaned on East Eighty-eighth Street, she had made beans and rice for dinner, and was nursing her son. She had turned on the radio because she knew Billy liked coming home to music. But the hours had fast gone by without her hearing his footsteps pound four flights of tenement stairs to get to their Edgecombe Avenue apartment. By ten, she wrapped the food in foil and placed it in the icebox, hoping she would have to wake later in order to reheat it in a skillet for him. By midnight, she was wondering which one of his buddies could have corraled him into getting drunk at Minton's Playhouse or St. Nick's Pub. By 2:00 A.M., she was in a cold sweat. By the next noon, when three New York City police officers knocked on her door with an excuse (not an apology), she was dead.

You know all niggers look the same to 'em, *one of the girlfriends who moved in with her after the shooting explained.*

Just count your blessings they ain't come looking for nobody here 'cause then you and your babies might be dead right 'long with your husband, *another girlfriend's mother consoled while she gave Tawana her first bath in days.*

It's just a shame they got a man who wouldn't hurt nobody 'less the government made him, *the elderly neighbor who came to check on her in the following days said.*

After everyone got back to their own lives and she got back to work at the urgings of a missus who desperately needed *her, she was relieved to have at least her son and daughter to cling to at night. She avoided her daughter's question of "Where's Daddy?" and began thinking of how she would explain things to them both, one day not today. Often and in panic, she wondered if a man had ever been there. She walked into the bathroom and it smelled like a woman. In it were her feminine things—her powders that smelled like spring, lotions and tonics with floral and fruity aromas, the things that made him fall in love with her. Decorative soaps were lined up perfectly for the guests who had stopped coming. Her bedroom held the softness of a woman. Plush pillows and throws rose above the height of the king-size mattress, completing the already perfect picture like the full breasts of a new mother. The wind blew lace curtains inward and made them dance like the hair of a girl running in autumn. Housedresses with Tawana's shape carved into them were draped across the back of the vanity chair, over the dresser mirror, across the bed like a bride waiting to be taken. The sun shining through the bedroom window heated the perfumes on the vanity and her smell came alive there too. Aunt Jemima smiled behind cabinet doors. The Bessie Smith album cover she used as a dustpan was propped against the pantry. The loose ceiling fan that whirled constantly throughout the poorly ventilated room sounded like a despairing mother's quiet lullaby. Tawana's breast pump dangled*

from the top of the refrigerator, ready for duty when her baby was
not. Inside the refrigerator were bottles of her milk, lined up by
hour so she always used the oldest one first. In the corner were
the size-seven holed-up house shoes that she slipped on to throw
the garbage over the window ledge and into the alley outside. Al-
ways, yellow gloves hung over the faucet; no man would ever
worry to preserve the softness of his hands.

She wondered if he had even existed. Had her memories only
been dreams? Could a spirit have impregnated her? In a blind
dash because tears were now streaming, she ran for the wardrobe
in her bedroom. As soon as she opened the door, the stale scent
of Old Spice rushed through her nose, and she was relieved. Sev-
eral of Billy's suits were hanging; some of them had not been
worn since the first few months after Billy had come home. His
derby hats were lined on top of the wardrobe's only shelf, and
she suddenly recalled the feeling she used to get whenever he
tipped one of those hats toward her after they had first met. His
work and play shoes were scattered randomly in a corner pile;
the familiar odor that emanated from them proved they had, in
fact, been worn.

Hopeful now, she remembered the top drawer of her dresser.
Through her dreams, she had often seen Billy open it late at
night. She opened the drawer frantically as if she had found a
dead relative's treasure chest. Loose change was inside. A tar-
nished silver necklace was neatly laid out, as well as a watch
that had ceased ticking. His father's Mason ring was also there.
Then closer, she noticed one of the imitation-gold hoop earrings
Billy bought her jammed between the imitation wood that made
up the drawer's base. She pulled it out and fingered it, thinking
of her man and the father she had wanted her children to have.
She had another one on the way, she knew, after finally realizing
that it wasn't grief staving off menstruation for two months.

Tawana was furious. Why why why had this happened to her,
to them? Why had they played it safe all this time, done it all

right, made everybody proud, got off to a good start in life only for life to end before they could cash in? For what? It was a furor so strong it closed her mouth rather than opened it. She would have to wait nearly a year for Blacks to rise up in Harlem and riot, and then she would be one of those in the streets screaming, fighting, cursing, chanting, breaking glass, acting out, celebrating the small victory of causing a small threat. Then, she would release the sound that welled up inside of her now and caused her head to pound all the time. That's what the inside sounds that have nowhere to go do. Her throat would be hoarse from screaming so loud. Her tongue would dry out. Her lungs would shrink from the release. Then, and only then, would she move on. For now, she let the sound become her until she was silenced.

Nobody noticed Tawana's depression. Those she kept house for had barely talked to her before, and after a few weeks of congenialities born of pity the family was right back to simply giving terse orders. They did, however, give her a quarter raise and allow her to take home even more leftovers than she had been taking before. They couldn't have known it still would never be enough. The few girlfriends she had tired of trying to get her out of the house, so they stopped coming by because they knew there was nothing more they could say. Her daughter often asked her why she was crying, but after a couple weeks of witnessing the same breakdown night after night, the child simply concluded it was actually nothing wrong, only something else new she had to get used to. The milk and icemen were genuine and honest; they didn't dare take advantage of a widow by offering their shoulders to cry on, even if it could have led them to her bed. So even they left her alone after she turned completely silent even whenever paying them. And that was just the way Tawana liked it.

She was still waiting on her "benefits," checking the mailbox every day after several visits to the local veterans' bureau. Because of the nature of the tragedy, there was runaround with obtaining Billy's death certificate from the coroner. She had run around for the couple of days it took to exhaust her bereavement time. The first time she had gone to the veterans' bureau, she was missing the children's birth certificates. The next time she went back, she found out someone had erred on the last digit in Billy's social security number. The final time, which would be the last time she could skip out on work for the long wait in the office, she was told to wait for the proper forms in the mail. Everyone in the building knew her predicament; even the whores who sometimes turned tricks under the stairs while everyone looked the other way wouldn't have had the heart to confiscate a check bearing her name. She was waiting for cold weather to use it as an excuse to spend a full day at the bureau to straighten the matter out. But the cold was several months away, and already her cabinets seemed to rest in a perpetual state of being starved for attention. If only she had taken advantage of the offer she received at Harlem Hospital after birthing her daughter. "Complete, total, and complimentary sterilization, to your own economic gain," a pink nurse had explained to her as the hell of labor took over her mind. But she wouldn't be bothered with signing forms whose words she was too drowsy to read. In misty Laundromats and crowded train cars, she had heard several women whispering about doing this exact thing—no more children no matter how much they enjoyed their men. And now how she wished she had stayed alert long enough to sign.

The night she decided to end it all, a simple thing had triggered her insanity. She was totally bored with the five-year-old, who now only hummed, or stared, had stopped telling stories, usually rocked back in forth in silence, and didn't laugh much anymore. The knowledge she would soon have another extinguished the newness and perfection and awe of the baby she already had. The doll-size clothes had shrunk and faded, she had mastered the art of fastening the diaper so the safety pin could not come loose and prick the child, the smell of its shit reminded her too much of the unpleasant odor of her husband's uniform. She used to enjoy the quiet moments when she nursed, but now the task simply infuriated her. Had she had her choice and the extra money to buy formula, she would have stopped a long time ago. She was sick of sharing her body with an infant and not a man. She wondered if she was crazy when the screams became so loud that she no longer heard them. She thought she was aging too fast when her daughter asked for something and she had forgotten what seconds later.

To make matters worse, the growing newborn now never seemed to know when it was full. The child's greedy and relentless sucking no longer thrilled her; it continued until Tawana, puzzled by the baby's persistence even through spit-up, one midnight decided to stop it. She was broke, tired, and cranky. She didn't know what she was going to cook for dinner or how she was going to pay for the milk tomorrow. She didn't know the pillow she smashed between her legs at night wasn't her husband. She was alone. She was lonely. She wanted it quiet so she could think. Not later quiet, but now quiet.

She slammed the baby down on the floor. She tore the child from her breast so fast if it had had teeth it would have drawn blood. She held it high above her head. With more strength than she knew she had left, she crashed the child into hard tile and afterward the baby didn't make one sound. She could still feel its tiny fingers pressed into the skin above her nipple, right below her own birthmark. She actually felt it more now. She hadn't planned it, though the force with which she did it would have made anyone think she had practiced long and hard for it.

The rest of that evening resembled the night she had waited for Billy to come home, though it ended in a terribly different way. She waited, while my little brother lay totally still on the floor, for movement that never came. But still she waited, not fearing the worst just as she had listened out for Billy's footsteps up creaky stairs. She waited, even though when she got up the *courage to put her hands on it hours later, the body was already ice cold. She waited, for the men in blue to come knocking at her door again, and this time they would be right. She decided not to wait for her daughter to wake up and discover what the mother who was no longer any use to her had done. A gospel quartet was singing on the radio when she made up her mind.*

> *No more weeping and a-wailing*
> *No more weeping and a-wailing*
> *No more weeping and a-wailing*
> *I'm goin' to live with God*
>
> *I want t' to meet my mother*
> *I want t' to meet my mother*
> *I want t' to meet my mother*
> *I'm goin' to live with God*

The crush of rushing water against the stained enamel tub soon drowned out the voices. The water was near freezing when she got in, as she had forgotten to turn both faucets, but she didn't notice the temperature. Her mind was occupied in memory, lost in a vision, of her husband coming home sweaty and rank from hauling garbage before lifting his son from her breast to make love to her. Insanity had overcome her and she didn't think to wonder what her daughter might do or see or feel when she had to pee in the morning; she had only locked the bathroom door and assumed the girl might just pee on herself. She waited, after Billy's razor had sliced softly into her wrists, for a sleep that was permanent for her and temporary for me. But though one child sat on her breasts already in death sleep, and another bled out of her into water filled in a dirty bathtub, Tawana thought nothing of what would happen to the one she was leaving behind.

TWELVE

THE LAVA LAMPS in Rasul's bedroom cast a psychedelic spell on me as tie-dyed colors danced across the walls, giving his dark room an orangish-red tinge. Only a couple of days after I had left, I was back, curling up under him to fill the void Nakesha had left by ending our friendship. Twista's latest underground mix-tape played low in the background while I lay on the bed against Rasul, my head resting on his chest. He chain-smoked Newports and listened to me breathe in the dark. I had shown up at his door around seven only to collect my clothes and money, thank him for his hospitality, and apologize for the mess I had brought through the front door. Surprisingly, he had invited me in. Real cool and relaxed, we just talked about things. By the end of the conversation, he was making fun of Hakim's accent. And we were locked in each other's arms. He pulled me into him tight, but I always pulled away. I knew what he was trying to do—hit it raw before my belly got too big to get in the way. All of this courtesy was an act, theatrics. What else could he possibly want with me? He knew he couldn't get me pregnant again, so he was just going to have his fun and throw me away. That's what they all did. So I kept my guard up, no matter how good it felt to have somebody this close to me. I was going to give him some, when *I* felt like it. When I knew Ma had arrived home from work, I did the right thing and called.

"I'm at my friend's house," I told her, being honest about something for the first time in weeks.

"Nakesha?"

"No, Rasul. The boy you met."

Rasul's aunt and uncle weren't coming home tonight, so if she tripped I could stay here if I wanted to. Because of the letter, I decided the time had come for me to be gentle—but truthful—with her.

"And I'm just supposed to accept that you laying up with some grown boy?"

"I'm not layin' . . ."

"Bring y'ass home."

"No." I was firmer than I had ever been with her.

"Shivana, bring your ass home right now. Don't try me 'cause I will come down there."

"Ma, I ain't doin' nothing but watchin' TV . . . having some fun for a change."

"You ain't over there just to watch TV otherwise you'd be watching it here. Now I'm puttin' on my shoes."

"Well can he come over our house?"

"He can stay his ass at home where he belong. Now don't make me come down there."

"I'm not coming then." My nerves had me shaking since I had never talked to Ma this way. But I was going to stand my ground.

"What the hell done got into you? I said bring your ass home!"

"No. I'll be home later. Bye, Ma."

I hung up the phone, cutting off the cussout she had started to give me. I would put up with a whipping later. Right now, I just wanted to smoke and chill.

"You know squares can be hazardous to a baby's health," Rasul said, holding a cigarette to my lips while I sucked in. Just two pulls because I didn't want to throw up because I hadn't had a square in a couple weeks, since Nakesha had stole one of her parents' packs out of a carton. I instantly remembered sometimes cigarettes were stronger than weed. I was immediately light-headed and calm, seeing through a clear haze that was nicotine's sedation.

"Not if the baby ain't gonna ever get here," I told him, lying on my side and staring at his face, right at the bright white spot on his cheek. I clutched the money that was still stuck in the jeans I had left at Rasul's, which he had returned to me that afternoon. All the money was there, and if he had noticed it at all he hadn't said anything yet. I hadn't told him about the appointment that was one week away. I reached out suddenly and traced the spot with my finger. I wanted so badly to ask him what these strange marks were, the one thing I always knew I would remember about him, but I figured he would have told me by now had he wanted to.

"Damn, so you really serious about this abortion shit?"

"Yep." I closed my eyes to enjoy the calm. I hummed to myself and wasn't the least bit embarrassed about my voice: *Soon we'll be done . . .*

"That's messed up."

"I don't need you to make me feel bad about it," I spat without opening my eyes.

"I ain't trying to make you feel bad about nothin'," he said.

"You don't have to tell me what's messed up. I know I messed up and all I'm trying to do is fix it."

Why was he trying to convince me to have this child? It wasn't like he was going to be doing anything to help.

"Maybe instead of worrying about me *you* should be trying to quit smokin'," I snarled, changing the subject and turning my back. "When your people coming back?"

"Why, you planning on staying again?"

"No, I'm leaving tonight. I just wanted to know."

"They should be back tomorrow."

"Oh." Damn, I had to go back home. And Rasul just couldn't drop it.

"You know, wasn't none of us wanted."

"Who is *us*?"

"Shit, Black folks. Look at me."

I hadn't ever thought about what it must be like for Rasul. It was one thing when your daddy stopped loving you, but it had to be something much more terrible when a mama gave up on you too.

"You think about them?" I asked.

Rasul just poked his lips, took a long drag, and shook his head.

"Not no more. I let them think about me." Then, "I think we was all accidents."

"Not everybody," I countered, turning to face him again.

"Shiiiit. Ninety-nine percent."

"Well see, then it's one percent that was like the Cosby kids."

"Man, that's TV," Rasul said. "I don't know nothing 'bout that."

"It's TV, but it gotta be real like that somewhere too." I hoped for myself because I needed to, otherwise there was no point to what I was doing if ten or fifteen years from now I was still going to be jammed back between a rock and a hard place.

"Guess so," he agreed. "*Good Times* was real so they put that shit on. So *Cosby Show* gotta be real too."

I wondered if too much nicotine had gone to his head because that last reasoning was so stupid I couldn't even call him on it. I only started giggling while he looked at me and asked "What?" and I ignored him as I reached across to his nightstand to pull my own square out of the pack.

MA LIGHTENED UP once she knew I had someone besides her to lean on. I came home Monday before ten and she just glared at me without saying a word. On Wednesday, Rasul stopped by, stammered "Hello Ms. Golding" when Ma opened the door with her hands on her hips, and I came in to get him like she wasn't even there. " 'Member Rasul?" was all I said. We sipped Kool-Aid and laughed in the kitchen. I totally forgot that by next summer, I could have another life to fight for besides my own. I relaxed and let it all go. Laughter was mine again. With Aunt Jewel gone, Rasul stepped in to become my refuge. And I couldn't, no matter how hard I tried, stop thinking about what he had said about the ninety-nine percent.

Can I do this should I do this what Ma gonna do when she find out how I'm gonna make money what it's gonna look like will it be a boy or girl whose hair it's gonna have will I see my daddy in its face

Over the next week I found myself in stolen moments standing sideways in my dresser mirror, pooching out my stomach wide as it would go, wondering what I would look like if I changed my mind and let it grow. Would I get fatter, and would my nose get wider? Neither scenario seemed possible to me then. As far as I knew, I was less than two months pregnant, but it felt like the baby was already born. My heart was beating for someone besides myself. I imagined myself with a child curled up inside of me: warm, snug, probably asleep. I wondered if it would be able to feel itself being ripped and bled out of me. If, before it figured out what was happening, it would pass all the nightmares it had planned on dreaming onto me. If I would be haunted until I died with something questioning me about why

I didn't want it to live. *Reproduction . . . genetics . . . cycles . . . life*. All of that shit I had learned in school started tugging at my brain. But the tug felt good, opened my mind and my eyes up. Made me think of how I had gotten here and how Ma and Aunt Jewel had gotten here, and even Grandma. And how we all were different but still so similar: the same kinds of coils in our hair, the same shared history on the South Side, the same lazy ways of cutting off the ends of words like *store* and *drawer*. And that's when I knew that I had generations of spirits and souls and lives sitting inside of me, waiting to take shape and show themselves to the world again, through me.

With all that on my mind, I forgot about Leroy instantly it seemed. For two days straight I woke up and Rasul was on my mind. I went to bed and he was still there. It was like I had an infection, a fever that wouldn't come down. He was all I thought about so there was no room in my head for the bullshit. I wanted to be with him whenever I could and do it without having to ask first. I guess I was "smelling myself" because I already saw where my nights out with him would become later and later, like a couple nights when Ma locked the door around eleven just to make me stand outside and bang for an hour before she let me in. Nakesha and I still weren't speaking; we had gone from just staring at each other to not looking at one another at all. Mrs. Carly had grabbed me Wednesday after the bell rang and asked if we were even friends anymore. I just hunched my shoulders and walked off before she could stage some "cry it out" intervention bullshit. I had a one-track mind, and mending past mistakes wasn't on that track. I had to look ahead to the future. I decided I wanted to get out of my ma's house. I wasn't that far along yet, and now I had my doubts. I needed to use what little money I had to start over in case Rasul's guilt trip had somehow swayed my mind. So I walked into New Horizons the day before Thanksgiving, without an appointment, to talk to the one person who I thought could help me—Sue.

"Well I'm happy you decided to come back and see me, but now I should know to expect you'll never make an appointment," she said once she finally called my name off the sign-in sheet I had bullied myself onto. As soon as I saw her, I regretted having an immature outburst in her office less than a month before. But then again, she probably didn't even remember it that much. I was just another one of the hundreds of brown faces smudged together week after week, day after day, time slot after time slot. Rasul had opened me up somewhat, cracked my hard shell enough that I was willing to actually share a little of what was on my mind. I dumped it all on Sue. I needed more time to figure out if I was ready to be grown, have this baby, and raise it. I needed to figure out what job I might want to do and if I would have to go to school after high school to do it. And I had to get the stress of Ma off my back if I was going to think about any of that clearly. I walked out of New Horizons with the name of almost every shelter, organization, and group home in Chicago for girls like me.

ON THANKSGIVING DAY, while my ma stuffed herself at the house of a great-aunt I couldn't stand, I secretly moved into The Haven of Christ's Temple Second Baptist Women's Shelter on Halsted Street. It was one of the only places I called where you didn't have to be a ward of the state or hiding from some man who was trying to kill you; you had to be a pregnant or parenting runaway, so on Thanksgiving morning I decided to run away. I called and found out that I would only have to stay in weekly contact with at least one person I knew. I also had to attend "home-school" in a group conference room because I didn't have a diploma yet. A woman named Gladys told me there were no beds, but I prayed if I showed up pitiful enough there might be a couch. While I helped Ma with the last of six sweet potato pies, I feigned a stomachache to get out of going to dinner with family who didn't care much about me and my life anyway. Then as soon as Ma was gone I left her a note telling her I was safe, I was going to live somewhere for girls my age and would call her later. Just that simple—there was no need to be confrontational. Rasul helped me catch a cab and carry all I owned in there: my boombox, cassette tapes, schoolbooks, shoes, hair stuff, and three garbage bags of clothes. I paid for the cab out of the money I had stolen. 8984 S. Halsted would be my place to call home until I could do better.

I was greeted by a stocky Black woman who reminded me of the Big Mama at New Horizons, only she had lighter skin. Framed by the light of a wide doorway, she shot Rasul a look above folded arms, letting him know he could leave. I almost didn't dare wave back at him. She looked down at me from the top step and bellowed, "Well I don't see no baby so you must be pregnant." She held open the screen with one hand while another sat on her hip. A big-boned woman, her generous hips could barely inch through the doors. They grazed each and every door frame we walked through. I followed her without saying a word. I would later learn this was Gladys, the oldest sister and the one who had gotten this place started.

We walked right on past my pile of stuff sitting in the middle of a huge vestibule lined with dark mahogany walls. Each doorway was accented with intricate wood carvings. Either a cross, picture of Martin Luther King, or painting of a Black Jesus centered every room. She led me through each floor: it was a four-story row house with two large bedrooms and one big bathroom on each of the upper floors. The only bed left was in a shared room with two other girls who had babies—there were six large rooms and about fifteen or sixteen of us girls total. The only phone in the whole damn place sat in this tiny booth near the front door, like a guard. There was supposedly one in an office that none of the girls was ever allowed into. The first level had a kitchen almost the size of me and Ma's whole apartment, with whitewashed cabinets so high up everyone had to scoot around the kitchen on stepladders. There were even some narrow steps by the back kitchen door that led to the upstairs, and the lady called them the old "servants' quarters." I didn't see one television or radio in the entire place. On the outside, it had looked like something out of an old black-and-white picture from the Harlem Renaissance or a Lena Horne movie. When I was bringing in my last garbage bag and Rasul was thanking the cabdriver, I had stared at the iron gate surrounding the house and imagined dragons were waiting inside.

The woman who had answered the phone hadn't told me much, but while giving me my tour explained just what my new home was. A bunch of old Christian Black ladies who didn't have a thing better to do were running it with Illinois state money and charity from rich folks. They weren't charging me to live there. None of the girls at the shelter had any money. Instead, the price was Bible study, prayer meeting, and getting saved, in that order. The application for residency consisted of me writing my full name, age, due date, last school, last address, illnesses, and food preferences in a tattered spiral notebook.

I was told the woman who cooked us breakfast and dinner every day was named Shirley, and she claimed all her ingredients were whispered to her directly from Jesus. With my stomach growling, I was left in the kitchen to wait for the next new person who would be telling me what to do from now on. Perhaps it was penance that I hadn't been offered Thanksgiving dinner though it was almost eight at night. Lined up on the counter were fractions of pecan pies, lemon pound cakes, and red velvet cakes. A couple of chicks eased into the kitchen in order to shovel out sweet wedges to wrap into paper towels, all of them staring at the new girl while trying to keep their cool. The kitchen still held the scent of every Black Thanksgiving delicacy there was—greens, ham, candied yams, corn bread dressing, even chitterlings. My mouth watered, and if it wasn't for pride I would have dug in without permission.

Then, a small woman named Sister Maureen came in and laid down the law under a sloppy head rag and over the best peach cobbler I had ever tasted in my life. If Jesus had come up with this recipe, then he had wasted his talents trying to save mankind. The Devil was definitely winning the battle for the world, but not everybody who thought they could could actually turn out a decent cobbler.

"Prayer meeting is Wednesday from seven to nine," Maureen told me in between bites, "and Bible study is on Tuesdays same time. Sign-up for washer and dryer time 'fore you even think about touching either one. You leave your clothes in the washer or dryer then the next girl got the right to take 'em out and set 'em aside. They get dirty again, oh well. Responsibility—it can make you or break you in this life."

I built up the nerve to interrupt her.

"Ma'am, I plan on getting a job soon. I can try to get Tuesdays and Wednesdays off, but you know how jobs are these days. If they don't let me have it . . ."

"Then you gonna have to quit. Jesus said, 'Therefore ye put me first and all other things shall be added unto you.' Priorities—that's what makes you or breaks you for the afterlife. Can I go on?"

"Yes, ma'am."

"Alright now. Bible study Tuesday, prayer meeting Wednesday. Church on Sunday—at Second Baptist of course—goes without saying. Sunday School is optional because I know you young girls get tired, taking care of yourselves all alone. You need your rest."

Maureen gave me a couple seconds to digest those rules before she kept going.

"No overnight guests. If you got a man friend you have to meet him elsewhere. Those doors lock at ten, so if you ain't here by then, you got to stay with him or find somewhere else to go. You got to go to your GED classes in the afternoon or mornings, whichever work around your schedule. Don't hang your panties or hose anywhere in the bathroom. That's why we took up a collection to be blessed with the washer and dryer. Draws and diapers and do-rags was hanging up like ghosts everywhere you turned."

This place had more rules than my mother's. I started to think I had made a mistake by coming here, but this situation was going to be temporary—unlike the future I envisioned if I had stayed at my mother's house. She devoured her last lick of cobbler with this final one:

"Oh, and if you still here by the time you have it, and you get back that *time* . . . you know—your monthly—just be kind to the rest of the girls and clean up after yourself. Discretion—that can make you or break you too. 'Specially if you a woman in this life."

Maureen sent me on my way with what was left of the cobbler, a plate of dinner leftovers, and a Bible that miraculously already had my name engraved on it in gold letters: *Shivana Golding.*

BEFORE I GOT settled into my room for the first night, I needed to make three phone calls. The first was to Rasul so he could psyche me up for the last two: Ma and Jewel.

Me and Rasul were quick. What's up what it's like where you sleeping and when I'm gonna see you again. We kept it moving. I dialed Hakim's number with trembling fingers, and had no pre-planned strategy in the event of an accusation. I spoke with a tongue gritty as a nail file as soon as I heard a voice on the other end.

A woman quickly said, " 'Allo?"

I wondered if Aunt Jewel had taken Hakim's accent along with his hand.

"Aunt Jewel?"

"Oh, no darling," the woman said. "One second."

She put down the phone and I heard music, laughter, and voices in the background. There was an eruption of hand-clapping before Jewel picked up.

"Hello!"

I could tell she was smiling.

"Hey, Aunt Jewel. It's me. Shivana."

For a couple of seconds, she said nothing. In my head, I saw the smile melt away to a less-decipherable expression. At least if there was company, she wouldn't be too long and stern.

"Happy Thanksgiving, Shivana," she said softly, and I wondered how to pick her smile up off the floor and put it back on her face. Unfortunately, absolutely nothing I had to say could do that.

"You too. You cook?"

"Oh, we had a potluck here. Hakim invited all of the friends and family he has in New York over. To meet me."

There was a funnel of silence I didn't dare fill with my latest scheme.

"What about you and Annette?" Jewel said.

"Oh, Ma ate at Glenda's," I said.

"Just your ma? You didn't go?"

I sucked in as much as I could before I started.

"Well, me and Ma don't live together no more."

"What? I thought all that shit had been settled—"

"It's not that. It's something else . . . I lied about being pregnant."

I heard Jewel gasp, then breathe a shuddered sigh where I could tell she was shaking her head. Probably leaning on something now. Probably with her eyes closed.

"Shivana," she moaned, her disappointment so apparent in the couple of extra seconds it took her to get out my name. "Baby . . ."

"Please, don't be mad, Aunt Jewel."

A cornrowed, plump-faced girl waddled close to me, but turned back around with her hands on her hips when she saw tears streaming down my face. As she rounded the corner, I was startled by her humungous belly with its huge brown navel poking through her T-shirt.

"How did this happen?" Jewel asked after several minutes where neither of us said a word.

"I don't know," I lied. "I just wasn't careful."

"With that boy Hakim caught you with?"

I figured no response to that would mean I hadn't lied.

"I never meant for this to happen."

"So Annette put you out?" Jewel asked.

"No," I said, finally calming down. "I left on my own. I knew it would be bad after I told her, so I moved into this shelter for girls."

"What kind of shelter? Where the hell are you . . . hey, I'll be off the phone in a minute!"

"It's not like the Salvation Army or nothing," I explained. "It's nice. These church ladies run it and I'm sharing my room. I still have to go to school. And they makin' me go to church. And I have to stay in contact with somebody so I figured that person could be you."

"So you telling me your mother has no idea where you are or what's going on?"

I couldn't answer her. Who was I kidding? I was going to be too terrified to make that last, most important phone call.

"I figured you could tell her," I suggested. "Just tell her I lied to y'all. I can't talk to her right now."

"Oh, so you grown enough to get pregnant and run off, but can't face your mama? You grown when you want to be?"

"I guess so." Wasn't no used to lying about it.

"How are you going to drop *your* responsibility on me now? And I *know* you stole Hakim's money."

"Jewel, I didn't know what else to do and you know I lost the babysitting job—"

"Well you need to apologize to Hakim," Jewel snapped. "You're lucky he's sympathetic that I got a family full of drama! You did me a favor by letting him know just why I keep my ass as far away from Chicago as I can."

"I'm sorry." It was a pitiful apology.

"I stay away so I can stay out of the middle of mess, which it seems like you all are always in," Jewel continued, letting the floodgates of anger loose. "Everybody's walking around in circles and nobody's standing straight. Now you sitting up here pregnant, about to be another Black teen mother, struggling your whole life. Because the odds are that boy is not going to marry you, Shivana. You know that, don't you?"

I didn't have the nerve to reply to her lecture. I had no idea what she would think about me killing the baby, so I didn't even tell her that was at the forefront of my mind.

"Well, what you gonna do?" she finally said, very softly. I had nothing to tell her at that time because I didn't know what I was going to do.

"Alright, fine," she finally said. "I'll call Annette for you. I'll do your dirty work—*this* time."

I gave her the address and number to the shelter, then the names of some of the sisters in charge.

"I guess you need more money," Jewel said as I hung my head low in shame. I was too proud to ask her for another thing, even though I didn't have much to live on if I was holding on to five hundred dollars for the abortion.

"I'll send you some," Aunt Jewel said. She hung up on me without saying good-bye.

"THAT'S NOT YOUR bed."

Someone had entered my room so quickly I hadn't heard. I turned around to see a girl who looked about six feet tall standing behind me. Almost the entire right side of her face was raised in an ugly, serrated, keloidal scar. She looked like she had a swollen jaw because of it. Standing right next to her was a petite high-yellow girl with her hair coiffed like a rooster's—red color and all. Thing about it was although she was bony as hell, she probably pulled men on skin color alone. She held a child wrapped in a puffy blue snowsuit, even though it wasn't snowing.

"That gotta be your bed over there," the tall one said gruffly.

"Oh, sorry," I mumbled, removing the one garbage bag I had lugged up on top of the fuzzy patchwork quilt. The shorter girl looked like she should be in middle school. Her baby had suddenly gotten fussy, and she began to bounce it in her arms while she paced the room. I noticed the tall girl's belly as soon as she took off her coat. It seemed to stick out as far as she was tall. I didn't know whether to introduce myself or not, so I just stacked my garbage bags at the foot of my twin bed and began to put other things in the nearest draw.

"I'm Janice," the tall one said. "That's Tiny."

She pointed at the younger girl, who didn't do anything but smile.

"I'm Shivana," I said softly, not knowing how cordial I should be around here. Women turned on women in the blink of an eye.

"You pregnant?" Janice suddenly asked, taking me off guard.

I didn't want or need people up in my business, especially since I hadn't yet decided that I definitely wanted to keep the baby. I needed to see how the next month would go and if I could figure out a way to make money. There was no use in me being pregnant one day and not pregnant the next, having to explain that to a bunch of folks I didn't know or care about. I wasn't like the rest of these girls. I wasn't going to be here past the season.

"No," I lied. They both looked shocked, though Tiny had yet to say a word.

"How you get in here if you ain't knocked up?" Janice asked so loud I'm sure the whole floor heard her.

"This was the only place for me to go," I said, making it up as I went along. I'm sure the sisters were too sanctified to gossip. They would tell any girl who came to them with questions about another girl to go somewhere and sit down.

"Oh, I ain't know they did that here," Janice said. "Well, it's just me and Tiny in here, and we got keys to the room so you ain't gotta worry about your stuff."

I didn't trust no damn body.

"Might as well tell you, puta man like to wake up hollerin' every night," Janice said, pointing to Tiny and the baby she had started to change. The room reeked with the stench of the child's shit. A playful stab at her son was all it took to get Tiny animated.

"No he don't!" she yelled, smiling. "He a good baby. You just a good little boy, ain't you, little man . . . ?" She brought her face close to the child's, beaming so that she seemed to turn shades lighter. I walked over to her bed and stared down into the yellow baby's face. An Indian baby, I thought. A little Pocahantas. The owl-like, black, slanted eyes and silky hair. One of the lucky ones whose mother was stopped in the grocery store or on the street by all the women she passed, even White women, who just wanted to marvel at how "be-yoooo-tiful" the baby was. With my luck, my baby would come out inheriting Ma's ugly scar and my hard knots of hair. I thought about asking to hold him, then changed my mind. No use getting used to those habits if I wasn't sure what I was going to do. No need to fall in love with all that now. I walked away from the baby and back toward my things, unpacking for about an hour before saying "Good night" and turning out the lamp near my bed.

WE FINALLY FOUND *what we been searching for all our lives, huh? A roomy house. A beautiful house. A safe house. An abundant house. A house with so many rooms and doors and closets and stairs one could lose their way. We made it, together, to the safe place. A place where the men stand far away while women and children play inside. A place where there is always food in the cabinets, on the stove, in our bellies. A place where we can sleep all night with both eyes shut rather than just one. A place where once the door is closed, whatever going on beyond it no longer matters. Where does all this come from? The sisters would say God, and we wouldn't argue. But I would add something. I would say it came from love too, wouldn't you? So this is what it could be like? None of that life's noise in here. Just soft sounds—water splashing, food boiling, forks clinging, pencils writing, women and children cooing in sleep. Pretty words hanging in the air all the time. Sister. Ma'dea. Lordamercy. Hallelujah. I feel different now inside of you—lighter maybe. I can* *feel you toss and turn less now, laugh more. Is it too late to invite the others? Might as well, before it gets too crowded here or folks who can't understand our peace come along to burn it down. We would stay inside though, while the flames danced around us, and we wouldn't burn. Not here, in this place. This is my house. This is* our *house. Finally,* our Cosby Show *house.*

THIRTEEN

I QUICKLY FOUND out that no one here was really friends. We got along, we spoke when spoken to, we were cool, and that was it. Not because we didn't want to be friends. But you didn't exactly come to this type of place to find a running buddy. With the mind-state most of us were in, friendliness *was* too much to ask for. We all had issues, or we wouldn't have been here. After washing up the babies and fixing something to eat and dealing (or not) with the babies' fathers, we were too worn out to stay up and giggle like we were rich girls in college dorm rooms. Once in a while me and Tiny would sit up with twice razor-sliced Janice; she would tell us all about New York where she was from, where Jewel had left me to go. We never talked about men. At night, everybody was tired—even those of us who didn't work. We were still tired. Tired of running, tired of putting up with men and the "man," tired of hoping, tired of being broke, tired of hopping from place to place. Most of the girls had a job, a few had two. I left only after my morning GED classes to look—hard. We were there because we needed to forget about a past and to think about a future. We weren't trying to get by on some once-a-month check that came out to be half of minimum wage on a forty-hour week. We wanted more.

That first Sunday it felt funny to be in a church where nobody stared or looked at you sideways because you had "fornicated," as all the religious women I knew liked to say. All us girls piled into the shelter van for mandatory Sunday service, and I thought it would be just enough to show up and try to look interested. My favorite part was the music, since the choir's singing reminded me of when I had braved the school choir and sang in two concerts. Then I realized I wasn't out of water until I stood up and endured that dreaded rite of passage for new faces at any Black church—"The Announcement of Visitors" is what it said in the program. Baptism and membership were the only exits out of visitor status, and not one of us was ready to commit to all that. The organist slowed down his bluesy rendition of "The Old Rugged Cross," inching the song along to make sure every visitor would have background music. One by one, we nervously patted down our hair and fidgeted with our shameful outfits before stating our names, what city we were from, what church we were coming from, and who had invited us here today. My roommates were given the cue by Sister Clara Walker, the shelter housekeeper, to go first.

"I'm Janice Clark. I'm from New York City born and raised—"

"Alright now," the congregation chimed.

"—I'm not currently attending any church but this one—"

"Praise the Lord Saints!" shouted a voice from the choir.

"—and Sister Maureen invited me here today."

Shiny black and brown faces stared back at us and smiled with approval. Then Tiny giggled nervously before speaking the first words I had ever heard her say to anyone but her baby.

"Hello, how you doin' . . . I'm Tiny but my real name is Monica Young . . ."

"*Take your time, sister . . .*" the man in front of us mumbled while Monica giggled again.

"I'm from Chicago," she continued once she took her hands from her face. "I used to go to Holy Trinity Fire Baptized Church when I was little, and I was invited here today by Sister Maureen."

The church exploded into thunderclaps, welcomes, and praises with each new announcement.

"I'm Geraldine, I'm from Gary, I ain't never been to no church but this one, and I don't remember the name of who invited me."

"I'm Catherine. I was born in St. Louis but I live here now. I was baptized at Ebeneezer Pentecostal Church and the ladies at the shelter where I'm staying brought me here today."

Finally, it was my turn. I took a deep breath and rose up, making sure to pull down my purple and black striped dress in the back, and hoping nobody noticed I wasn't wearing stockings. For a quick minute I was scared my nipples were showing through the fabric stretched tight across my chest. Then I remembered I had on dark colors so maybe nobody would see that. I had never spoken to a large group of people before, not even in school classes, so I just concentrated and stared at the large vase of fake flowers blocking out the altar.

"I'm Shivana Golding, and I'm from here. Right now I don't belong to any church, but I like this one so far."

The organist hit a few notes and almost everyone shouted, "*Amen!*" When I went to sit down, I heard the whole church start to chatter. I was so nervous from talking that I couldn't make out what anyone was saying. Then Tiny tapped my leg and mouthed, "Who invited you?" I quickly jumped back up, forgetting about the back of my dress, and said, "Oh. *Sister Maureen* invited me here."

There. I had done it. *By the grace of God,* as all the sisters liked to say. From then on, I would just have to show up and look like I was trying to be saved in order to meet my requirement. I know me and the other girls must have looked a mess sitting in the back of that church, dressed like we were going to the club. Tarnishing rings on every finger, because we were the type of chicks who always had to be ready for a fight. Earrings hanging down to our shoulders. Feet stuffed into cheap, open-toed shoes. Dresses low-cut, tight, and so short we had to sit down with our hands pressed against the back. Nails long, bright, and fake with fairy-tale designs on them. Hair curled, finger-waved, and braided in styles so high and wide the ushers probably sat us in the back so everybody else could see the preacher. None of us were really looking to become holy and sanctified; we knew too many who hadn't gotten anywhere living that life. We were there for two reasons only: a dollar in the collection plate was cheaper than rent, and the shelter had staff to watch the babies while their mamas were off being saved. It was mandatory and it was a break. That was it. There were times though, when the music swelled and the minister was sweating and the members started getting happy. The tambourines would sing like a thousand doorbells ringing at once and the organist would be playing so hard he had to stand up and thump his feet. Then, we would all jump up—clapping and dancing and laughing like we were at a club in a city we never ever thought we'd get to.

IT ONLY TOOK me a couple of weeks to discover the wounds of all the girls who stayed in the house, and even those of the women who ran it. Not one of six or seven girls ever dared speak a word as we sat around a first-floor conference room, in front of a chalkboard, while a different sister gave us a GED lesson each morning. Information was shared at the edges of mealtimes—when the first few girls were arriving or the last few were finishing up. Over bountiful breakfasts of eggs and pork, and desserts incomplete unless they were à la mode, runaways itching for some neutral conversation for a change were content to talk to me about others. No evil was intended, only the maintenance of harmony, as most assumed me knowing the gossip would keep me from creating it. The stories were leaked to me piece by piece, with the essential details left out because no one knew them of course.

"Sister Maureen ain't that damn holy shit she used to hoe."

"Well don't tell her I told you, but Shirley learned how to cook in the joint."

"That chick on the second floor bipolar—she laughing in your face one minute and tryin' to cut it up the next."

"Your roommate Janice a dyke and she only pregnant 'cause she been raped."

"The one with the lazy eye pregnant by her own uncle."

"They say she got three kids already in foster care, just won't stop having 'em."

"Sister Clara couldn't never have no kids so that's why she here cleaning up after ones ain't her own."

But there was one tidbit I couldn't let just pass me by. Late one night while another fifteen-year-old named Nicole and I were finishing up on dish duty, she kept staring at me in her periphery until I called her on it.

"Is there a problem?" I asked, my sudsy hands resting on my hips.

"Naw, why you ask?"

"I feel like you starin' me down," I answered, returning to wash before she rinsed and dried.

"I was just wondering if you knew," she said, facing me.

"Knew what?"

"About your roommate," she said. In the background, one of the sisters locking doors for the night announced herself with a verse of "The Old Rugged Cross." We quickly turned back to the dishes until her voice withered to a distance in the house.

"Which roommate and what about her?" I asked as soon as I heard the voice fade out completely. Nicole chuckled.

"Damn . . . they ain't even tell you," she said, shaking her head. "That's messed up."

Now she just had me irritated. I couldn't stand when somebody wanted you to beg them to taste something you didn't even know existed until they opened their mouth.

"Tell me *what,* Nicole?" She sensed the exasperation in my voice. I was halfway through that first trimester, when I heard all women want to do is fall down and sleep every chance they get. I didn't have the patience for juvenile games, and I was surprised I had to come up in here to play them.

"Tiny. Redbone . . . you know she got AIDS."

My mouth dropped open. How the fuck were they going to room me with her, knowing I was pregnant, and not tell me some shit like that?

"No she don't," I said. "Quit lyin'!"

"I ain't lying," Nicole said, with her lips poked out. "That's why don't nobody talk to her. Why she ain't trying to work and why she got them doctors' appointments all the time. Ain't you ever noticed that? Homegirl got HIV. Baby got it too. I hope you ain't been kissin' all on him . . ."

I remembered how I had had urges to pick him up, especially when Tiny quickly left him on the bed while she went to the bathroom, yet somehow the urges vanished. Must have been the Holy Spirit talking to me. What if some of its spit had leaked into my mouth?

"Messed up they couldn't even tell you," Nicole said, as I continued to robotically wash the last few pots and pans. No wonder it had been so easy for me to get in here. Nobody else would take a room with somebody who had AIDS. Mother-fuckers! As if I didn't have enough to worry about. What were we supposed to do if she got really sick and started coughing all over the damn place? Janice looked like she had nowhere else on earth to go, that she'd sleep with wolves to avoid sleeping outside. No wonder Tiny never asked anybody to hold or change or burp that baby. Even its spit-up was crawling with a virus. Then when I thought about it, she never even kept her trash in the room but took it downstairs each and every night. No wonder she was so damn bony. Come to think of it, she had a pretty face but it was messed up because she had a tooth missing. And there was this funny sore on the side of her right temple that she kept covered with a bang. There was no telling what I had touched in there that had their germs on it. How dare they not give me a choice in this matter?

Nicole and I finished up in the kitchen, and I washed up for bed before returning to my room. Thankfully, Janice, Tiny, and her baby were sleeping when I got up there, so I didn't have to be phony. I would go ahead and sit next to her in morning classes. I didn't want her to know I knew. But right after that I was going to go to the head sister—Gladys herself—and beg to have my room changed.

"YOU GOT SOME nerve coming in here with nothing but the clothes on yo' back and talkin' 'bout who you share a room with."

Gladys's arms were folded across the hump in her chest. Nerve wasn't the least of my problems with a Black woman stout as this in front of my face.

"It's just that I'm worried if I touch something or—"

"Well, quit worrying!" The force in her voice not only shut me up, but made me sit straight up as if I had been struck by lightning. "You can't catch no HIV or AIDS or just 'bout nothing else 'cept the flu just by standing next to somebody, breathing the same air. She got just as much right to be here as you. You girls need to all mind ya business and focus on gettin' right with the Lord. Spreadin' gossip is shameful, it's blasphemy, and

I ain't allowin' it in my house. Where the Bible you got when you first moved in here? 'Cause I know you got one."

"In my drawer." She could barely hear me because my head was down.

"Where?" she bellowed, squinting her eyes and pressing her chin in her chest.

"In my top drawer," I answered, feeling my stomach churning as if I was about to throw up.

"Well go upstairs and open it to John 8:7. Or Matthew 19:19," she said. "You got that? Think you can remember that?"

"Yes, ma'am," I said, "I can remember that."

"John 8:7 and Matthew 19:19," she repeated. "If more people in this world just paid attention to them few couple a sentences, this world wouldn't be in the shape it is now. Don't take but one least lil' thing to make folks turn on one another."

I kept my head bowed during her sermon, suddenly feeling pressure in my pelvis, having to pee but too afraid to interrupt her. I wasn't trying to get kicked out of the house as soon as I got here. But she kept on talking, in a daydream that had nothing to do with me.

"I bought this house with my own money some years ago, what I had saved and worked for all my years. Now you wanna come up in here questionin' me? Who up in here and how I'm doin' thangs?"

"No ma'am."

"Well that's what it sound like to *me*. You settin' there with a baby in your belly and not a pot to piss in nor a window to throw it out of, yet you wanna act funny 'bout who you sleep next to? You lucky you got somewhere to rest your head."

"I'm sorry, I didn't mean to be disrespectful . . ."

"Just 'cause you didn't mean it don't make it alright. Like I said, this here my place, started with my money. I married an army man, just like my own mama did, and when he died I had enough money to do what I wanted to do for a change. So I wanted to come to Chicago and dance and carry on, be young, you know . . ." She smiled and leaned back a little, before the scowl came back.

"So when I got too old to dance in the clubs I wanted to dance in church. And when it was time for me to set down in church, I decided to do something to help somebody out. You young girls runnin' round out here, in these streets carryin' on like the devil can't come up from hell and bite your butt. Well, he can and he do whenever he get the chance. Soon as you open that door you done invited sin in to set right on down. Problem with y'all young girls nowadays is you bringin' babies into this world and don't give a damn—forgive me, Jesus—'bout the devil bitin' their little behinds too. Like they just fall out your thang and all of a sudden grown with a paycheck. So what y'all do when you find out that ain't the way of it? Huh, what y'all do?"

I just hunched up my shoulders as if I was talking to Ma.

"I'll tell you what most of y'all doin'. Leaving, half doin', goin' on to live your own lives and not carin' what happen to these babies. I could be making a lotta money renting out this house, but I decided to try to do something to make more of these girls want to stay. Used to be just our mens leaving us, gettin' killed and gettin' themselves killed, now women trust to do the same. We in the last days, yes we is."

I didn't dare fidget or squirm.

"But Psalms 27:10 say, 'When my father and mother forsake me then the Lord will take me up.' You hear that. The *Lord*. That's all this house is right here, to you and any other gal out there who need it. This the Lord's work. I ain't had nothing but the Lord when I was growing up. Just five years old when my daddy was shot in Harlem and not even six when my mama drowned herself in a tub. Now, that was my lot, my hand in life. Try being five years old with your mama dead on the other side of the bathroom door and you can't even get in, nobody tellin' you what happened, after you done came to school with piss running down your legs. Try that! And you wanna set here in my face and complain 'cause somebody you ain't even got to ever lay hands on might have something you can catch you just sharin' a room not having sex with her gal get on out my face with this nonsense."

I had been dismissed, and couldn't wait to get out of the tiny, cramped office which had gotten stuffier with each one of her remarks.

"What you supposed to be going upstairs to read?" she called out to me as I walked out.

"John 8:19 and Luke—"

"No. Matthew 19:19 and John 8:7. Read it right now. And you think about that 'fore you think about twisting your lips to say one thing wrong to that young girl ain't got nowhere to go."

NOW, TINY'S PRESENCE simply unnerved me. Her light skin became more than a complexion and more of a pallor, her thin frame looked too much like a skeleton's. As she moved about and around us, her aura had faded to something almost ethereal in my eyes; whether the glow fringing her silhouette was from life or death remained to be seen. There was no way Janice could know what was up with Tiny; matter of fact, Janice acted like she was sweet on Tiny—always offering to do things for the baby, sharing anything sweet, fixing flyaways in her hair. Just like a butch for a femme.

"Damn this shit is good," Janice squealed one night as she passed a carton of corner-store Neapolitan back between her and Tiny, something me and Nakesha would have done. They were only using one spoon—Janice, Tiny, and that baby. There was no way Janice could have known. But we didn't have any drama in our room. We all respected each other's privacy and bedtimes. We made casual conversation about music and the weather. I didn't plan on being here forever, so there was no need in me causing any drama in the short time I was here.

"No thank you," I said, as cheerfully as I could while I slathered Palmer's cocoa butter on my feet before I went to bed.

"Mmm mmm," Janice said, scooping out her last spoonful before passing it along to Tiny. "Damn, what was we supposed to read for Bible study? I don't never do that shit on time . . ." She scratched her scalp between her cornrows and lazily flipped through the leather-bound Bible bearing her name.

There was no way I could forget the assignment, since I was positive it had been handed down by the powers that be because of me.

"Matthew 19:19 and John 8:7," I told them before shutting my eyes for the night, finally accepting that maybe Tiny wasn't so bad and maybe the sisters were right.

THE FIRST SNOWFLAKES of winter are always the sweetest. Not yet polluted, not too stubborn to melt, just light and soft, teardrops without the salt. Rasul and I had gotten back just in time to watch Chicago's first winter snowfall. We sat in each other's arms on the shelter porch, both listening out for the door to creak and announce one of the sister's prying eyes. We had been out all afternoon—rode the train downtown just to walk around a couple skyscraper blocks then come right on back. I had gone inside only to get my Bible and show him the verses that were supposed to make me feel bad about being pissed that I had to share my room with an AIDS victim.

" 'Thou shalt love thy neighbor as thyself.' " He grinned, then flipping to the next passage, " 'Let he who is without sin cast the first stone.' "

"What that got to do with me?" I asked. "I ain't casting stones, I'm just saying I don't want no AIDS."

"You wouldn't be able to put your mouth on mine no more," he said, obviously making fun of me.

"I'm serious, Rasul. And I don't want my baby having no AIDS if I decide to keep it."

"You decided yet?"

"Don't ask me." There was a part of me still hoping that it would all go away on its own. But then there was a part of me wondering what it would be like to be married and have a family. Rasul seemed open to the idea. I could stay here, pretend to stay pregnant even if I got rid of it, get myself together, then move out on my own. Or I could have it and still get myself together and move out on my own. Or I could move in with Rasul in an apartment like his. The future was wide open. It was a shame that it had taken me getting knocked up to learn to search for options in life.

"Shivana, it's about to be three months soon, right?" Rasul reminded me.

"What you care?"

"Well, I would like to get to know you better," he said, his face stone-serious.

"Get to know me how?" I grinned, knowing exactly what he meant. Sneaking feels on the train, stoop, and restaurants was getting played. He just grinned back, and I pulled away.

"You just think I'm not gonna make you use a condom 'cause I'm already pregnant," I snapped.

"Why would I think that? We sitting here talking about somebody with AIDS."

"Why you want me, Rasul?" I finally asked, something I had wanted to ask for a long time.

"What you mean, why?"

"Rasul, don't play with me. If I keep this baby, you gonna have a pregnant girl. Then a girl with a baby."

I just took it upon myself to assume I was already his girl. He didn't correct me, so my assumption became fact at that very moment, as the snow fell harder. We shivered inside our down jackets and our old sneaks, all of them already in need of a washing and the season wasn't near over.

"Guess I just ain't thought that far yet," he said. "Shit, when you done moved around much as I have, you just take shit day by day."

"Well, a baby ain't day by day, that's every day for the next eighteen years no doubt."

"You actin' like you want to keep it. I mean, you missed the first appointment. You running out of money and ain't been back down there to the clinic yet."

"I ain't running out of money," I snapped, feeling no need to tell him about the fifty bucks Jewel had sent me every week since Thanksgiving. One thing I had heard from too many women was to never let the right hand know what the left is doing. "I just been thinking, maybe I could do better somewhere else. Sometimes all you need is a change." At least that's what I used to tell myself all those years I was stupid enough to think my daddy had just left to make some money, and would be coming back to us.

"I hate this country stuff too," Rasul said. "Ain't no jobs here. Just factory work and driving people around. And I'm sick of getting stopped by the police all the time. Plus, my uncle's wife starting to get on my nerves." His breath smelled like Wild Passion Alizé. We had been drinking that all afternoon. I had to be sure not to speak to any of the sisters with alcohol on my breath.

"Wish I could go stay with Aunt Jewel," I suddenly said.

"In New York?" Rasul lit up and held me tighter. "Now that's what I'm talkin' 'bout. Shit, New York? That's where all the MCs are—the good ones at least."

"You could be the next," I said, not realizing where my mind was going. "We should go."

"To New York?"

"Why not?" I had never been far out of Chicago, and all I knew of New York was what I had seen in movies like *Juice* and TV shows like *21 Jump Street*. It just looked like Chicago with more people, traffic, and buildings. I was sure I could adapt to it like I had adapted to most everything in my life—quickly.

"And stay with Jewel and that big gorilla mothafucker? No way . . ."

"He ain't so bad. He was just mad."

I had his interest.

"You think they'll let us stay with them?"

"Jewel wouldn't turn me away. Not me."

"Yeah, but what about me?"

"She wouldn't turn you away either, not if you came all the way with me. Maybe Hakim would let you work in his barbershop . . ."

"Shivana, you just talking shit . . . you ain't trying to go to New York. Your auntie would have your ma on the phone in a minute shutting that shit down . . ."

"We just can't tell her we coming," I cautioned. "We just gotta show up. I mean, we might have to sleep on the floor when we get there, before we get our own place, but who cares . . . sleeping on her floor better than sharing a room with somebody got AIDS."

The porch lights flashed on and off several times, the sisters' signal that the doors would be locked soon. See, I was too grown for all that. At least I thought I was. I focused my attention on my man and some little girls across the street, determined to keep on jumping rope even as the ground became slippery from snow that was reluctant to stick. They didn't stop until they were called inside like I was now being. I realized The Haven wasn't the place for who I was trying to be. I was sick and tired of being a girl.

"I bet it's all kind of fun jobs I could get in New York," I fantasized as the snow fell harder. I didn't even care about my hair getting puffy. I was only thinking about the moves I could make if I left all I knew behind. "I could be one of the girls dancing in the videos."

"My video," Rasul said, laughing, seeing it with me for the first time.

"I got enough for the train."

"That's a thousand miles from here . . ." He kept talking, stuck in his own dreams. Who knows if I was even still in them.

A thousand miles from me, I thought.

We stared at each other, long and hard, me and him, friends for no other reason than we didn't have much of anybody else, lovers soon as we could find a quiet, private place to make love. A warmth filled my chest, so strong I was sure I was alive, and like magnets we held on to hearts turned steel and refused to let go. We paid no mind when the porch lights flashed again, as the snow blanketed everything around us in determined sheets. We were too busy holding each other, smiling because it was all we had to do, looking up to the sky through the falling snow, searching for our own light.

FOURTEEN

THE NEXT SUNDAY, I quietly handed Sister Gladys the keys
to my room at the shelter. I did it while everyone else was at
church, so there would be no questions and no gossip. I hadn't
even said good-bye to Janice and Tiny. I had thought about calling Ma and Nakesha, then had changed my mind about both.
The next time either one of them heard from me, I would be in
another state.

"Well, you always welcome back if we got room," Gladys
said, hugging me in the Haven of Christ Temple's vestibule.
"Long as you don't get fussy 'bout who you sharing it with."

I had many emotions about leaving. This was the closest
thing to a family I had ever had the privilege of living with. I
had not spoken with Ma, especially after hearing from Jewel
that she was completely irate with me, so much so that Jewel refused to confess my location for fear my own mother might slice
my throat. I did not know where we stood, if she had "forsaken"
me as it said in Psalms. I loved my ma, would always love her,

but I just needed some time away to discover what I was truly made of. I wanted to know if I could make it beyond King Drive and Chicago, my tiny world in which I had always felt like I was drowning.

Sundays on the South Side of Chicago belonged to the church folks: old ladies stood at the bus shelters in their ornate hats, saggy-jeaned thugs took cover as saggy-suited boys followed their grandmothers into church, old men crawled out of the bars and into the pews. When a shiny, 1980-something chocolate Eldorado pulled up on Halsted, I wasn't expecting Rasul to get out. I thought it was going to be one of the deacons from Second Baptist, picking up the few stray girls who were sure to be late each Sunday. Tupac, not gospel, blasted from the stereo as he partially rolled down the window, wearing dark black sunglasses, to let me know it was him. He had on a leather jacket I had never seen him in. His fade was lined just right. The new car, clothes, and cut made him look brand-new—more like the man he was always claiming to be. God, he looked fine that day, in the Sunday morning sunlight, leaning out of that car window like he was picking me up for church. I patted my hair down nervously like I was seeing him for the first time.

"Hello, Ms. Gladys," he said, then gently pulled the ride up to the curb. He hit a button inside to lift the trunk automatically.

"Hmph," Gladys grunted. "Looks like somebody got them a new job . . ." In her mind, he had to be just one of the many dealers who dropped their teenaged lovers off at the shelter once they had used them up for another night.

My stuff was waiting on the stoop. Rasul had put the car in park and was rushing forward to help me.

"Just get in . . ." he mouthed as soon as he saw I was about to question him about the whip. I guess if I was going to ride or die with my man, like Bonnie with Clyde, the first thing I had to learn was to not ask questions when he ordered me to do something. I jumped in and sat tight while he loaded up the trunk with my things.

"Rasul, what the hell is this?" I yelled as soon as he got back in.

"Just a little something for the trip . . . we ain't riding no train," he said. "We coming to New York in style . . . we gonna be ballin', baby, so it's time to look the part."

The car had a new money shine on the outside, but the inside revealed a different story. The foam lining the ceiling had started to hang down. The leather seats cracked in jagged, crooked lines. The ashtray held caramelized soot and wouldn't turn back in no matter how hard I pushed. I knew enough about hoopties from my cousins to recognize a slow starter, squeaky brakes, and a ticking engine.

"Rasul, where you get this car?"

"I bought it," he said, without looking at me, lighting a Newport on the dash. He took a long drag, fidgeted at the wheel, and wouldn't look my way.

"Where you get the dough?" I knew he had a little filing job, but there was no way he could have saved for this.

"My uncle used to let me keep all my money, so I just saved and saved and saved," he continued. "Shit, I figured now was good a time as any to put that money to use."

"You got a license?"

"No, but shit I know how to drive. I don't plan on getting stopped." He turned up the radio. I quickly turned it down.

"Did you drive it first? It sound like something wrong with it . . ."

"Naw, I just bought a ride without test-driving it first. I bought this from my uncle friend—I told them I was ready to leave and be on my own, and they sent me off like a man."

The rearview mirror was turned his way and he wouldn't look in mine, so I couldn't tell from his eyes whether he was lying or not.

"Rasul, we ain't gonna need no car in New York," I snapped. "They got a subway there. We coulda rode the train and used that money for something else."

Soon as those words slipped out of my mouth, I wanted to look around for my mother. I sounded just like her right then. She and Daddy were always arguing about what she wanted to spend money on versus what he wanted to. Usually, she favored business while he fought for pleasure. Rasul looked crushed that his effort to impress me had failed. This wasn't the foot I was trying to start us off on. The time to start relaxing was now. I didn't need to put stress on myself, especially being pregnant and with a long, strange trip ahead of me. I had no idea how long this would take. There were a couple of maps wrinkled in the backseat, letting me know Rasul had pored long and hard over them. What was the point of me leaving to start fresh if I was going to take a worrying head with me? I relaxed and leaned back as Rasul made it down Halsted to get to 57 South, which would soon lead us to 80 East; I knew from Hakim that from there it was a straight shot east to New York City. All I needed was my man like Hakim at the wheel and gas money for a thousand miles. And I had both.

"I'm sorry," I said. "I guess you got it covered then."

"I got you faded for the car and gas," he said, "but not for the eats and shit. How much you got left?"

"Oh, we straight," I said, not wanting to be totally honest just in case I wanted to keep a little put away for myself.

I hadn't spent much of anything while living in the shelter. From the cabby, Hakim, and Jewel I had saved up almost six hundred dollars. I estimated that should last a good couple of weeks in New York, until I got a job at Micky D's or somewhere. Rasul looked at me for the first time since he had gotten into the car.

"You got enough for a hotel?"

"Why we gotta stop? Shoot, I can take over when you get tired; we need to be saving that money . . ."

"All your ass do is sleep. How you gonna take over shit? And I don't know how you drive."

"My daddy taught me how to drive!" I shouted, indignant. "I bet I got behind the wheel before you did."

This wasn't going well. I had read in one of Jewel's women's magazines that you knew you had your soulmate if you could survive a road trip together. We hadn't even made it out of Chicago's city limits.

"Well, we'll talk about all that later but right now I gotta pay attention to get us out of Chi." He gave me the silent treatment for a couple minutes before suddenly saying, "I was thinking we could get a hotel tonight. You know, do something romantic."

I knew exactly what "romantic" meant. And I couldn't deny I had a familiar ache. I had felt Rasul between his jeans several times. He had pressed up against me the last time he had lain in his bed and moaned—that's when I knew I had him. He wasn't going nowhere until he felt what it was like inside and up against. I had learned something from Nakesha before we stopped being friends. I felt that tiny pinch of electric, just thinking about what we could do when we were truly alone and on our own.

"We might could do that," I said real sweet. "Maybe . . ."

After that, neither one of us could stop smiling. We had started out listening to Chicago radio, and when that faded out we put DJ Jazzy Jeff and the Fresh Prince into the tape player. We had stuffed our bags in the huge trunk—most of what we owned was clothes, shoes, and music. I probably had the most stuff—a portable TV Jewel gave me, a small Panasonic stereo, and a few books from my English classes. Earlier, I had been so worried about the black smoke coming from the back and the rusted pipes hanging from the bottom of Rasul's "Ramobile" (as we had playfully dubbed the Eldorado) that I just knew I wasn't setting foot in it, even if Rasul was bragging about the new engine his shade tree mechanic uncle had put in. But right then, I didn't care how reliable that car was. All I was thinking about were the exciting things Janice had said, things like: *Shivana, you fine enough to get one of those dress-up jobs downtown . . .*

Rasul was actually a controlled, calm driver; I had relaxed within minutes of him zipping past the roaring semis and massive vans that shared the early Sunday morning road. This real trip was an adventure for me, the first adventure I think I ever had. For the first time in my life, I was leaving Illinois. I was going somewhere else. I was leaving my mama behind. I think I thought I was proving something, but I didn't know what. I was going to be a real mother. I was almost sixteen. I wasn't in jail. I could read. I could write. I could get a job at a bank, or a telephone company, or a day-care center, or a building dropped in a distinguished word like *downtown*. I was in a big brown car going down a big highway with my man driving me.

I was so happy—holding a duffel bag full of Vitner's potato chips and cans of Old Towne pop that Rasul had bought for our trip. All we needed was some good weed—not the brown dirt full of seeds and sticks, but the fluffy, bright green kind that smelled like rainwater when you smoked it. When we finally escaped Chicago city limits, the fields of Indiana started passing us by like swirls on a record playing. In the front seat, Rasul turned up the tape player so loud that I couldn't help but sing along to "Real Love" by Mary J. I made him rewind that song three times while I simulated dancing like the girls in the videos. We laughed back and forth until my lips slowed down and my eyes got heavy. The last sign I saw before I fell asleep with my baby on my mind said "Cleveland, 396 Miles."

WE BOTH HAD been too hungry for each other to wait for night. Around noon, Rasul had nudged me awake outside of a

Travel America where he had planned on getting gas and snacks. A Howard Johnson's was attached to a sprawling gas station and rest center. It was the first large motel he or I had ever seen, apart from the huge ones downtown, that didn't charge folks by the hour. Riding inches away in a roomy car whose windows blocked out the rest of the world, we had been filled up with a new sense of each other. The heavy scent of our excited youth had hovered between us like another passenger. The Eldorado was a tight pressure cooker, forcing us captive to imagine the possibilities that accompanied our new freedom. Just two hours into the trip and already we had gotten lazy, weighed down by anticipation and the desire to have one another for the first time. The fire in our groins had made us docile and sullen. When I leaned against the car and stretched from head to toe, adding a short yelp to dramatize how stiff I had become, Rasul fell into me and held me tight. He smiled toward the Howard Johnson's neon-orange sign, and my eyes crinkled as I just shook my head without saying a word.

We were obviously ready to be hustlers in New York; Rasul had to give the bucktoothed, carrot-topped front desk clerk forty extra dollars of my money in exchange for letting us check in without ID. But forty extra dollars was a small price to pay for the heaven of four walls closed around just us—no other diners, train passengers, or neighbors stomping on and off the stoop. We had rustled through garbage bags for lotion, deodorant, and clothes to change into in the morning. Neither of us had thought about night clothes, but it was too cold to go back out and my guess was we wouldn't need them.

For two hours, I stared at the granulated ceiling and tried to count all the tiny spots. I always got messed up around 120, either because Rasul would change position or the channel. We weren't ready to get into it just yet. I liked that he took his time, didn't feel the need to devour me as soon as I walked through the door like Leroy always had. The pillow play before the act was a sign of the pillow talk to come after. But he came back from the Travel Center with foot-long sandwiches and pop, spreading one of the hotel towels in between us on the bed like a picnic blanket, and with our stomachs satisfied it was time to satiate the part below.

"You ain't scared is you?" he asked me.

"Shit," I spat, defensive. "What I look like scared of something? You know I been with a grown man."

"I'm grown," he assured me.

"Prove it then."

He was now undaunted by the sass that had arrested his interest from the moment we met. We had begun a new chapter in our young lives together, and I thought that type of commitment warranted him not using a condom. He felt light on top of me, so much so he didn't bother to raise up once. Plus, while he caressed me, and hugged me for what seemed like hours before and after, he said strange things that I thought I only heard because I was high off cigarettes. He teased me with talk of the future, and "*our* baby." All that sweetness Ma had warned me against. The type of talk men used to get our noses open to get what they wanted. But it sounded so good as we pressed into each other underneath the scratchy covers, the blinds shut tight to close out the fading daylight. It sounded so good as he pushed deep inside of me, so much slower and gentler than Leroy. It sounded even better when his words muffled my own promises, whispered in the midst of a passion I could finally be unashamed of. I stretched myself as wide open as my body would allow, letting him stay on top of me the whole time. I was fine with him being in control. While he whispered my name, I enjoyed his surrender to me. I escaped inside my own head to have a talk with my child.

I wish we could start this all over again . . . me, you, and him just wipe the slate clean. Forget Leroy, forever, and pretend this happened today, right here, right now, anew. Then maybe I could feel better about you. Maybe this situation wouldn't be so sour. My heart wouldn't be so heavy, my future wouldn't be so uncertain. See Ma was wrong she got me blaming you when I should be blaming them—these men, the ones who don't know how to love us. But I got me one right here in my arms, right here on top of me, loving me because it's what he want to do and not what nobody forced him to do, and my heart tell me he ain't going nowhere. So I think it's okay for me to think about you now to let you in my mind and make plans about the both of us while this man on top of me making me feel so good I can start looking for you some nice clothes all pink 'cause like Nakesha said I hope you a girl but I know he gonna want a boy I really don't care what you are I just know I'm gonna keep you looking good I'm gonna shine your face up with Vaseline every single day like my grandma used to do me you gonna wear shiny patent leathers to church and boy or girl I'm braiding your hair and putting beads with Africa's colors on the end because I'm gonna raise you to think you a king or queen so no matter what happen to me you don't never let nobody come along and steal your light and pride. So let's just pretend it's happening all over again. Let's just pretend me and you start fresh, again, brand-new, today, and we all a real family. You can rest easy now, baby . . . I ain't getting rid of you.

WHEN IT WAS all over and we were both sweaty and satisfied, I wondered if he was going to say "I love you." I lay on my stomach while he lay on his back, our shoulders lightly pressed together and our breathing in harmony. I waited to hear him say it, because I wanted to but I wouldn't do it first. He fell asleep.

That next morning—later than we should have—we emerged from the hotel room refreshed as newlyweds. Our next destination was McDonald's, then the road. Finally, I understood the sparkle that could mark a woman in love from miles away. Rasul wasn't the finest thing I had ever seen—his lips reminded me of a bird's, he was rail thin, and his face was so skinny you could see all the little bones in it. Not to mention the funny white spots in his face. He wanted to wear cornrows, but his hair wouldn't grow in thick no matter how much Bergamot and African Pride he saturated it with. The most he had going for him were his eyes—they were kind of green, but his skin was so pale that his eyes seemed to fade away along with the rest of his face whenever he was in bright light like today's. But I swear, he could look at me and make me feel soft faster than the coldest brother on the block. He had a way of looking at my eyes and putting his hands in my hair that made me feel like I was the only girl he had seen all day—not just the latest one to catch his eye. I wondered if that look was part of what the old ladies at Second Baptist meant when they had talked to us about "heart love," not "hot love."

I turned around and smiled at him after I had taken a few steps out of our hotel room, daring him to chase me to go farther, but he only rolled his eyes at me and headed toward the "Ramobile." For the first time since we had pulled over, I looked around in all four directions. I turned, and the wind blew my hair around with me. We weren't even that far from Chicago, really out in the middle of Indiana's extensive nowhere, and yet I had never seen so many trees in my life. On Monday morning, the Travel America was busy with all those heading back after weekend getaways. An older White man walked a little toy dog while his wife followed behind with a cane. I noticed they wore crisp white shorts and short-sleeved striped tops; it wasn't *that* nice outside. A dark Mexican family—two little boys, a man, woman, and maybe a grandma—made sandwiches and laughed out loud at one of the picnic tables. Spanish music played inside a van nearby where they sat—the grandma soon got up to dance with her hips while the rest of them laughed louder. I always liked their music. It seemed like what you would listen to when you owned a big house and had to spend a whole Saturday cleaning it, but you didn't mind because it was yours and not somebody else's.

The entire scene invigorated me. I suddenly felt more alert and alive than I ever had in my whole life. My senses were so sharp I felt like I could hold a conversation with God. I felt like there were invisible people around me that I couldn't see, but somehow, I wasn't bumping into them. Maybe it was because they could see me. My vision took on a heightened clarity as if I had just slipped on a pair of rose-colored glasses. The air seemed to crackle with energy. Rasul laughed at me when I held a comb up above my head. Jewel had showed me how to make my hair stand up if the air felt right—crisp and burnt like it did now. I patiently looked in the tinted Eldorado passenger side window and watched a few strands rise up like Alfalfa from the Little Rascals. It seemed like ever since I had left Chicago all I wanted to do was sleep and laugh. Matter of fact, that's all I was going to do for the first month that I was in New York. I had some savings; fuck a job. When we piled back into the Eldorado I had MTV, Times Square, Harlem, and the Cosbys on my mind.

FIFTEEN

INDIANA WAS EASY.

I slept most of the way. The even ramble of country road hypnotized me into weariness, and it was inside my dreams where I reignited. I dreamed of Daddy, cotton candy, Ferris wheels, dandelions, and trains zooming underground. I would occasionally stir and open my eyes to stare out the window with its fleeting scenes, quickly deciding that what went on in my dreams was more exciting. A very ordinary milieu of cornfields, barnyards, high grass, and open space was decidedly unordinary to my city eyes. The cotton puffs torn loose from withered dandelions floated throughout the air, a couple even shooting through the window and landing on my lap. Chicago was a fantastic, light-filled mecca for the rest of a state held captive by unbroken darkness at night and unbroken horizon in the day. To the rest of the Midwest, I was a virgin when it came to country. Less so was Rasul, who had vagabonded through Southern states and cities by the time I was just starting school. Within a couple of hours, the adrenaline rush of escape had worn off for both of us. The radio volume had been turned down—by who I couldn't remember. We no longer had the mental tolerance for hip-hop's angry noise. This was a calm journey.

I woke up several times in between naps, once using the bathroom while Rasul refilled. The South Side of Chicago was my territory—I never saw any White folks but the teachers at school. But that's all there was at the one stop we made. Plaid-clad, leather-faced White folks. "Crackers" is what my daddy used to call them. Fat men and skinny women all stared at us while we filled up and took bathroom breaks at a Shell with a sandwich shop inside. I listened to the twang of country music as I squatted over a funky toilet. Even the wild-haired, fat-ass truckers with their butt cracks peeking out had the nerve to stare. Rasul had wanted squares, but decided against them.

"We should both try to stop smoking, I mean, if you might have the baby and all," he explained. I nodded my head shyly, and grabbed his hand in agreement.

I was impatient once we left the shop and Rasul took a couple of extra minutes to look under the hood of the Eldorado. He had never mentioned knowing much about cars to me, but then again I was running away with someone I barely knew. When he slammed the hood down, the entire car shuddered and I glimpsed a veil of concern over his smile.

"We straight?" I asked.

"It's cool . . . I just had to open the radiator cap and put a little water in . . ."

"I thought I had smelled something burning."

"We gonna get there," he assured me. "Don't even worry about that. We ain't stoppin' 'til we get there. Even if I gotta carry you on my back."

He and I both knew neither of us wanted that. Just like a woman, I was already thinking ahead as one hand rested on my belly—slightly harder and rounder now. Worse came to worst,

if the car broke down we could hitchhike to a gas station. I
wasn't going to breathe easy until we cleared Indiana. All them
White folks in one place meant we would have to walk to Ohio
or back to Illinois to get anyone to pick us up. But at the gas station, we could call a cab to a train station. Then, we could sleep
on our garbage bags of clothes until the next train came. Or
maybe we could hibernate in a motel room and make love for
two days until we felt like riding the train. With just six hundred dollars to my name and a baby on the way, no one could
tell me I wasn't rich. And it felt *good*. Seemed like that money
in my bra gave me the gift of arrogance, the power to say "Fuck
you" if I felt like it, the option to both make plans and have a
Plan B for a change.

Ohio was a little more complicated. I searched for signs to
cities I had heard of before: *Cleveland, Cincinnati, Toledo*. It was
a wonder to me that I was finally within miles of places I had
only heard about; that meant all the other places I had heard and
read about were actually in the world too, I just had to get close
to them. People lecturing you about all the things you can do and
places you can go in your life don't mean shit when you don't believe that these things and places are there. But now, I believed.
About a hundred miles into it, I saw a sign for Cedar Point. I
knew there was a huge amusement park in Cedar Point that
Aunt Jewel had promised to take me to, but we had never made it
there. I wondered how nice it would have been for me and Rasul
to stop there. We could ride that Ferris wheel. But there was no
time. I was ready to get to New York, and Rasul claimed we
would be there before the sun set. It didn't matter that it was
nearly four and we hadn't even officially escaped the Midwest.

A four-lane where everyone surpassed the speed limit was
enough to get Rasul flustered and cranky. He never drove past
the speed limit, and sometimes didn't even reach it. The burn I
thought I smelled had intensified, and he had slowed down as if
he was obeying its silent command. At one point, an angry man

mouthing curse words shot past us when we were only going forty-five miles an hour. Rasul had retired his sunglasses when the sun began to dim around six, actually five our time since we had lost an hour soon as we crossed the Indiana state line. I feared a rainstorm coming. I took a catnap and woke up to find him listening to his own juvenile, underproduced songs recorded on cassette tapes—mouthing the words to himself. *We ain't your slaves no more or your Uncle Toms, just niggaz raised in broken homes with single moms, keep walking down the street and don't look us in the eyes, pop pop pop we ain't nothing but soldiers in disguise . . .*

"What's up, sleepyhead?" he teased after he caught me staring and was embarrassed.

"We almost there?" I asked, as if New York City were around the block. I was sore from our lovemaking the night before. I almost wanted to stretch out in the backseat, but I thought that would be selfish and cruel.

"We almost at the end of Ohio . . . then it's Pennsylvania." Like the genius I now believed he was, he had memorized the map. "We should be there around midnight."

"Okay," I mumbled, drifting back into sleep, believing Rasul was Everyman, he could do anything, and I could rest easy with him at the wheel. But he was getting tired. And though I wasn't doing much but sitting down, so was I. So I decided to talk though it was clear he didn't want to.

"Man, I can't wait to get there. Wait 'til I tell Nakesha. She's gonna be so jealous."

I imagined the news spreading at school. This time, it wouldn't be gossip. There would be no talk at the lunch tables or in the bathrooms or at the lockers about Shivana being bald-headed, or stupid, or fat, or getting pregnant by some old man who was locked up. No one would know. They only would know that I was no longer at school because I had made it somewhere they probably would never see—the Big Apple.

"I wonder what everybody gonna say when they see us on the BET Music Awards?" I thought, out loud. Rasul perked up as I stroked his ego and his dreams.

"Don't forget the Grammys and the American Music Awards," he exclaimed.

"Oh, and the MTV Video Awards, 'cause you know your first video gonna be the one everybody can't stop talking about." I started laughing. "Damn, Rasul, you gonna be bigger than LL Cool J!"

"I wonder if we gonna see him," Rasul asked.

"Hell yeah! We gonna be in New York. We gonna see everybody—LL, Tupac, Queen Latifah. I bet we gonna see Mary J. Blige too. They all live in New York."

"Yeah, but where? You know New York way bigger than Chicago. There's Brooklyn, the Bronx . . ."

"So what? We gonna find out where they live, and we gonna go, and we gonna give 'em your tape. Matter fact, turn that shit up!"

He cranked up his tape. When I heard his voice muffled in static and bass that was turned up way too loud, I didn't care. I imagined it was coming from the radio.

"What you think your mama and daddy gonna say when they hear you on the radio?" He trusted me now, I knew, believed that I was the woman who could bandage his wounds rather than throw salt in them.

"Shit, I don't know," he said with his eyes locked on the road ahead. "You know they probably gonna come out the woodworks and shit. After all this time."

"What you gonna say if you see 'em?"

"I don't know." He was silent for the entire bridge. "Shit, I guess I'm gonna say, 'What's up?' I don't care. I ain't mad."

I ain't mad either, not no more, I thought, thinking of my own daddy. Maybe he was in New York. I remembered from the letter my mother had written me, which was packed among my clothes, that my grandmother had said he was in California. If he could get to California, then he could certainly get to the other coast.

"I got my own kids and family to think about," Rasul suddenly said. I didn't dare ask if he was talking about me. He still hadn't told me he loved me. I didn't know how long this was going to last. I had been warned by too many that love faded. In my head, I cautioned myself the way Ma had with the man who came after Daddy, the way her few female visitors had whenever they talked about a new man: *I'm just gonna enjoy this until it's over.*

"So do I," was all I said, not giving away that I hoped that he was going to be in my family, forever. "I gotta think about my education. And my big house. 'Cause I'm having a big house, with a dog and white fence and clothesline in the back and everything. No, fuck the clothesline. I'm having a washer and dryer in my house. Fuck washing shit out in the tub and hanging it up like everybody else. Or spending all day at the Laundromat. I might just pay somebody to wash my clothes! I'm gonna be rich."

Rasul didn't respond to my dreams the way I had wanted him to.

"Man, this is stupid," he said, turning off his own song.

"What's stupid?"

"Us. This. Going to New York and shit. I bet we gonna have to come back. Tail between our legs and shit."

"No we ain't!" I was rejuvenated by his doubt. It gave me a way to talk myself out of my own. "We ain't coming back, Rasul."

He didn't look so sure. For once, our roles had reversed.

"We gonna make it there," I said. "And we gonna stay. And I'm gonna have my baby."

He took his eyes off the road for the second it took to stare at me with his mouth open. I just nodded my head to let him know he had heard right.

"You sure?" he asked.

"Yeah," I said softly. "I'm sure. I think it deserves to be here, just like I did. I mean, who am I to stop it just because shit ain't perfect?"

"It's never perfect," Rasul said.

"I know you mean what you said," I continued. "Last night, about us. I know you weren't just saying some shit to fill my head."

He looked at me again, this time a little longer, and nodded himself because I needed convincing now. I had said aloud what I wanted to do, something I had avoided doing because I was never sure. But I was sure now. We would use all the money to get set up in New York. I had no idea how much that really would cost, but I didn't care. I was sure that we would make it.

"We ain't never coming back to Chicago," I told Rasul. "We're gone from that life, and everything in it. Just like Jewel. Folks wanna come see us, that's fine. But we ain't coming to see them. Half of 'em didn't give a fuck we was there anyway. Fuck 'em."

He just shook his head and listened to the radio, looking for the next place to stop as the car suddenly began to shudder and spit.

WE STOPPED IN a place called Clearville, Pennsylvania. I had never heard of it. The only place in Pennsylvania I knew of was Philadelphia. I had learned in History that the Liberty Bell or some shit was there. Before I realized how long this trip was going to take, I had wondered if we could stop and see it. Just so I could say I had seen something once that I had only before seen in a book. But I knew there would be no time. There were no signs at all for Philadelphia on the Pennsylvania Turnpike, still called Interstate 80-East on the map. Thankfully, we did see signs for New York City, but it was still almost four hundred miles away. It had taken us forever to go the first four hundred miles. If there was something longer than forever, I feared that was how long it would take us to do the last four hundred. Road signs had been announcing Clearville for miles, so we figured that it was a major place where we could feel safe pulling over at night. We turned off and came upon a Shell gas station with a Dunkin' Donuts. We both were hungry, having sustained ourselves off the McDonald's breakfast and potato chips. I noticed a pay phone on the side of the station. I decided to use it while Rasul went inside to pay for more gas and grab sandwiches.

I dialed "0" for the operator, hoping that my mother was home. I was halfway to New York now, so nothing she could say to me would convince me to come home. It would take just as much time to get back to Chicago as it would to get to New York, so I was better off going forward and not back. Ma had nothing better to do on a Monday night after work, so I was alarmed when the operator came back and said no one was answering the phone. I hadn't spoken to Ma in a couple of weeks, ever since I had left home. Aunt Jewel told me she was mad at me, and that was all I had needed to hear. My one letter to her had been returned because I had forgotten to put a stamp on it. I asked the operator to try again, and she returned with the same report—the telephone just rang and rang. I couldn't talk into the answering machine without charges accumulating. Since there was no one there to accept them, the operator wouldn't let me do that. Rasul came out of the station just as I was about to hang up. Then, I had another idea. I shooed him away when he came toward me holding sandwiches and juices in the air.

"Gimme a minute," I said to him with my hand up. He walked back to the car to dig in. The operator was still there, impatient. I asked her to try one more number. I hoped Mrs. Murray would accept my charges so I could talk to Nakesha. Her little brother Darion was on the line once the charges were accepted.

"Darion, it's Shivana," I said to him.

"You in jail?" he immediately asked.

"Hell naw, I ain't in jail!" I shouted. "But I'm far from Chicago, so that's why I had to call collect. Nakesha there?"

"Yeah, lemme go get her."

Darion came back to the phone a couple of seconds later.

"She said she busy."

I sighed. That girl was the most stubborn person I had ever met.

"Look, Darion, this is important. Would you tell her to come to the phone, please?"

"Damn, I'm trying to watch cartoons!" he yelled before I heard his footsteps stomp off. After a couple minutes of waiting and fearing that Nakesha would never come to the phone, I heard crackling on the other line. She was picking up.

"Hang the phone up in there, Darion," she said. "I *said*, hang the damn phone up! Dawg! I'm sick of sitting here every night with y'all getting on my nerves I just ask you to do one thing and you can't do that you selfish little heathen don't ask me for no more money . . ."

"Nakesha," I interrupted, "it's Shivana."

"Yeah, I know," she said. "I only picked up the phone 'cause you calling collect. What, you in trouble so you want me to help you out? And why you ain't been back to school? Everybody been asking me if you dropped out."

"I'm not in trouble," I said. "But I'm not in Chicago."

"Where the hell you at? You still pregnant?"

"Nakesha, I can't get it into all that right now."

"It's a yes or no question," she said dryly.

"Okay, yes," I answered, hoping she wasn't so mad that she

would tell the whole world, if she hadn't already. "I'm still pregnant, but I'm going to stay with Jewel in New York."

"When?"

"Right now. I'm almost there. I'm in Pennsylvania."

"Pennsylvania?! Where that at?"

"Far away. You gotta go east. I'm driving there with my friend Rasul."

"Who the hell is Rasul?"

"That guy I had told you about, in my building."

"You ain't never told me about no Rasul . . ."

"Nakesha, I gotta go. We gotta get back on the road. But I just wanted to tell somebody where I was and where I'm going. I'm in Pennsylvania now, and we should be in New York later tonight. Can you call my mother and tell her?"

"Oh bitch you gotta lot of nerve asking me for shit . . ."

"Nakesha, please!" I yelled. Impending motherhood had made me more brazen. "Look, I'm sorry about what happened. I don't know how many times I can tell you. But I was going crazy with all this stress and drama. Come on, you know you my girl."

"If I'm your girl how come I ain't heard from you since you left school? You ain't called me or thought about me. Now you need something, and here you come calling my house collect. Now *I'm* gonna get in trouble."

"I didn't have nobody else to call," I confessed. "And, you wasn't talking to me, so I was like fuck it."

"Well, I was mad."

"I know, and you had every right to be. But can we just forget about that now? Damn, Nakesha. I'm trying to tell you I'm going somewhere else. I'm going to New York City, by myself, with my man."

"Oh, he your man now?"

"Yeah, kinda." .

"When did all this shit happen? So what, you ain't getting no abortion? I knew you wasn't gonna do it! And can I come visit in New York over the break? Girl, I could get my hair done real fly like the video girls, go shopping . . ."

I knew we were cool again because she had started running her mouth.

"Nakesha, Nakesha, we'll talk about all that tomorrow, when I get to New York. I'll call you then."

"Don't forget."

"I won't. And don't forget to call Ma for me."

"I won't."

"Cool. Peace out girl."

"Peace out mama," Nakesha said, with a giggle on the end. I walked back to the car smiling wide, relieved to have my sister back in my corner.

THAT LAST MORNING had begun with us both on a high from the previous night. I wasn't worried once we left Clearville. Seemed like the stretch of road was one big movie screen—and I was the star. How imagination filled the sky of open road. Yet our destination wasn't my subject. Instead, I thought of the peaceful times: Grandma dressing me in bright yellow for Easter Sundays, Ma and Daddy in his cab, me and Nakesha walking home from school on a sunny day when no fights broke out. And Jewel—any time I had of her was enough. My thoughts merged with the open road until they became as tangible as the horizon now seemed, my extant memories persisted as day gave way to a night that would be thick with fog.

No one had told us about Pennsylvania, because we hadn't asked. We hadn't planned, we hadn't thought, we hadn't read, we hadn't consulted others who had taken the trip before. We hadn't taken the time to interpret the color gradations and sinewy lines on the maps, signs that would have alerted us to a thing or two about its geography. We hadn't checked the weather. We didn't know about the fog that would haunt us for a hundred miles before a windy snowstorm took its place. Like most people chasing dreams, we had just taken off without forethought or pretense. Raised betwixt Midwest plains, we knew nothing of hills and mountains so curvaceous we felt our stomachs plummet mile after mile. As soon as we crossed the Pennsylvania state line, we found ourselves at the peak of hills we didn't even know we were on until we started going down, or looked to our side and saw jagged cliffs below. The weight of reality was an avalanche.

The concrete monstrosities of the city were manufactured, man-made structures that could not compete with the threatening brilliance of nature. I had never seen a mountain, let alone looked down from one. I was overwhelmed and overcome with my own smallness in the middle of sky-high trees and steadily rising altitudes. People fell quickly out of project windows; way up here I wouldn't do anything but flutter, giving me extra minutes I didn't need to think about what was going to happen when I finally hit the ground. Rasul was just as jolted as I was, but there was no way he was going to show it. Especially not after the show he had thought he put on that night. He was the first to suggest we stop, for cigarettes no less. I didn't want anything but to get to NYC. I put in my favorite CD—*What's the 411*—but even that couldn't calm my nerves.

"I think we should get a hotel room again tonight," I suggested, as the snow picked up. It wasn't until we needed the windshield wipers that we figured out they weren't working. Rasul had to pull over a couple of times to wipe the windows with a T-shirt he had gotten from the trunk. I had noticed a furrow of worry in his brow, but last night had him pumped up and feeling like a man.

"Naw, 'cause that's gonna be another hundred dollars when you add in the bribe," he said. "We gonna need that dough when we get to New York."

I decided to let him be the man and get the last word.

"I think we can make it tonight. Maybe round midnight, but we gonna get there."

I shook my head, but I knew I wasn't going to sleep no matter how much my head pounded or my eyes strained.

LOOKING BACK, SEEING the first deer should have made us pull over. The hotels and rest stops were scarce now, not at all like on the Midwestern interstate. Around eight we had gone an hour without seeing one bathroom, and I had to go so bad I was squirming and almost got my butt out on the side of the road.

"Damn, this shit like *The Shining,*" Rasul had joked, referring to the wooded surroundings that appeared eerily within minutes after leaving Ohio behind. It seemed like even the cars had disappeared. But I wasn't in the mood to giggle about these strange, surreal surroundings. I was a city girl. I was out of my element. I figured we were now closer to New York than Chicago, so I wasn't about to turn around. But I would definitely stop. Aunt Jewel wouldn't leave us stranded in the middle of Pennsylvania. She would come get us if we couldn't make it out of this maze.

The first one had been killed—ripped almost in two most likely by a semitruck. I had never seen a real deer, up so close like that. But I had also never been in the middle of fog where the things immediately before you seemed to show up only after you'd passed. That's how we ran into the scene at the side of a narrow crooked road right outside a town called Sharon. The scene should have disturbed us enough to turn around and go back to the hotel we had seen about thirty miles back. Rasul hit the brakes as soon as the three figures appeared. We skidded across the highway dividing line, and fortunately, there were no cars coming in the other direction. My heart pounded as I looked back. Two burly White men, wearing shades even at night, worked together to lift the cumbersome animal onto the bed of a pickup truck. Its head seemed to be hanging on by just a few cords connecting at its neck. Its tongue hung lazily to the side. Had it not been for the antlers, I would have thought they were lifting a horse.

"Damn . . . ," Rasul whispered, in awe of the sight.

Though two men were now struggling to throw it in the back of a truck, I could tell the animal had been a strong one. Its muscles bulged and stretched tight against a rich coat. The road directly ahead of us was smeared with its blood. By morning, the snowfall would have covered all evidence of the accident. As Rasul drove on—slow at first while we were caped in the fog—I turned back to watch them until a white mist suddenly cut the scene like a movie reel had stopped running. I was rooting for the men I didn't know, and the deer too, I guess. But the last thing I saw before the mist cut them off was the massive animal slipping out of their shared grip and crumbling to the ground one more time.

"Where all the signs letting us know where we at?" I asked Rasul, teary-eyed. The neon-green billboards stating the number of miles to New York City had disappeared.

"I don't know," he answered, easing up on the gas as we approached another dense patch of fog. Soon as we made it through, he pulled over, completely silent. He reached over my thighs into the glove compartment to pull out the maps we hadn't needed to make it through Ohio and Indiana.

"Damn, this shit ain't flat as before," he mumbled. "It's like we in a whole other country."

"I know," I agreed. The clock on the dash read almost 10:00 P.M. We hadn't stopped much, yet it seemed we had so much farther to go. But my man disagreed with me.

"I think we almost there," he said softly, unsure.

"How you know?"

"I don't know," he answered, putting the car back into drive and checking behind us for oncoming traffic. "I just got this feeling we almost there."

IT WAS THE second deer that did it. Just as soon as we got way back high up, where mountains faced each other on opposite ends of wide valleys, the fog started messing with us again. Only the valleys of land were now giving way to valleys of water as well. I always noticed how men got quiet when they knew they were just plain wrong, as I'm sure Rasul suddenly realized now that we could barely see several feet in front of us. The windshield wipers did nothing for the condensation that collected in thin sheets, and a headlight had gone out about forty miles back. In the misty fog, as I now recall, it *was* just like things came up on us right after we passed them. Once it was behind us, be it another car or a pulled-over traveler or a tree that looked out of place, that's when we noticed it had been there. There was no time to react, take a good look, figure much out, or absorb the details. There was only the time to notice it had been there and move on. But that huge deer's timing couldn't have been more perfect. I felt the Eldorado bump her slightly, like maybe we had only grazed her hindquarters. I had always heard people talk about being scared like a deer stuck in headlights. I would have imagined a stunned glaze of terror would take over in their eyes. But she didn't look scared at all when her eyes met ours as she galloped across the snowy, rocky, narrow road. Maybe she had babies waiting on the other side. Because her black eyes looked calm, as if she was in control of it all. She had more control than we, because she kept running even after being hit.

It was Rasul and I who were decidedly out of control, more at this moment than we had been in the past couple of weeks when we made the mistake of allowing pipe dreams to become real. I know Rasul was screaming "Shit!" though I couldn't hear it above my blood pumping hard and fast in my ears. He hit the brakes hard, and maybe they gave out or maybe they just gave up. We spun on a slick of ice that covered the road about ten feet ahead of the deer. I saw Rasul's mouth moving but didn't hear one word. I had stopped breathing so I couldn't scream or cry. I didn't even get a chance to steal a look at him before the chocolate Eldorado tipped over the flimsy guardrail only experienced drivers should have expected to protect them. As we tumbled down the rocky side of a jagged hill whose altitude I didn't know, Rasul vomited against the dash and I pissed myself. I reached out ahead of me to hold on to something, but nothing was there but clear glass mired with dirt, twigs, water, snow, and brown leaves. Like cloth playthings I had watched through washer and dryer doors, we rolled from ceiling to floor and back to our seats.

But none of it hurt. Not one knock or hit made me cry out. I was only wishing I had told Rasul I loved him, and I imagined that's what he was now saying to me though there was just too much commotion for us to say anything now. My world suddenly became a cube of gravity suspending. I didn't wonder when the ride would end or where it was taking me. I was only wondering in those last few moments if this was how Ma felt when she was tumbling out of the Ferris wheel.

WE SANK INTO *the water you me and him and because you were poor neglected black boy and girl you had never frolicked in the froth of the ocean or journeyed to the caribbean or the hamptons or martha's vineyard or idlewild or even an overcrowded pool someone paid for you to be in at the ymca so you could not recollect the instinct of the womb in which you once thrived where you made your own rules accepted the liquid breath in amniotic fluid the possibility of gravity's suspension for in the womb you were the master and no weight was too powerful for the lightness of innocence to rise above but you have lost that and you never regained it once you shot out of your hopeful but doubtful mothers who succumbed to defeat like you now succumb to the weight of water the momentum of waves the sudden terrifying choke of oxygen when it meets hydrogen the adrenaline of fear which keeps you fighting but also contemplating the end the dark the worst the futility of trying to learn to swim or float now because it only takes seconds for a human or object to sink when it falls in water* *at the magical nearly impossible perfect ninety-degree angle if you had had minutes maybe you might have saved yourselves if someone had once instructed you to fill your lungs as deeply as you could before the water closed over you so quickly and evenly like an onlooker could have second-guessed the river's parting after blinking just once fancy that after just one blink water can heal its wound and become whole again maybe if people and hearts and souls were made of water you would have done the same in life maybe you wouldn't have panicked so maybe you wouldn't have given up like you had done with everything else in your lives up until this heroic end you would have done so much more you would have thought so much more you would have fought so much more but you only looked at each other as the headlights gave way to hell's light then you looked for each other as the water rushed in and divided your embrace I felt you Ma dying on me stubborn ass just like all others you closed your eyes but I grabbed you shook you rocked you heaved with you the same thing your ma would have done had she been here or there or back then way back when she would have found you like I now seek you without a guide compass lantern lighthouse or map she would have jumped into the deepest most frigid part of the ocean after you with her shoes still on if she had any in the first place or with grand stones for anchors tied to her ankles by middle passage crew who decided she really was not worth the trip she would have jumped in after you even if someone just shot the hole in her heart through which the water would flow rush swoosh preventing any float but still she would have jumped in without first reaching for a plug she would have excavated her baby like you were a precious artifact her evidence proof of the underworld the spirit world the better world then she would have fought you slapped you mouth to mouthed you said you fass heifer don't die on me don't leave me now you all i got you all i really ever had but she was not there I was I had always been there would never leave where else have I had to go since eternity but your womb your heart your soul your body your dinner table your hard wooden sunday church pew your nest made in a field where you watched me with eyes in back of your head your underground cave house of a negro settlement your bed in a one-room hovel your lap on silent crowded bus your seat the only one left while you stood patiently for hours at the free health clinic inside your coat in the government cheese line in between your legs on a saturday hair press day in your stained but immaculately scrubbed bathtub in your embrace when your own Ma died or in your arms when a daddy left so we were already used to listening out for each other's breath in the dark and the black of night water only became the dark so we have disappeared like a frosty handprint on a rattling window in a bad winter a moment too divine to freeze in place a vision too spectacular for permanence an impression unimpressed with a world where the good times are fleeting we are destined for the fate of those unafraid to vanish we demand something better the second time around and there is always a second time waiting to become a third so bitch don't you die on me don't you sleep stop sink rest bloat give up drop out settle for a grave at the bottom of a dirty river tainted with this life's piss I will punch your eyes until they open again pound your chest till your heart beats once more snake the blood through your veins with a single hair from my newborn head if I have to battle the whites the men the man anybody who gets in my way and tries to stop me I will fight them off cause I love you I need you I am you I life you I birth you I grab you I hug you I hold you I lift you I raise your head to the light of the moon leading our way it looks like a big Ma's white head wrap and the string of clouds make out our mother's face her smile her life creases she has followed us you know she will carry us to life beyond itself I want to go I want to go I want to go there with you and only you always you forever you no matter what with you so I clench your fingers in mine and say, "Come on, Ma. Let's go."*

AND SO I went. And haven't gone back since.

I could have never imagined my name, let alone my face, in anybody's newspaper. In my small, insignificant life I would have never felt the pride of one-sixteenth of a page in the *Chicago Sun-Times,* my life known and thought of by too many people to count, many of them staring at my freshman class photo while riding the same bus my mother was too grieved to continue to drive. The processional in my honor would have made King proud, joyous that footsteps had pounded a street bearing his name and turned a funeral into something of a march. The people—mostly Black, some White, old, young, sad, outraged, puzzled, or just plain bored on their day off—came not because they knew me but because they did not. The people came to be a part of something, but no one thought to ponder their part. There were no apologies for our passing, no widespread knowledge of the third life lost, no word of me after a media storm dissipated like the first jolting and stimulating fizz of a gulp of soda pop.

Eventually from their conversations and consciousness, as soon as I had come, I and my story settled blandly like what was left at the bottom of the bottle someone was just too thrifty to throw out. I had wanted to tell them, in some way, not to weep or wail—just like the song had said. I had wanted to tell everybody that I and my child were alright, as we always had been. We would be moving on to another life, a greater life, a better life, maybe even an eternal life. At least, that's what I hoped as I looked down from the other side with my baby in my arms and my man at my side.

After Ma passed and Nakesha joined the service, it was Aunt Jewel and Hakim who traveled from Brooklyn to Chicago once a year. Not to visit the relatives who no longer or perhaps never knew her, but to lay flowers on the headstone of the only one besides her big sister who truly had. I was surprised by others who did the same, if only once or twice. Maureen, Gladys, Shirley from the shelter. Janice and Tiny before Tiny went down. Mrs. Carly. Patty-Cake. Renelle. My love, Leroy. The kids, grown-up. My daddy, too late. But in time, visitors would come to my headstone and be surprised, then search for me in Oakwood Cemetery, then question their memory before accusing the undertaker of reselling my plot, then soon abandon the task and cost of exhuming a Black body to be sure the right one still lay there, finally explaining everything unexplainable the way Black folks always had—as *God*.

An unaware and free young girl had been a prankster. In death, an aware and freed woman becomes one once more. Slyly, slowly, mysteriously, my epitaph etched in soft pink granite shifts, words painstakingly selected change their minds, new letters suddenly rebel above atrophied lilacs or begonias or gladioluses or roses laid just once a year, before dried out by trouble and time, they crumble and give in to the gentlest breeze. Until finally my headstone announces what I might have named it had we made it, the most certain act in an uncertain world, the miracle actualized amid chaos and fury, the destination of orgasm, the beauty forgiving all life's ugly, the greatest thing I had ever achieved: *Conception*.

"Baby, the first thing I need to know from you is do you believe I killed my father?"

Winner of the Terry McMillan Young Author Award

KALISHA BUCKHANON

A NOVEL

upstate

Seventeen-year-old Antonio and sixteen-year-old Natasha face tragedy when Antonio finds himself in jail, accused of a shocking crime. Over the course of a decade, they share a desperate correspondence. Despite being apart, they turn to each for support, advice, and love. All the while, they can only wonder if they will ever be reunited.

Reading Group Guide available at www.the-blackbox.com

St. Martin's Griffin   www.stmartins.com